About the author

Louise Emma Clarke's blog, 'Mum of Boys and Mabel', has over 100k followers. Having moved to Dubai with her family she's now back in the UK and is enjoying writing. *From Mum with Love* is her debut novel.

From MUM with LOVE

LOUISE EMMA CLARKE

HEAD
of
ZEUS

First published in the United Kingdom in 2019 by Aria,
an imprint of Head of Zeus Ltd.

This paperback edition first published in 2020 by Aria.

975312468

A CIP catalogue record for this book is available
from the British Library.

ISBN (PB) 9781838930646
ISBN (E) 9781789541908

Printed and bound by CPI Group (UK) Ltd,
Croydon, CRO 4YY

MIX
Paper from
responsible sources
FSC® C020471

Aria
an imprint of Head of Zeus Ltd
5–8 Hardwick Street
London EC1R 4RG

Dedicated to my husband, Charlie,
and our three babies: Stanley, Wilfred and Mabel;
without whom this novel would have been written
at least six months earlier

Prologue

How it all started…? It was pitch black and very nearly silent, bar the occasional roar of a car passing on the street below. Her left arm was now completely numb and her left leg, which was taking most of her weight, was starting to prick with pins and needles. But she didn't dare move an inch. A small human being lay below her, its breathing soft and shallow. Squinting in the darkness, she didn't take her eyes off the child, waiting patiently until she saw the rise and fall of her chest grow deeper, accompanied by the gentle snuffles of sleep.

Now came the escape plan – and she knew it wouldn't be easy.

She slowly removed her hand from the rising chest, finger by finger.

Thumb, then forefinger, then index finger, then ring finger, and finally her little finger. As that last finger gently lifted, she paused and held her breath, listening to the sound of the breathing.

She exhaled quietly with relief as the snuffles continued, undisturbed in their rhythm.

Now to escape. Taking a deep breath, she glanced at the sliver of light coming from underneath the door behind her – and carefully dropped to the floor, beginning a slow, steady crawl in its direction. There were a couple of floorboards that squeaked with too much weight, so she made sure her hands and knees avoided them. *Slow and steady,* she thought to herself, as she danced to the left and then to the right, towards the promised sliver of light. *Don't blow it now.*

But as she placed her left knee back on the floor, touching distance away from the door, she felt pain sear through her leg. Every part of her wanted to scream 'FUCK!' and roll around in agony – but the consequences would be dire. She gritted her teeth so hard that the pain flooded into her head and roared into her ears, before pulling a small Hello Kitty toy out of the skin on her kneecap. She wanted to rip its head off, but instead she glared at it fiercely and tossed it onto the chair by her head.

I'm winning this battle, she thought to herself, as she crawled awkwardly towards the door. Reaching it, she climbed slowly to her feet and gently pulled the door open.

And it was then that she heard the unmistakable clatter of metal in the lock of the front door.

'No!' she muttered under her breath, lunging for the door. 'He'd better not… No… Please… He'd better not…'

But it was too late.

'Honey! Bella! Daddy's home! Where are you?' The shout echoed up the stairs, followed by a loud clunk as he threw his keys and phone onto the sideboard in the hallway.

'Shut up!' she hissed. 'I've just put her down!' She raced towards the top of the stairs, adding, 'please… shut up!'

He was starting to climb the stairs now: 'Sorry, honey? What was that? You OK? You both upstairs? Is she in the bath?'

And just as his right foot hit the top of the stairs, a trill scream was heard from the nursery.

And that was that. A wasted forty-five minutes, contorting her body over a cot, numb limbs, and an imprint of Hello-fucking-Kitty on her knee – and he'd blown it all with yet another badly-timed arrival home and yell up the stairs.

It was 6.45 p.m. Bella was usually asleep by 6.30 p.m. – after all, she was fourteen months old – and despite Chris requesting endlessly that they move bedtime back so he could see his little princess when he made it home from work, Jessica had always had quite enough by then. If he wasn't home by 6 p.m., he didn't see Bella; it was as simple as that. Unless he woke her up, that was, which was becoming a bit of a habit. Just as he caught sight of his wife standing on the landing with a face like thunder, Bella called out again from her cot – and his face dropped with realisation. 'I'm sorry, honey. Did it take a while to get her off?' He pushed open the door to her nursery and made his way to her cot, while looking back at her. 'Has it been a tough day?'

'Has it been a tough day?' she echoed hollowly, while rubbing her bruised knee. 'You could say that, yes.'

She considered pushing past him and heading downstairs to pour herself a large glass of something cold and alcoholic but had second thoughts, and followed him into the nursery instead, standing alongside him as he scooped Bella into his arms. 'Do you want to know how our day went? Really? It started at five-thirty this morning when you woke her up getting into the shower. Well, that was fucking brilliant, because I'd already been awake four times in the night while you lay there snoring.'

Bella was smiling up at her daddy, who was gazing adoringly back – but as Jessica paused, he turned his attention back to her. She wasn't finished. 'I tried to get her back to sleep, but she wasn't having any of it, so while you sat on the train to London, probably flicking through a newspaper in peace and drinking a coffee you could actually get to the bottom of before it went cold, I was watching the *Teletubbies* on the living room rug, wearing a donkey puppet as a hat. And after doing that for what felt like an eternity, I looked at my watch and it had been fourteen minutes, Chris. FOURTEEN MINUTES. Can you imagine? No, you bloody can't!'

She took a deep breath before she continued. 'So next on the day's fun agenda was feeding her breakfast. A simple task, wouldn't you think? Well no, it never bloody is! I offered her cereal first. She threw the whole bowl on the floor. I offered her banana next. She smeared it over the high chair, over her face, over her clothes, and as a crescendo, over my pyjamas too – which I only washed yesterday, so you can imagine my delight... I then decided that was enough mess for one day and I made her some dry toast. But, as you can probably guess by now, that wasn't bloody right either – so I spent the rest of the morning veering between feeling outraged at how incredibly headstrong our child is and worried sick that she is deliberately starving herself. And let me tell you, Chris, asking Google didn't alleviate any of those worries...'

'OK, honey, I get the picture,' he interrupted, as Bella started struggling in his arms to get down.

'You get the picture? You get the picture? No, you don't, Chris!' she shouted. 'Keep with me because there is more. There's lots more!'

Chris leant down and placed Bella on the floor of her nursery. She immediately toddled towards Jessica and attached herself to her legs.

'Moving onto her morning nap, where I tried unsuccessfully to get her to sleep for a grand total of fifty-three minutes,' she continued, leaning down to scoop up Bella. 'What were you doing at 9.35 a.m., Chris? Having a leisurely breakfast at your desk? Making a coffee in the kitchen and comparing fantasy football results with John? Well, I hope it was fun, because I was lying on a bed being repeatedly whipped around the face with a cuddly bunny rabbit!'

Chris' mouth curled into a smile, which he tried to hide by leaning down to pick up Hello Kitty from the chair below him. 'Ah, here's Hello Kitty, Bella!' he said. 'We were looking for her last night, weren't we? She was here all the time!'

Bella cooed and reached out to grab Hello Kitty, while Jessica exhaled deeply.

'I'm sorry, Jess! I'm really sorry,' Chris said, reaching down to stroke his daughter's hair.

5

'Are you?' Jessica snapped back. 'Are you *really* sorry?'

'Yes, honey. Of course I am,' he replied, smiling down at his daughter.

'You don't bloody sound it,' she said, feeling the rage bubble.

Chris looked up at her. 'Let's not do this now, Jess. Not in front of Bella. I'm exhausted.'

Jessica sighed loudly, plonked her child in her father's arms, and stormed out the room.

'You're exhausted! *You're* exhausted! Ha! That's brilliant!' she called back at him, running down the stairs.

'We're *both* exhausted,' Chris replied quietly. He kissed the top of Bella's head gently and took a deep breath, before calling after Jessica. 'I'm sorry you had such a crap day! But do you know what?'

'What?' she called back, making her way to the fridge.

'I've told you this before, but you really should write everything down in a blog!'

'Well, maybe I will!' she shouted back

And as the wine glugged noisily into her glass, she added under her breath: 'At least somebody might bloody listen to me.'

I

Followers – o

Dear Bella,

This is my first letter to you, and as I write it, you are asleep next to me. Tiny, and curled, and peaceful – which is a relief after the night we have just had. You are three weeks old and I think it's time to start writing. When you were born, I promised to tell you everything – and I don't know whether these letters will make much sense, given how groggy I feel with lack of sleep, but I will try. I will keep writing.

And where better to start, but at the beginning? I am Jessica, and I am your mummy. I grew up in South East London with Granny, Grandad and your Auntie Fran. Grandad worked on the railways and Granny made curtains, filling our living room with giant swathes of fabric that we all had to tiptoe around. Auntie Fran is ten years older than me, but she has always been my very best friend in the world, even when I was a goofy teenager with my head buried in books and she was a cool, sassy student with boyfriends who rode motorbikes and smelt of cheap aftershave and musty leather. Our family didn't have a lot of money, but I don't think we ever noticed. We were close and very happy. And that's exactly what I want for you.

I always wanted to be a writer, Bella – so everyone was so proud when I packed my suitcase and headed to Leeds University on the train to start a degree in English Literature. My dream was to graduate and start a job as a journalist in a bustling newsroom, with my own desk and a slimline laptop, rushing out of the office when a story broke. But I soon came to realise that life doesn't always follow the course we imagine – and after a year of rejection letters landing on our doormat with depressing thuds, Granny turned to me and said: 'Apply for something different Jess! Anything! Just get out there and earn some money. You can still write one day, but you need to do something now!'

I gave her the silent treatment for a few days after that, but I knew she was right. I quickly accepted a job as an office manager at an insurance company in the middle of Blackheath Village. There were only fifteen of us in the office and I enjoyed my job. I made cups of tea, I ordered stationery, I processed invoices, and I managed diaries. Gradually, my dream of being a writer fizzled, faded, and disappeared without so much as a pop.

I was careful with my money and before long, I had enough to move into a small flat in the centre of the village, where I wandered back every evening after a drink or two with the team. And it was on one of those nights out that the course of my life changed forever. The whole team were out celebrating Tom McGee's fiftieth birthday – and I had definitely drunk too many glasses of white wine (and definitely not eaten enough nibbles to soak it all up) when I quite literally bumped into a tall, dark, and handsome stranger at the bar. And as he looked down at the crotch of his suit trousers, which were now drenched in the contents of my wine glass, the world stopped spinning. Just for a second, it stopped. He was older than me, I guessed around forty at the time, but he was very handsome. About 6ft 2, with tanned skin and dark hair, a few greys at his temples, and eyes a bright, surprising green. 'I'm Chris', he said, offering his hand. 'And I'm Jessica,' I replied, shaking it. And since that moment in that bar, your daddy and I have been inseparable.

He worked in the city by day – and by night, he came home and we snuggled under fleece blankets and watched TV boxsets, whilst taking it in turns to knock up feasts in the kitchen. He soon decided to sell his flat in North Greenwich, given it was pretty much always empty, and we started looking for places to buy together. And when we stepped through the door of a house in Westcombe Park on a sunny autumn afternoon, with its duck-egg blue front door and lavender bushes scenting the path, we knew we'd found our forever home. We moved three months later – and as the sun set over our new garden on a crisp December evening, Daddy got down on one knee, opened a small turquoise box, and asked me to be his wife. 'Thank God I poured that wine over you!' I cried, as I fell into his arms and cried happy tears.

That was the beginning, Bella.

That was the beginning of us.

But I have so much more to tell you.

Just wait.

Love from Mummy x

Jessica's fingers rested on the keys of her laptop. Leaning back in her chair, she moved her eyes down to the notebook lying open on the table in front of her and traced her finger across the page. Once smooth, the paper was now filled with the indents of words scrawled in a blue biro. She'd carefully typed the letter word-for-word, allowing her mind to wander back to the day she first wrote it. The tiredness, the newborn cuddles, the emotions. It felt like yesterday, but a lifetime ago, all at the same time. Shutting the book with a snap, she pulled it towards her and sniffed the leather. There was something very comforting about this notebook, with its sunshine yellow cover and gold monogrammed initials.

JDH. Jessica Dawn Holmes. Her married name.

It still gave her a thrill nearly two years later.

The notebook had been a gift, handed to her on the last afternoon of her hen weekend in Cornwall a few weeks before her wedding. The small group of friends and family were gathered in the lounge, and Jessica unwrapped parcels one by one.

'Right,' Fran had said. 'I've saved mine until last. Here you go, little sister!'

She held out a small package, wrapped in colourful polka dot paper and tied with a silver bow. And as she untied and pulled, those gold initials were the first thing Jessica saw. Her new name staring back at her. She was the first of her friends to have a serious boyfriend, let alone get married, but she didn't have a single doubt. And as she smiled up at her sister to thank her, she was filled with nervous excitement about becoming JDH for real.

Jessica blinked now and glanced down at the same notebook in her hands, the gold initials fading in places and the pages filled with letters to her daughter. The idea to share the letters in a blog had come to her a few weeks ago. She'd been avidly reading parenting blogs since Bella was born and she'd often thought of starting her own, but every time she opened her laptop to start typing, she just couldn't find the words. *What should she write about? And how should she start?*

And then she remembered the notebook.

She already had the words.

Jessica's eyes shot back to the screen of her laptop, speed reading the letter she'd just typed in her mind – but there was something stopping her from publishing it. *Did she really want to become a mummy blogger? Did she fit the mould?* She didn't have a troop of perfectly turned out kids, her house was never tidy, she didn't have a glamorous home in the South of France to spend her summers, nor a team of photographers to capture her in fabulous outfits against cool backdrops. She didn't have long glossy hair to flick, nor a lounge of monochrome prints to photograph, nor the bank balance to take her daughter to different over-priced attractions every day of the week.

She was just Jessica – a thirty-one-year-old, mummy-of-one, and wife to forty-four-year-old Chris. She had an average wardrobe in average size twelve, an average three-bedroom house on an average street in South East London, and an average career as the office manager of an insurance firm (before she gave it up to become a mummy, that is). She wasn't anything special.

But she did love to write and she thought, possibly, she might even be quite good at it. She would just stick to writing letters to Bella, telling the story of how motherhood happened for her.

She felt comfortable with that. It felt right.

And even if she wasn't quite ready to send it out into the world just yet, that was the moment she knew she was really going to do it. Sat at her laptop, with her notebook in her hand, and memories of early motherhood drifting in and out of her mind.

But first, dinner.

'You ready, honey?' Chris asked, loosening his tie as he walked into the lounge.

'Yep, let me just grab my lipstick,' Jessica replied. 'Where's Mum gone?'

'Chatting to your dad on the phone in a very loud whisper, but all quiet from Bella Boo. We can escape as soon as you're ready.'

Jessica smiled at her husband, as he pulled off the tie and undid his top button. She didn't often stop to look at him any more – *really* look at him – but standing in front of her now, he was very definitely still the man she fell in love with that first night in the bar. She, on the other hand, looked vastly different. As she smiled at him, her hand subconsciously skimmed her stomach.

'You look beautiful,' Chris said, reading her mind. 'Is it a new dress?'

'Oh this? No, I've had it for years,' Jessica replied, looking down at the black shift dress that fell past her knees. 'But thanks, birthday boy!'

She walked towards him and kissed him on the lips, before unhooking her handbag from the banister at the bottom of the stairs to find her lipstick (that pre-baby handbag was so rarely used these days, it was always a packed nappy bag that she dragged around with her).

Standing in front of the mirror in the hallway, she painted the cherry red hue carefully onto her lips, pursed them, and applied another layer. After checking her teeth, she stood back and admired her reflection.

'Right, I'll just say goodnight to Mum. Is the cab outside?' she asked, making her way to the kitchen.

'Yes, just arrived,' Chris replied.

And two minutes later, they were pulling the door quietly behind them and making their way outside.

Jessica had made Chris promise he wouldn't be late home from work on his birthday, and although she'd been hoping he'd make it back in time to kiss Bella goodnight, she was thankful they wouldn't miss their 8 p.m. dinner reservation. She'd bathed Bella, got her to sleep, and managed to escape back downstairs ahead of schedule. And, just as she finished typing the letter, which she'd started during Bella's naptime that afternoon, Chris had walked through the door. Her mum had arrived minutes later to babysit. Everything was set for their date.

It was a treat to be heading out on a Monday evening, especially as Chris had chosen their favourite Argentinian restaurant in Blackheath. It would be just like old times when they used to stroll to the restaurant hand-in-hand, feeling like two lovestruck teenagers – except this time, they'd be bleary-eyed from a broken night of Bella standing up in her cot and screaming at the injustice of being behind bars.

It wasn't until their starter arrived that Jessica decided to bring up the blog. 'So I typed up the first letter…' she said, pushing her chilli prawns around the plate with her fork.

'Really?' Chris replied, taking a sip from a wine glass nearly as big as his head. 'So you're going to do it?'

'I think so. Even if nobody else reads them, the letters will be safe for Bella when she's older. And I get to keep my notebook…' Jessica winked.

Chris smiled. 'I'm pleased, honey. I think it's going to be a big success.'

'I'm not sure about it being a success, but I'm going to enjoy sitting down when Bella is asleep and typing them up – and it gives me an incentive to keep going when I finally catch up,' Jessica continued.

Chris nodded. 'You've always wanted to write, and you're bloody good at it!'

'I used to think that being a writer was all about working in a busy newspaper or magazine, but there are so many bloggers doing it from their sofas now,' Jessica replied. 'I should've started years ago.'

'Well, you know I'm behind you,' he said. 'You're always glued to your phone reading those blogs, but I know you can do a better job than any of them...'

'Well, I don't know about that' Jessica cut in. 'Some of them have hundreds of thousands of followers. And I will probably have a loyal following of, well, just you!'

Chris raised his eyebrows in shock, as he took a bite of his toast. 'Hundreds of thousands?' he asked as he chewed. 'Wow.'

'Part of me is a bit embarrassed to put myself out there,' Jessica continued. 'It scares me that strangers might start to read the letters – but on the other hand, it scares me that they won't... What if nobody cares? What if I press "publish" and nobody reads it?'

'I don't think you have to worry about that, honey. You need to stop worrying about everything,' Chris replied, before pausing and looking around the room. 'Where's our waitress gone? Do you want another glass of wine?'

'Well, that was dismissive,' Jessica said, rolling her eyes.

'What was?' Chris asked.

'You don't seem hugely interested,' Jessica snapped back, refusing to make eye contact.

'In the blog?' Chris asked. 'I'm totally behind you, honey. I'm just trying to order a glass of wine and eat my bloody starter.'

Jessica sighed. For a while, the two of them ate in silence. Jessica, spearing each chilli prawn with her fork before popping it into her mouth, accompanied by sips of Sauvignon Blanc and the sound of Chris crunching his toast, all to a background hum of other diners chatting away at their tables.

After ordering another glass of wine for them both, Chris looked across at Jessica and smiled. 'Do you remember when we used to come here on Friday nights after work?' he asked.

Forcing herself out of her mood, Jessica nodded and said: 'You'd come and meet me and the rest of the team in Cecilia's Wine Bar and we'd try to escape without anyone noticing...'

Chris nodded, swirling the wine in his glass. 'Now we need a babysitter scheduled for at least a month before we can head out to dinner!'

Jessica laughed. 'God, do you remember how easy it was? We didn't have to think about anybody but ourselves! We used to lie there on a Saturday afternoon for hours reading papers and sipping mug after mug of coffee – and we'd only get up when we needed a wee or wanted to raid the fridge!'

'And the funniest thing is that I remember thinking life would always be that way,' Chris replied, laughing.

'Imagine if we tried it now... Bella would be climbing all over us!'

'Or raiding the cupboards in the kitchen in an attempt to fend for herself,' Jessica said.

'She has to do that anyway!' Chris said with a wink.

'Oi!' Jessica squealed, kicking him under the table. 'Don't be so bloody rude!'

'But seriously, honey,' Chris continued, 'I don't say this enough, but you are a brilliant mother. I know you've found things harder than you imagined and that we've argued more than we did before. It's been bloody exhausting, to say the least, but our daughter is a credit to you. She's happy, and clever, and gorgeous, and on the whole, well-behaved...'

'Except when I'm trying to get her to sleep...' Jessica cut in.

'Well, there is that... but I'm proud of you and I know you're going to do just as good a job with your blog. You didn't belong at Dellware Insurance. Writing is your passion and you're going to show the world what an amazing writer you are!'

Jessica smiled, pausing as the table was cleared around them.

'Let's have a toast!' Jessica said, lifting her wine glass as the waitress walked away. 'Happy birthday to my dashing, brilliant, and really quite ancient husband!'

'I'll toast to that!' Chris laughed, clinking his wine glass against hers. 'Cheers!'

'Cheers!' Jessica replied, feeling like the luckiest girl in the world as she leant across the table to kiss him on the lips.

He was right; it had been a difficult fourteen months. Tougher than she'd ever imagined. She had thought long and hard about returning to the familiarity of her desk, alongside the same colleagues she'd worked with for years, having the same conversations in the kitchen every Monday as she waited for the kettle to boil. And in the early days, she'd fully intended to go back there, imagining herself heading to Blackheath every morning, ordering her coffee in her favourite café (black, two sugars), and then climbing the stairs to her desk alongside a window that overlooked the heath.

But life moved on, and with a tribe of new friends by her side, each armed with a toddler the same age as Bella, she stumbled blindly but happily into a new routine. And soon, she couldn't imagine life any other way. Her agreed maternity leave was quickly coming to an end, but suddenly she knew she couldn't go back to that job. She just couldn't. She had a discussion one evening with Chris, which resulted in them sitting together tapping numbers into a calculator and chatting about how it would all work – by midnight, the result was a mutual decision for Jessica to stay with Bella at home (for the time being, at least).

'You know, I can't imagine going back to work now,' Jessica said, as they walked hand-in-hand out of the restaurant. As they strolled towards their waiting taxi, she glanced up at her office window across the street. She'd sat next to that window for years, struggling to envisage a life beyond it. She'd watched mothers walking children to school, pushing strollers with tiny babies inside, and taking children to classes in judo outfits and powder pink tutus. But as her bump grew, she still struggled to imagine a life beyond that window.

'No regrets then?' Chris asked as they climbed into the car.

'I don't think so,' Jessica replied, squeezing his hand across the back seat. 'No.'

Thirty minutes later, with Jessica's mother on the road towards home, they huddled around her laptop on the dining room table. Jessica clicked, and scrolled, and watched as her first blog post flashed onto the screen.

With the help of her university friend Becca, now a web designer at a cool advertising firm, the WordPress blog was stylish in design. The words 'LETTERS TO MY DAUGHTER' ran across the top in large pink letters, with a banner of images flashing slowly through photographs of Jessica, Chris and Bella underneath. In the first photo, a heavily pregnant Jessica beamed at the camera. In the next, Chris was sitting on a hospital chair, cuddling a tiny Bella on the day she was born. A family selfie followed, taken in the early days in their garden. Then there was a picture of Bella crawling, smiling up at the camera as she reached out to grab it. And finally a photo taken on Bella's first birthday, with crumbs of rainbow cake dotted around her mouth.

'I'll leave you to read it,' she said, making her way towards the kitchen. She wanted Chris to read it before she published it. No, she needed Chris to read it before she published it. His support and approval meant everything to her – but still, she felt embarrassed and vulnerable to know that the words she'd written to Bella were now playing in his mind.

Flicking on the tap at the kitchen sink, she shook her head and laughed quietly. *You can't be embarrassed about him reading it*, she thought to herself, as the water ran noisily into the wine glass in her hand. *You'll never make a blogger.* Deep in thought, she squirted washing-up liquid into the glass and used a sponge to work it around the rim, watching the bubbles fly back into the sink as the sponge squeaked.

So when Chris walked up behind her and kissed her on the shoulder, she jumped in shock.

'Fucking hell! You scared me!'

Chris laughed. 'Well, as expected Mrs Holmes, that was bloody brilliant,' he said

'Really?' Jessica asked.

'It's great. And I know I'm biased, but my eyes may have started watering towards the end. And you know me honey, I'm not a crier.'

'So you think I should publish it?' she asked, placing the wine glass on the draining board and turning off the tap.

'Yes definitely. And there is no time like the present...'

'Well, I guess I could do it now,' Jessica said. 'The wine at dinner has probably given me a bit of confidence I won't have tomorrow...'

So once the second glass was washed up and left to dry on the draining board, Jessica made her way back to her laptop and took a deep breath.

'You're definitely OK with me using pictures of Bella, aren't you, babe?' she asked Chris, as she pulled over a chair and sat next to him.

Chris shrugged. 'I don't think there's any harm in it. Maybe if your blog suddenly got really popular, we'd have to reassess, but I don't think we should be worried about the odd picture for now...'

'I agree...' Jessica replied. 'Let's see how it goes.'

She took a deep breath and hovered her finger over 'PUBLISH POST' on the screen.

This was it.

'Oh, fuck it!' she said out loud. 'I'm doing this. I'm going to be a blogger.'

And with that, her finger clicked, and she snapped the laptop shut.

2

Followers – 81

Dear Bella,

It was 10.34 a.m. on the 6th August 2016 that I found out you existed.

It was my wedding day – and after heaving over the toilet bowl for an entire week beforehand, it suddenly occurred to me that my period was late. I had quickly added a pregnancy test to my online shopping order, which had arrived with bottles of prosecco, slices of smoked salmon, and half a dozen bagels the day before. I whipped the test away before anyone could see it (up the sleeve of my jumper, just in case) and stashed it in the bathroom in a carrier bag, behind a pyramid of toilet rolls. I tried to forget about it the next morning, as I danced around in my white velour robe, swigging glasses of fizz, and sobbing happy tears when I read the card Daddy had left propped up for me in the kitchen.

But with a fresh wave of nausea later that morning, I couldn't wait any longer. I made my excuses and dashed upstairs to the bathroom, my stomach flipping with nerves as I ripped the box open, tore the foil inside, and pulled out the plastic stick. As I sat down on the toilet and peed clumsily over the end (and all over my hands, as it happened) I could hear my mum (your granny) and my bridesmaids (your Auntie Fran, my school friend Callie, and my cousins Leyla and Emily) singing along badly to Beyoncé downstairs. And then I stood up, placed the cap back over the end of the test, kind of revolted by the sight and smell of my own urine, and paced the room for two minutes, trying not to look down. My heart was beating so fast inside my chest that I could hear it as the seconds ticked on – and as soon as two minutes passed, I leant down and snatched up the test.

And there you were.

Two bright blue lines staring back at me.

I didn't tell Daddy that day. I just couldn't. I knew you were there, hidden deep underneath the lace of my wedding dress – but selfishly, I didn't want his memories of that day to be about anything but the two of us. At the time, I envied him that – because every time I felt waves of happiness that day, my mind immediately turned back to those blue lines and I felt sick all over again. I wished I could forget it had happened at all; for one day at least. Just for one day.

It was the next morning, lying in our super king bed in the most amazing bridal suite that I finally plucked up the courage to tell him. I don't know what I expected your daddy to say but I expected some kind of hesitation, a few doubts at least. I didn't get it though. As I uttered the words, 'I've got something to tell you…', he interrupted to say: 'You're pregnant, aren't you?' It turned out that he'd suspected it all along, hearing me heave in the bathroom for days beforehand, as I tried my best to stifle the noise. He pulled me into a kiss and told me everything was going to be wonderful – and from that very moment, I believed him Bella. I really did.

I didn't find pregnancy easy and if I'm honest, sometimes I was angry that I didn't get to enjoy the first weeks and months of married life without the presence of nausea, heartburn, and haemorrhoids. Pregnancy isn't glamorous – at least mine certainly wasn't. We found out that you were a little girl at our twenty-week scan and I sobbed with happiness. I would have been just as happy if you were a boy, but finding out who you were suddenly made it all very real to me. After the scan, we walked straight into Greenwich for a celebratory decaf coffee (for me) and pint of beer (for your daddy). I wandered around a local baby boutique afterwards, choosing the softest powder pink blanket as a memento of the day we found out we would be getting a daughter. You still sleep under that blanket now, and when I look at it, I remember exactly how I felt that day. The excitement. The happiness. The promise.

It seems a long time ago Bella – but I only have to unzip the bag covering my wedding dress and you are the first thing to come flooding into my mind. We didn't come face-to-face for another seven months, but that was the moment we first met. Right there in the bathroom, to a soundtrack of Beyoncé and my heart jumping into my mouth.

And I will never forget it.

Love from Mummy x

'Fucking hell!' Jessica exclaimed loudly, as she rolled over in bed to show Chris her phone. 'Look at this!'

Chris pulled his attention away from Sky News, which was playing quietly on the TV in the corner of the bedroom, and took her phone. He was quiet for a few seconds as he panned down the page. '81 social media followers? How did you do that, Jess?' he replied, with a big smile on his face.

'Thanks for the vote of confidence!' she laughed. 'I shared the blog to my personal page before we went to bed last night and it seems everyone has followed it. Shit Chris! What do I do now?'

'It's not surprising, honey. Your friends and family know it's going to be good!'

'I think they're probably just being kind, babe, but even so, I wasn't expecting so many people to take an interest...' As she spoke, she clicked through the likes on her phone, recognising the faces of friends and family as she scrolled.

'I knew they'd like it,' Chris said, heaving himself out of bed. 'You'll have to type up the next letter when you get the chance. You've got to keep up the momentum now you've started!'

And even though it was still six in the morning and she'd been disturbed by Bella in the night, Jessica felt a thrill at the thought. She couldn't wait to sit down at her laptop in a quiet moment, open her notebook, and start typing.

But it was Tuesday, which meant they had a busy day – once she'd tackled breakfast, dressed a squirming toddler, and packed her bag for every possible eventuality, that was.

It was 9.45 a.m. before she finally made it out of the house that morning. She'd been ready to leave twenty minutes beforehand but had smelt something ominous as she was about to step out the door. 'Oh, you haven't, have you?' she said, as she bent down to sniff the bottom of the child already strapped into her buggy. With the culprit identified, she sighed loudly, unclipped the straps, and scooped Bella into her arms.

Ten minutes later, with Bella now dressed in her second outfit of the day, Jessica was standing by the front door again, mentally ticking off things in her head.

Nappies? Check.

Wipes? Check.

Drinking cup? Check.

Snack?

'Crap!' she said out loud, as she ran into the kitchen to cut some grapes. But spotting a stash of mini raisin boxes, she paused.

'Oh, sod it,' she thought, as she grabbed a box and threw it into her bag instead.

Bella's music class started at 10 a.m., and Jessica found herself walking at double her usual pace, trying to make sure she made it in time. Bella looked sleepy (not surprising, given how awake she'd been at 3 a.m. that morning) and Jessica didn't want her to nod off just as they were arriving. Plus, getting there a few minutes early meant she could have a quick chat with the girls before the class began – and that was the bit she enjoyed the most.

Because those girls – Mel, Deena, and Henny (and their children, Lara, Finley, and Tallulah) – had been keeping Jessica sane since she'd first rocked up to this class when Bella was six months old.

Jessica was the first of her friends to get married and have children, and she'd been surprised at how quickly she'd slipped off everyone's radar. The first few months of motherhood had been lonely without friends by her side, but she accepted that their lives were busy too. Amongst her school friends, Callie had moved to Southampton for work, Nicola had moved in with her boyfriend and now had a long commute to the school she taught at, and Frankie had been doing her best to squeeze in auditions between the shifts she worked as a waitress. There really wasn't much time left for baby cuddles. And whilst Jessica had stayed in touch with some of her university friends since they'd graduated, most were still based in the North, which meant that meet-ups were sporadic even before she became a mother.

She knew she needed to get out the house and meet people, but it hadn't been easy walking into a church hall full of strangers back in the autumn after Bella was born. And she'd thanked her lucky stars that she found the courage ever since.

Today, however, there was no hesitation.

'Oh look, it's the mummy blogger!' a voice called out, as she pushed Bella's buggy inside the wide double doors and stepped inside.

Jessica rolled her eyes and smiled, parking the buggy at the side of the hall and unclipping Bella. And as she toddled off to join the other children in a playhouse behind her, Jessica slipped off her ballet pumps and walked towards the colourful mats in the centre of the hall to sit down with her friends.

'So,' Mel said, 'how does it feel?'

'What? You mean, the blog?' Jessica asked, feeling her cheeks flush.

'Of course!' Mel replied. 'Or do you have another exciting hobby you forgot to share with us?'

Jessica laughed. 'Honestly? Well, I'm a bit embarrassed you're all reading it, but…'

'It's bloody good, babe!' Henny cut in, smiling widely. Mel and Deena nodded along, until the four of them turned to the sound of wailing inside the playhouse.

'Oh God, is it one of ours?' Jessica asked, as they started to get to their feet.

'Don't worry, it's mine!' a mum on the other side of the room shouted in their direction as she made her way over. 'We're having a problem with sharing at the moment!'

The girls all smiled with sympathy, secretly relieved it wasn't their turn - and back on the mats, the conversation resumed.

'Well, I loved it, girl,' Deena said, re-clipping her fringe out of her eyes as she spoke. 'Are you going to write all of them as letters to Bella? I really like it. I feel like I'm getting a glimpse into something private. It feels kind of nosy.'

'Ooh, that's right,' Henny said, nodding. 'That's exactly how I feel too!'

'I think that's why it works so well,' Mel chipped in. 'I didn't know that's how you met Chris, by the way. I mean, I knew the tall, dark stranger bowled you over the second you set eyes on him, but I didn't realise you'd soaked his crotch in cheap white wine!'

'Oi, what makes you think it was cheap?' Jessica asked, raising her eyebrows and laughing. 'The worst bit was that I grabbed a towel on the bar next to us and tried repeatedly to mop it up myself...'

As Jessica put her head in her hands at the memory, Mel, Deena, and Henny laughed loudly.

'But thanks girls, I really appreciate your support on the blogging thing,' Jess continued, trying to compose herself. 'It'll probably end up being just you lot and my family reading it, but that's OK. I'll keep going anyway.'

'Well, no,' Henny said. 'I clicked onto the social media page before I left home and you've got loads of followers already.'

Jessica felt herself blushing. 'Thanks, Hen, but I had a look earlier and it's only my friends and family. Everyone is just being supportive as it's early days, but that's fine...'

'My neighbour Cathy has followed it. You don't know her, do you?' Deena cut in.

'No,' Jessica replied quickly, looking up. 'Well I haven't looked since first thing this morning, but I had 81 followers and I'm sure...'

'81?' Henny interrupted, laughing. 'No way, babe! It was over 200 when I left the house.'

Jessica could feel her jaw drop. 'No,' she eventually managed to mutter. 'Your phone must be doing funny things. Hang on, I'll check...'

She stood up to make her way to her bag to find her phone but was stopped in her tracks by a voice at the back of the hall. 'RIGHT LADIES AND BABIES! SHALL WE START? WHO'S READY TO HAVE SOME FUN?' And with that, she turned back, scooped Bella up from beside the playhouse, and sat back down with her friends.

The class passed slowly for Jessica that morning – though her body was present, dancing around to tribal music and drumming as per the day's theme, her mind was somewhere else entirely. *How was it possible that she could have so many followers already?*

When the class finally came to an end and Bella was safely strapped in her buggy and happily munching away on her box of raisins, Jessica grabbed her phone and clicked her way quickly onto her page stats to have a look.

266 followers.

'Holy shit!' she said out loud, searching for the girls in the crowd of mummies, toddlers, and buggies leaving the hall.

Henny appeared out of the crowd, with Tallulah struggling under her arm. 'You OK?' she asked, looking concerned.

'Yep sorry,' Jess replied, bending down to pick up a couple of stray raisins on the floor. 'It's my social media page,' she said, gesturing to her phone. 'I mean, who are these people? And why do they want to read my blog?'

Just like every Tuesday morning, the four friends strolled over to Mel's house after class to chat, drink coffee, and let the toddlers play. It was only a five-minute walk from the church hall, and they made their way two abreast on the pavement, with Jessica, Henny and Mel pushing buggies and Deena carrying Finley in a carrier on her back.

Deena was the youngest of the group at twenty-seven years old. Originally from Sri Lanka, she had arrived in London as a teen and now lived with her partner Ian and their son Finley on the outskirts of Greenwich, managing an Italian restaurant in the evenings. Today she was wearing her dark fringe pinned back, a floaty maxi dress in swirls of purple, and a black leather jacket.

Then there was Henny; thirty-five years old, blonde, bubbly, originally from Cardiff. By chance, she lived on the road behind Jessica with her children, Thomas and Tallulah, and her husband Dan. A stay-at-home mum, Henny lived in leggings, long tops, and cardigans – all styled with flip-flops and a braid in her hair.

Mel was the eldest of the group, in her early forties with shoulder-length dark hair. Naturally slim, she was wearing a grey jersey T-shirt, skinny jeans, neon pink lipstick, and metallic sandals showing off her perfectly pedicured toes. A lawyer by trade, she'd lived in this part of London her entire life, but had only called her beautiful, three-storey house 'home' since she'd married Steven a few years beforehand.

And the house really was beautiful. As they pushed their buggies through the front gate and towards the front door, Jessica looked up and admired the white climbing roses across the façade. At three stories high, the house was big too – especially when it was usually just Mel and Lara filling it, given the long hours Steven worked in the city.

'Everyone for coffee?' Mel asked, as she released Lara from her buggy in the hallway and watched her toddle into the lounge.

'Is the Pope Catholic?' Deena replied, unclipping Finley from her back.

'On it,' Mel laughed, as she strolled into the kitchen.

One by one, the girls followed. As Mel started scooping, pouring, and plunging to make coffee in a large rose-gold cafetière, the four friends chatted away. There was a large bright breakfast room to their right, complete with a giant wooden table and eight modern white chairs around it. Behind it, a huge mirror with a gold frame covered the entire wall. To their left was the open-plan kitchen, decorated in muted hues of pale wood and turquoise blue, right down to the blue leather radio that was quietly playing Capital FM. A large window ran the length of both rooms, looking straight out at the garden, which looked deliberately and beautifully wild.

'So let's get this straight,' Deena said, as Mel handed her a mug of coffee. 'There are four of us here and we don't have a single baby wipe between us?'

'I made sure I had a pack in my bag,' Jessica explained. 'I thought there was a few left, but it turns out that it's empty.'

'I have a supermarket delivery coming this afternoon. I'm waiting for that!' Mel replied.

'But what if Lara shits between now and then?' Deena asked, raising her eyebrows.

'Well, I guess I'm buggered, aren't I…' Mel replied dryly. 'Henny, you having sugar in your coffee today or not?'

'No thanks, babe. I'm on a diet again. I know it's boring,' Henny said. 'I always forget wipes. I just assume you girls will have them with you.'

'Well, I *did* remember,' Deena said. 'But I lent them to one of the ladies at class this morning and she never gave them back…'

'What a bitch!' Mel replied in a mock horrified tone, prompting laughter from the other three.

'Right, what can we do?' Henny asked. 'Is it definitely not a flusher?'

'Ew Hen, that's vile,' Deena replied. 'And after a quick peek, the answer is very definitely no.'

'Cleaning wipes?' Mel asked, pointing to a pack of kitchen wipes by the sink. 'Just spare me a couple as I need to give the surfaces a good bleach later…'

'Great suggestion,' Deena said, rolling her eyes.

'You got any kitchen roll, Mel?' Jessica asked.

'Of course,' she replied, reaching for the roll behind her.

'Right, I'll try and create something close to wipes, Deena. You go and get Finley ready.'

And that's pretty much how these mornings went. Chat about poo, and projectile vomit, and sleepless nights, and Googling strange rashes and symptoms (nearly always coming to the conclusion that it was 'a growth spurt' or 'teething'), interspersed with strong coffee, moans about husbands and partners getting home late from work, and reminiscing about the old days before they had kids. And while they chatted, the babies toddled around, dropped trails of raisins, and had the odd fight over who was the rightful owner of the prized orange building block which, for some reason, was so much better than the identical one in red.

Today, however, Jessica's blog was a point of conversation, too. And once Finley was cleaned up, the girls gathered back in the kitchen.

'Your page has nearly 300 followers, babe!' Henny said, pointing to her phone.

'Really?' Jessica asked, sitting back down at the breakfast bar. She shook her head and stared out to the garden for a moment, deep in thought. 'This is crazy. What's going on?'

'Do you think somebody shared it?' Mel replied.

'They must've done… I'll investigate when I get home and see if I can work it out. I'm still learning with the social media stuff, but hopefully I can find out who it was.'

'300 followers is pretty impressive girl,' Deena added. 'My mate Finty has been blogging about food and wine for years and I still don't think she has that many people following her.'

'Really?' Jessica replied. 'I don't know… I didn't expect anyone to read it…'

'I'll be honest,' Mel said. 'I don't really know much about blogging. How many followers do the biggest bloggers get?'

'Some of them have hundreds of thousands,' Jessica said. 'I imagine they make a fair bit of money, too.'

'But how does that work?' Mel asked. 'I mean, who pays them?'

'They team up with companies and advertise their products,' Jessica replied. 'It might be nappies one minute, bubble bath the next, then a hotel that's really good for families. It changes all the time. Sometimes they do a whole blog post and sometimes they just post a picture on their social media. I'm sure it's way more complicated than that, but all the bloggers I follow seem to be doing adverts now…'

'Is that what you want to do, babe?' Henny asked, lifting Tallulah onto her lap.

'Oh, I don't know… I guess it'd be nice to earn a bit of money eventually, but I just want to share my letters to Bella for now,' Jessica replied, leaning over to pick a raisin out of Tallulah's white-blonde hair.

'I bet it doesn't take long,' Deena said. 'I mean, if it carries on at this rate… When will we be able to read the next letter?'

'I'm hoping to start typing it up when Bella sleeps at lunchtime. If she bloody sleeps, that is...'

'On that note,' Henny said, 'I'm going to get this one home, as she's yawning. Do you want to walk together, Jess?'

'I probably will, actually,' Jessica replied. 'I don't want Bella to fall asleep in the buggy or I'll miss out on naptime altogether. When are we next seeing each other, girls?'

'Greenwich Park tomorrow?' Mel suggested. 'Henny and I were just starting to make a plan...'

'Oh crap, I can't,' Jessica cut in. 'I'm seeing my sister.'

'How is she?' Henny asked.

'Well, she's leaving the house again, which is a big step.'

'It's great she's heading out,' Henny said. 'I mean, wow, I can't even imagine...'

'Poor, Fran. Jesus. She's had a shit time,' Mel said, shaking her head. 'Don't worry, we can do another day. Does Friday work for everyone?'

One by one, the girls nodded.

'It's a date,' Jessica said, as both she and Henny kissed their friends on the cheek and grabbed their bags.

'Yep, see you then,' Mel replied.

'Bye girls, see you Friday!' Deena called after them as they started pushing the girls down the road. 'And for fuck's sake, can everybody try and remember baby wipes?'

3

Followers – 382

Dear Bella,

I wasn't ready for you.

I was thirty-five weeks and five days pregnant when I walked away from my desk for the last time, clutching a hamper of pink baby clothes and a giant bunch of roses. I glanced back at that seat, that computer, and that window one last time – and then walked away. Your daddy met me right outside the office door, taking the hamper from my arms and planting a giant kiss on my lips. He didn't need to say anything; he just needed to be with me, as I walked away from the only adult life I really knew. The team had wanted to take me out that evening in the village for a bite to eat ('The Last Supper', it had been coined for comedic value) but I wasn't feeling well enough to do it. I was exhausted, my back was hurting, and I felt far more emotional about leaving than I had expected. So, we called it off and a rushed celebration in the office was organised instead, complete with so many bad jokes that I actually did wee myself a couple of times. And, after gathering up my things, walking out of that office, and climbing into a taxi, I sobbed into your daddy's chest as we wound our way towards home.

I spent that night lying lazily on the sofa, but I couldn't shrug the back pain. At about 10 p.m., I stood up awkwardly and tried to breathe heavily through a fresh wave of pain. And it was then that we both realised that something wasn't right. 'Jess, you're in labour!' Daddy suddenly blurted out – and I didn't have the energy to reply, let alone disagree.

The rest passed in a blur. We still didn't have a car (that was on the 'to-do' list for the next few weeks), so my parents rushed to pick us up in the Volvo – a twenty-minute journey, which apparently takes half that when the driver is being shouted at hysterically by his terrified wife. Minutes after that car screeched to a halt, at the hospital, I remember being whizzed through the corridors, faces coming into view and then out again. I remember panic in the room as they realised how quickly it was all happening. I remember pain like I've never felt before, softened occasionally with a desperate gasp of gas. I remember pushing. I remember burning. I remember your daddy beaming at me proudly with tears welling in his eyes as he watched things happen down the business end – quickly followed by a big gush of water and an angry cry. I remember being handed a warm, slippery baby and pulling her tightly to my chest. And I remember gazing down at your wrinkled face and puckered lips as you slept there so peacefully – and wondering if it had all been a dream.

No, I wasn't ready for you, Bella – and it took a few days to truly believe you were mine. You were little and kind of yellow and they didn't want us to go home straight away. So I lay in that hospital bed for a few days, feeling shell-shocked, nauseous, and delirious with tiredness, as family and friends stood above my bed cooing, smiling and handing me envelopes marked 'Baby Girl' because we still couldn't think of a name.

My bump had disappeared before I even had a chance to take a last picture – and in its place, lay an empty, jelly-like paunch. I remember touching it occasionally and feeling revolted. And I remember that when you latched onto my nipple in the early days, which sent pain searing through my body, that jelly-like paunch suddenly decided to join in the pain party too, cramping so tightly that I yelled out, 'WHERE'S THE BLOODY GAS NOW?' to a midwife who stood by the bed with her hands on one of my tits.

And then there were the bodily fluids. Nobody tells you about that at your baby shower, do they? Nobody tells you that you'll need to wear nappies, or that your nipples will dribble down your stomach when you take off your bra to climb into the shower, or that you'll wake up in the night drenched head to toe in sweat, wondering if you've somehow caught a tropical disease. Nobody tells you any of that. And it was a shock.

Oh, Bella; it wasn't easy. But we made it. Two days after you screamed so angrily when you were first plonked on my chest, we were on our way home in Grandad's Volvo (and this time, he drove at about five miles per hour).

No, I wasn't ready for you, Bella – but suddenly you were mine.

And life was never going to be the same again.

Love from Mummy x

Chris was late home. Jessica had been picking up her phone every few minutes to check for messages, getting more and more irritated by his lateness. He'd missed Bella's bedtime by a long way – and having promised to pick up a takeaway for dinner on his return, her tummy was growling in solidarity too.

She wished she could be more relaxed about the nights he was late home from work, but she found it hard. Knowing that he would be walking through the door close to Bella's bedtime kept her going on even the hardest afternoons – and that afternoon had been particularly hard. Bella had woken up from her nap after only twenty-three minutes and had taken over an hour to stop screaming with tiredness. When she finally came around from her groggy anger, Jessica had found the hours, the minutes, and the seconds dragging past depressingly slowly. It didn't help that it was throwing it down with rain outside. She really didn't have the energy to waterproof Bella from head to toe (or herself, for that matter). So, when a message pinged through from Chris that said he wasn't going to make it home for Bella's bedtime, she felt like throwing the phone across the room.

She hadn't expected to turn into *that* wife – but here she was, only a couple of years into marriage, filled with rage that her husband was late home from work. Especially when she had half-expected him to come swinging through the door with a bottle of champagne at lunchtime when she'd shared the news of her amazing new blog following – after all, he'd encouraged her to start this blog from the beginning! A half-hearted: 'That's great honey! Sorry, will be late tonight. I'll get dinner on my way' was not only frustrating on the parenting front, but massively underwhelming on the husband front, too.

But there was no point wasting precious childfree time brooding – so once she had got Bella to sleep and successfully commando crawled out of the bedroom, she had made herself comfortable on the sofa, pulled a blanket over her knees, and opened her laptop. Clicking straight through to social media to check on the latest stats, she couldn't resist re-reading the comments underneath that morning's post.

Laura Cunningham: I've just discovered your blog and you have another follower! I can't wait to read the next one!

Louise Henry: I found out I was pregnant on my wedding day too! We should start a club! Great post. Looking forward to more

Elena Smith: I never usually read blogs, let alone comment on them – but your post really resonated with me. Thank you for writing it.

Georgina Wright-Cooper: I love this. In fact, you just made me cry. Finding out I was pregnant with my little boy was one of the best days of my life and you took me straight back!

Coming to the end, she replied to each reader to thank them for taking the time to comment (she didn't know if that was blogging etiquette, but it seemed the polite thing to do). In all the time she'd spent wondering whether anybody would actually read her blog, it hadn't occurred to her that they may comment too. And if she was honest, it gave her a buzz to read them.

When she was done with social media, she moved onto finding a photograph to illustrate her next letter. Enjoying the excuse to scroll through pictures of the night Bella was born, she quickly settled on a photo taken just minutes after she had been handed to her by the midwife. Jessica was lying in her hospital bed, with a tiny Bella curled sleepily on her chest.

Before she saved it to her desktop and uploaded it to the post, Jessica paused for a moment to study the photograph. Her hair was stuck to her face, her skin was blushed red, and her hospital gown was less than flattering – but her smile and tear-filled eyes said it all. It seemed such a long time ago that she had been in that hospital bed, studying those tiny fingers and breathing in that milky-sweet newborn scent.

Deep in thought, she jumped when the front door banged open and Chris appeared with a soggy paper bag stashed under his arm, drenched from the rain. It was 8.27 p.m. and despite wishing she had the strength to grit her teeth and smile, she just couldn't hide her anger.

'Finally!' she blurted out, shutting her laptop with a snap.

'Sorry, honey,' he said, walking towards her to kiss her.

But as he leant down, Jessica turned her head. 'Oh, fuck off, Chris – as if I want to kiss you!'

He looked stunned. 'What's wrong? Jesus, what have I done *now*?'

'It's 8.30 p.m. Chris, and I'm starving,' Jessica replied. Even as the words came out of her mouth, she knew they sounded ridiculous, but she couldn't stop herself. She was too angry. 'Don't offer to get a takeaway if you can't manage to get home at a decent hour. I could have cooked a bloody full roast dinner by now if I'd known! Seriously, why can't you ever get back in time to see Bella? What is your problem?'

Chris sighed. 'You want to do this now?'

'Yes, I want to do this now!' Jessica spat back at him in a loud whisper, desperate to scream, but equally desperate not to wake up her daughter. 'I'm sick of it! I'm sick of putting Bella to bed without a cuddle from her daddy! I'm sick of waiting on this sofa for you! I'm sick of the messages telling me you're going to be late again! I'm sick of the excuses!'

'You're sick of it?' Chris shook his head. 'What about me, Jess? Do you ever think about me? Do you ever wonder what it feels like to rush home to see my daughter and miss her by a matter of minutes? Do you know what that feels like to go days without seeing her? It's shit! Do you think I care less about her, because I have to go out and work every day? Do you not think I'm jealous of the time you two get together?'

Jessica flinched, but refused to look away.

'I can't win, can I? If I try to get home early, I end up waking her up. If I stay a bit late at work because my boss emails me at 5 p.m. and tells me he needs to chat over a pint, I am in trouble too. What am I supposed to do, Jess? Tell me! What the fuck am I supposed to do?'

'You had a pint?' she asked, shaking her head in disbelief.

'That's the only thing you pick up on?' Chris asked, still looking straight at her. 'Why does it always have to be about you, Jess? It's always about you!'

'Well, funnily enough, Chris,' Jessica said, grabbing the takeaway bag from under his arm and taking a step towards the kitchen, 'it mainly *is* about me, yes. Because I'm the one that's sleep deprived, I'm the one that's running around after a toddler all day, I'm the one that's feeding her, and bathing her, and entertaining her! I'm the one that never gets to go for a drink after work any more! So yes Chris, it is always about me! And that is the problem! I'm exhausted!'

'SO AM I!' Chris shouted back, so loudly that they both turned to look at the baby monitor. And when the hum of the white noise continued undisturbed, he added quietly: 'I'm exhausted too, Jess! Please start realising that!'

He sighed and turned towards the stairs to change out of his wet clothes. As Jessica unpacked containers from the soggy brown bag onto the work surface in the kitchen, tears pooled in her eyes.

The next morning, the rain had finally cleared, and as Jessica opened the doors to the garden, she paused for a moment to feel the sunshine on her skin. She didn't want to be stuck inside all day, so hastily sent a message to her sister to ask her to meet at Greenwich Park, rather than head to her house as planned. Fran typed back within seconds:

No probs, 10 a.m.? Usual place?

Jessica quickly replied:

Perfect, see you there.

She stashed a picnic blanket under her buggy, did a quick mental checklist that she had everything she needed in her bag (nearly forgetting a spare nappy, which could have seriously challenged her mothering skills later on that morning), and was out of the door ahead of schedule.

Jessica couldn't help feeling cheerful as she strolled

down their street. With her feet in her favourite flip-flops, the sound of birdsong in the trees, and sunlight dappling the pavements, she felt far happier and more optimistic than she had the night before.

It was the kind of weather where she knew she would be constantly pulling Bella's cardigan on and off as the sun weaved in and out the clouds, so she had thrown several spare layers under the buggy to keep them both warm. She had a thermos of coffee in her bag to drink as she chatted to her sister. She'd even remembered Bella's doll pram for her to push down the paths, which she'd collapsed and stashed under the big one. And, after a brisk fifteen-minute walk in the sunshine, she walked through the heavy wrought iron gates of the park a full five minutes ahead of schedule. She wasn't going to lie; she felt like Super Mum.

The park was busy for a Wednesday morning. Tourists milled around, pointing up at the Greenwich Observatory above them and then walking like a line of ants in single file up the hill to reach it. Students played frisbee on the lawn, yelling to each other as it flew through the air and they lunged to catch it. Dogs bounded off their leads after balls, then returned to their owners with tails wagging and tongues lolling. Passenger planes glided silently through the clouds above their heads on their way in and out of London.

Jessica always found the energy of the park a tonic for the mind. In fact, this park had been a place of solace in the early days of being a mother. Long before the days of making mummy friends, she had often felt so lonely and isolated at home – but as soon as she stepped through the gates of this bustling part of South East London, she felt like herself again. She would climb the path to the top of the hill until Bella dropped off into a content sleep, then sit on a bench and sip a thermos of coffee as she watched life carry on below her. She always left that park feeling more buoyant, reassured that the world hadn't stopped turning on the day she'd given birth.

Jessica usually met her sister by the big gates on the south side of the park, as Fran liked to grab a coffee in her favourite café before she met them. Bella was happy in her buggy for the moment, but Jessica knew she had very little time before she would be struggling to escape, so she had her fingers firmly crossed that her auntie would arrive on time for once. As they strolled down the path, past the pale grey façade of the Naval College on her right and the park on her left, she quickly realised her luck was in as she spotted her sister leaning against the gate drinking her coffee.

Fran was wearing her usual skinny jeans, black leather jacket, and pretty gold sandals. At forty-one, she was slim and stylish and easily looked fifteen years younger.

But as soon as she spotted Fran, Jessica noticed her sister wasn't alone. Her parents were beside her, deep in conversation as they gesticulated at a tree in the distance. 'Oh, bloody hell, they're all here today,' she muttered under her breath, just as Bella clocked her family ahead of her and squealed in appreciation.

Whilst Jessica loved her parents dearly, she couldn't help feeling disappointed they'd decided to gatecrash. Fran found it hard to talk openly when her parents were in earshot and Jessica had been looking forward to a good catch-up as they watched Bella play.

It wasn't long before a shrieking Bella had alerted everyone within a ten-mile radius that they were approaching and right on cue, the three family members at the gate turned in their direction. Her parents smiled widely as they strode towards their grandaughter, giving Fran the opportunity to silently mouth 'Sorry!' as she gestured to her parents behind their backs with laughing eyes. As they met, she pulled Jessica into a big hug and whispered in her ear: 'They insisted on coming. Sorry! It's the blog – be warned! They're obsessed!'

'Here she is!' her mother said loudly, standing up and beaming at Jessica broadly. 'Our family blogger!' Jessica could feel herself blushing, as her mother glanced around to see if anyone was listening (which no doubt she was hoping was the case). A couple of Japanese tourists shuffled in their shoes uncomfortably as they felt her eyes on them, but the coast was otherwise clear.

'Hi Mum,' Jess replied. 'No need to make a fuss. It's just a little blog!'

'A little blog!' her mother bellowed back proudly. 'I don't think so darling! You have hundreds of followers! That's not little darling! You are a superstar!'

Her dad, generally quieter than his larger-than-life wife but equally enthusiastic, stood alongside her, smiling in agreement. 'Come here,' he said as he hugged her. 'We're very proud, Jessica! Very proud indeed!'

Embarrassed, Jessica diverted attention back to her daughter by bending down to unclip and release her from the buggy. Bella toddled down the path with impressive speed, with Granny chasing her closely behind. And as Grandad strode off after them, Jessica finally had the time to turn to her sister.

'How are you, Franny?' Jessica asked, searching Fran's face for clues.

'Oh, you know…' Fran said, looking down at her coffee in its black quilted takeaway cup. 'Life is a bit shit, but I'm OK. Don't need to worry about me.'

Jessica sighed. She reached into her bag for her thermos, unscrewed the lid, and took her first sip. The coffee was still scorching hot and shocked her throat as it slid down, but she felt comforted by a moment of distraction.

'Of course, I am going to worry about you,' she replied. 'I always worry about you!'

Fran turned to her sister and smiled, linking arms as they strode along the path. They walked silently for a few minutes, before it became obvious that Bella was giving her grandparents the run around. Jessica stopped and reached down to grab her little buggy, opening it with a quick flick of the wrist. She ran it over to her parents, calling her daughter's name to try and distract her from another escape attempt.

The sun had disappeared completely now, and as Jessica walked back to her sister, she noticed her teeth were chattering. *She needs to eat more,* she thought to herself, making a mental note to cook a casserole that evening and get Chris to drop it round to her parents.

'Do you want to chat about Cornwall?' Jessica asked, turning to look at her sister.

Fran exhaled loudly. 'What do you want to know?'

'You don't have to talk about it if you aren't ready, Franny,' Jess said, turning back to watch their dad chasing Bella across the grass.

'It was horrible. I mean, fucking horrible,' Fran replied, staring ahead. 'But I'm pleased I didn't take Freddie with me. He would've hated it. It was much better for him to stay at home with his grandparents.'

'I think you're right,' Jessica replied. 'He was worried about you though. We hung out a lot that week. We looked after him, don't worry.'

'He was probably even more worried about me when I got back and didn't get out of bed for a week. Shit. I feel like a terrible mother,' Fran said, taking a sip of her coffee and turning to smile sadly at her sister.

'He knows how strong you are! And you've got each other! You'll both be OK,' Jessica said, putting her arm around her sister.

'We've got no bloody choice, have we?' Fran replied, resting her head on Jessica's shoulder.

And for a while, they stayed like that. Watching Bella running, their parents laughing loudly as they chased her on the grass, and tourists dodging around them as they walked on the path. As the sun reappeared, warming them up for a moment, Fran sighed and sat up straight, ready to take on the world again.

'So, tell me about your blog, Jessy,' Fran said, squinting at her sister.

'Oh no, don't be silly, we don't have to talk about that!' Jessica replied.

'I *want* to talk about that Jess!'

'Well, what do you want to know? I've been writing letters to Bella since she was born – in that notebook you bought me before we got married actually – and starting a blog seemed like the perfect way to share them with other people. Chris thought it was a good idea too, so it was decided.'

'I had a feeling you'd do something amazing with that notebook,' Fran replied, smiling. 'How's it going at home? Is he getting home any earlier?'

Jessica laughed dryly. 'No, not really. We had another big argument last night. We never used to row like this, Fran. And half of me hates myself for it, because I know deep down that he doesn't really get a choice when he leaves work in the evening, but the other half just doesn't understand why he doesn't make more of an effort. Bella goes days without even seeing him. That can't be normal, can it?'

Fran sighed and took a sip of her coffee. 'I'm pretty sure there are thousands of parents having exactly the same argument every single night. Babies do that to you. It's not easy. And yes, I do think it's pretty normal for a lot of babies not to see their dads during the week.'

'Do you think?' Jessica asked, turning to look at her sister.

'Yes, when do you think Dad got home to us every night? He worked afternoons and evenings down on the railway – and Mum just had to get on with it. I remember you being a newborn, don't forget!' Fran said, winking at Jess.

'Well, that makes me feel a bit better I guess,' Jessica replied. 'But I still wish he got home for Bella's bedtime every now and again...'

'I'm not saying he's a saint, Jessy. In my opinion, men rarely are...'

'He went for a bloody pint after work last night! Can you believe that?' Jessica snapped back.

'So what? He isn't allowed to have friends now?' Fran asked, smiling.

'I didn't mean that... It wasn't even his friend, it was his boss, but it's just frustrating when he's promised to be home and I'm sat there waiting for him,' Jessica replied, her eyes to the ground.

'I know, I remember it well! It's bloody hard work! But that's maybe why this blog is a really good idea, because then you have something else going on too. Maybe even a career, if it goes well,' Fran said.

'I don't know whether I'll be successful enough to turn it into a career, but I'm enjoying it,' Jessica replied, sipping the dregs of her coffee.

'You should send a message to Tiggy. Do you remember her?' Fran asked.

'Tiggy from our street in Mottingham?' Jessica asked.

Fran nodded. 'Yep, she's Tiggy Blenheim now, but she was Tiggy Lewis back then.'

'Yes I remember,' replied Jessica. 'They only lived a few doors down, didn't they? Her brother caught the same bus as me every morning for years after you both left school and moved on. Do you still see her?'

'No, she moved away years ago. But I still see her parents

every now and again,' Fran said. 'Have you seen her blog?'

'No,' Jessica replied quickly. 'What's it called?'

'I don't read it,' Fran replied. 'Something like "Motherhood and Tiggy"?'

'"Tiggy Does Motherhood?"' Jessica snapped back, her eyes wide open in surprise. 'Is that *her* blog?'

Fran shrugged. 'That sounds right. You've seen it then?'

'Yes!' Jessica replied. 'I haven't followed it that closely, as her children are a bit older, but I've seen a few posts. I had no idea that it was the same Tiggy that lived on our road! Wow, she's changed!'

'Yep, a completely different person to the girl I used to hang out with… I think she's got about seventeen children now!' Fran replied, laughing. 'But seriously, I think she's been quite successful with her blogging and she might give you some tips.'

'Do you think she'd even remember me, though? I mean, I was quite a lot younger than you both…' Jessica replied, biting her fingernails.

'Jess! She'll probably remember the day you were born! We were always together, that gang on the street. She even babysat for you a few times when I was away at college. Do you remember that?' Fran asked, turning to her sister.

'Shit yes…' Jessica said, shaking her head. 'I can't believe I hadn't worked out that it was the same girl.'

'Send her a quick message,' Fran replied, smiling. 'I'm sure she'll be happy to help you.'

'I will, thanks Franny,' Jessica said warmly. 'Now come on, let's go play with your niece'.

4

Followers – 824

Dear Bella,

I had time for lots of reading when I was pregnant. I read mainly in the evenings, cuddled under blankets on the sofa, popping ice cubes in my mouth and crunching as I turned the pages. I read books cover-to-cover, I scrolled websites, I flicked through magazines, and I devoured the information leaflets handed to me by the midwife. I genuinely believed that the more I read, the better a mother I'd be when you arrived.

When it came to your birth, everything I read told me that you'd be handed over to me and I'd feel a deep, over-whelming and very instant love. I imagined a thunderclap and flash of lightning in the hospital room, followed by a warmth spreading quickly from the tips of my toes to the top of my head. My heart would instantly swell to double its usual size, and I'd mutter things like 'I've never felt a love like this before! It's incredible!' to anybody who happened to be in earshot. I looked forward to feeling it; this amazing kind of love. It's what got me through those last achey, heavy days.

But do you know what Bella? It doesn't happen like that. At least, it didn't for me. I knew you were mine and I needed you close to me from the beginning, but I didn't experience the sudden, gushing, overwhelming, toe-warming love that everyone talks about. Maybe it was because you were early and I wasn't ready, or maybe it was because I was so tired and I was struggling to remember my own name, or maybe it was because I was in so much pain from those stitches that I was preoccupied trying to imagine the relief of plunging my nether regions into an ice bath. I don't know, Bella – but in the days and weeks that followed your speedy birth, I worried about it.

'Does it make me a bad mother?' I mused, as I pressed the button on the coffee machine and inhaled a whiff of caffeine, watching it stream into the mug.

'Is everybody else just lying about it? Or does this epiphany really happen?' I thought to myself, as I stood in the shower in the morning, barely noticing the milk trickling down my tummy.

'Maybe it did happen, but I'd had too much gas to notice,' I wondered, as I sat feeding you in the darkness at 3 a.m., urging you to go back to sleep.

The truth is, Bella, that those first few weeks at home were hard. I found it really difficult to breastfeed, recoiling in pain each time that you latched on. I cried a lot of big, ploppy, hormonal tears, feeling shell-shocked by the tiredness. I quickly realised that none of those books, or magazines, or leaflets, or websites could prepare me for the whirlwind of having a newborn. One day, while trying to find a chapter on the colour of newborn poo to determine whether we should be worried, I flung one of those books so hard against the wall in a fit of rage that a handful of pages detached from the cover and slowly danced to the floor in a messy heap.

But, as the days ticked on, the fog started to lift. I still sobbed occasionally but my tears weren't so big and ploppy. I still felt deliriously tired but it was nothing a few coffees couldn't fix. I still found it all incredibly overwhelming (especially when Daddy went back to work just a week in), but I started to understand your cries, your habits, and your routine. I was getting to know you, Bella; a little more every single day.

But the moment I realised things had really changed was when Granny and Grandad suggested they took you for a walk around the streets on a sunny morning, so I could have some time to myself. I agreed hastily, thinking I'd hop into the shower, have time to apply some make-up for the first time in weeks, and maybe even have a few spare minutes to enjoy a hot drink before they returned. But I did all that, and they still weren't back. Panic started to bubble in my tummy, as time slowly ticked on. Various natural disasters, freak accidents, and kidnap attempts flashed through my mind. Messages were delivered to their phones, but not read. And when I decided enough was enough and picked up the phone to call them, hearing the sound of their forgotten phones ringing in the hallway was pure torture. So when they finally delivered you home (an hour and thirty-seven minutes after they'd stepped out the door), I ran to you, pulled you out of your basket, and took the deepest breath of your milky scent in relief.

And that's when I knew Bella.

That is the moment I knew.

I loved you.

Even though I hadn't experienced fireworks, or lightning strikes, or a symphony orchestra breaking into tune at the very moment of your birth.

I loved you.

I really did.

And from that moment in the hallway, we never looked back.

Love from Mummy x

As Jessica sat at the dining table, light streamed through the living room window. Her fingers were dancing on the keys of her laptop, copying the words of her letter word for word.

She hadn't published a letter for a few weeks. The gap had been intentional at first, because she didn't want to post too quickly and run out of letters, but with the pain of new teeth burrowing through Bella's gums rocking her world (and in turn, rocking Jessica's with a fresh wave of sleep deprivation), she simply hadn't had the time to focus on the blog. But when Chris had turned to her the night before and asked: 'You are going to keep going with the blog, aren't you? It's too good to stop now!' she had the incentive she needed to sit down, open her notebook, and start typing.

As she tapped, she could hear Bella's breathing through the monitor propped on the table next to her, heavy and sleepy. Her coffee mug sat next to it, the dregs at the bottom now cold. The crumbs of a hastily eaten sandwich lay on a plate by its side.

Jessica had chosen a photograph of Bella sleeping in her basket to illustrate this letter. It was one of her favourites from the early days at home, and after pausing to admire it for a second, she cropped it to the right size, pressed 'ADD MEDIA', and uploaded it to the top left corner. The words wrapped around it neatly, and after admiring her work for a second, she pressed 'PUBLISH POST'.

Right on cue, the monitor flashed red and within seconds, a call of 'MAMAMAMAMA!' followed loudly. Jessica carried her mug and plate into the kitchen, dumped them in the kitchen sink with a loud clunk, and started climbing the stairs.

It was now the middle of July and the weather was disappointingly overcast, so she had made a plan to head to Henny's house that afternoon to keep the little ones busy. After pulling an angry, sweaty-haired Bella from her cot, making a start on packing her bag, and dabbing a bit of concealer under her eyes to try and hide the fact they had all been awake since 5 a.m., she picked up her phone to check whether Henny was ready for them.

Hey, Hen, let me know when Tallulah is awake and we'll head over xx

But as she pressed to send it, another message flashed onto the screen.

Fran: Hi Jessy, if I noticed something bad about the blog, would you want me to tell you?

She tapped back quickly.

Yes of course. What is it?

She held her breath as she waited for a reply. When a message popped up, she jumped.

Henny: Hi babe, I'll wake her in 10 minutes and send you a message. See you soon xx

Jessica swiped away the message to wait for a reply from Fran, her foot tapping impatiently on the floor. Seconds later, it arrived.

Fran: Check the comments under the new letter you just put up! Do you know her? What a bitch!

Glancing quickly in Bella's direction to check she wasn't up to trouble (which she wasn't, if pulling every shoe off the rack in the hallway didn't count as trouble), Jessica made a beeline to the dining room table and opened her laptop. Clicking straight onto her social media, she found the link she'd just posted.

'Holy shit,' she said out loud, noticing there were already 163 likes on the post. '163 likes in less than ten minutes? That's crazy.' And with that, she started scrolling through the comments underneath.

Rebecca Atkinson: OMG somebody has finally said it! Why does everyone talk about this amazing moment when a baby is born. IT DOESN'T HAPPEN LIKE THAT!

Alexandra Young: A symphony orchestra didn't break into tune at my birth either! I just love this. So honest! Keep writing!

Lucy Thompson: I'm so happy that you have written another letter! I've been checking constantly! And it's the best post yet! Can't wait for the next one!

She continued to scroll… and there it was.

Felicity Macdonald: Well, this is just delightful for your daughter to read in later life isn't it?! You didn't love your daughter when she was born and you want to tell the world about it? You should be ashamed of yourself! How about you forget the blogging and concentrate on your daughter?!

Jessica froze in shock, forgetting to breathe. 'What the fuck?' she finally blurted out loud. 'What the actual fuck!'

She clicked on the name and a profile picture enlarged on her screen. Felicity Macdonald. Blonde hair, dark plum lipstick and the hint of a pregnancy bump. Clicking the arrow next to it, another photo appeared, and there she was smiling in a family photo with her husband and a young son. In the next photo, the little boy held a baby scan photo up to the camera. No, she didn't recognise her. She was sure of it. Felicity Macdonald was a complete stranger. A complete stranger who was so outraged, disappointed, and offended by her words that she had taken the time to write a comment telling Jessica that she should be disgusted with herself.

She didn't know what to do. *Should she delete the comment? Should she just delete the whole blog post? Should she try and ignore it? Or should she reply?*

Her attention was suddenly pulled away by Bella, who was trying to climb up her legs. Lifting her onto her hip, she paced the room for a moment. 'Why did she write that Bella Boo?' she said to her daughter, who was more interested in the box of raisins she'd spotted on the kitchen surface. As she gesticulated and shrieked loudly, Jessica gave in. She handed her the box, put her down, and watched her toddle away.

She suddenly knew what to do. Grabbing her phone, she scrolled down the list of her last dialled numbers and found 'Chris Mobile' in seconds. Three rings later, he picked up.

'Hi, all OK?'

By the tone of his voice, she could tell he was at his desk with his colleagues around him. 'No, not really. Can we talk?'

'Sorry, not now. Speak later, OK?'.

As the line beeped and then disconnected, Jessica felt winded. What did she do now? She was expecting him to have the answer and make it all OK. As she chewed her fingernails, the comment played over and over again in her mind.

How about you forget the blogging and concentrate on your daughter?!

Sitting down at the table, she made a snap decision. Her fingers moved quickly across the keys, forming words on the screen as her mind simultaneously screamed them:

> Haven't you got anything better to do with your time than leave vicious comments? Maybe you should forget the online trolling and concentrate on your son?!

It was her blog and she had the right to defend herself. After a deep breath, she pressed 'send' and watched the comment pop up underneath Felicity Macdonald's. She wasn't going to sit back and let people talk to her like that.

But as she was re-reading her comment, a reply suddenly popped up:

> How do you know I've got a son?

Her stomach plunged. How could she explain why she'd been clicking through her photos? She exhaled loudly and moved her fingers back to the keyboard.

> I was trying to work out whether I knew you – or whether it was a complete stranger telling me I should be ashamed of myself...

As she watched the comment pop up, she held her breath. She was angry now, and her heart was beating fast in her chest. Quick as a flash, Felicity's reply appeared:

> And I'm the troll?!

Jessica felt like she'd been punched in the stomach.

How could she reply to that? She'd dug a giant hole for herself and managed to jump straight in. She put her head in her hands and sighed, only sitting up when the loud clatter of a full box of building blocks was turned upside down onto the living room floor.

Within seconds, her phone rang.

'Hi honey', Chris said. 'Sorry about earlier, I was with a client.' Jessica could hear the background noise of a busy London street as he made his way back to the office.

'Fuck. Fuck. Fuck,' Jessica replied, pushing the palm of her hand against her forehead repeatedly. 'I need some help.'

As she spoke, she glanced back at the words 'And I'm the troll?!' and could see three people had liked the comment. Her readers were turning against her!

'What's up?' Chris asked, his tone changing.

Jessica spoke quickly, her heart beating with an increasing sense of panic. She explained how she'd published the blog post, seen the comment, and then made a flip decision to reply. She felt so silly now for thinking she could handle it on her own. She should've waited to speak to him first. He was always so calm and collected, always the voice of reason.

'OK, stop, Jess. Wait a minute. Let me go back to my desk and I'll have a quick look and get back to you. OK?' Chris suggested.

Jessica took a deep breath. 'Yep, OK. Fuck. What do I do?'

'Bear with me. I'll call you back!'

Jessica hung up and stood still for a moment, deep in

thought. She had always shied away from controversy, and now suddenly she had hurtled face first into it. She felt like deleting the whole blog. Forgetting it completely. Putting her laptop into a drawer and never opening it again. She clearly didn't have thick enough skin to take one nasty comment on the chin, so starting a blog had probably been the worst idea she'd ever had.

But before she could think any more about it, her phone jumped into life on the table and a picture of Chris' face lit up on the screen.

'Hi,' she said into the phone, just as a couple of stray raisins on the carpet caught her eye and she bent down to pick them up.

'Hi honey,' he replied. 'Now listen, I've read it and I just think you should just leave it. It's slipping down the comments now, so very few people will see it anyway.'

'You think?' she replied, staring down at the two furry raisins now in the palm of her hand.

'Yes, just forget it,' he replied. 'Did you really look at her photos?'

'Well, yes,' Jessica stuttered. 'But only because I was trying to work out whether I knew the bitch!'

Chris laughed. 'And I take it she's a stranger?'

'Yes!' Jessica said loudly. 'Are you sure I shouldn't just delete it?'

'I don't think you should bother. Listen, you have over 600 likes on that post now!' he said, prompting Jess to swallow with shock. 'So just ignore it, OK? Focus on the hundreds of positive comments. It's going *viral*, honey! It's amazing! I've got to get back to my desk, but stop worrying. It doesn't matter. Felicity Macdonald is obviously just having a bad day.'

'And she's not the only one,' Jessica said, turning her eyes to Bella, who had managed to find the pack of oatmeal cookies she had stashed under the buggy to take to Henny's house and was doing her best to break into the packaging. 'OK, see you later. And babe?'

'Yes?' Chris asked.

'Thank you,' Jessica replied. 'Can't wait to see you later.'

As she hung up, she already felt stronger and calmer. Chris always had the answer, and even though she doubted she'd be able to scratch Felicity's words from her mind for a while, she was going to try her best not to dwell on them.

She hung up and made her way straight to Bella, confiscating the cookies and putting them out of reach on the kitchen surface. Time was ticking and Henny would message any second. While she waited, she reloaded the social media page, clicking and swiping on her phone until the page re-loaded and the stats lit up.

634 likes, and she'd only posted the link thirty-two minutes ago.

634 likes in half an hour.

She'd made a mistake biting back, but Chris was right. In the grand scheme of things, it didn't matter. There were so many wonderful, supportive comments, but she'd zoned in on the one negative.

Still, the last half an hour had taught her one thing; she needed to talk to someone who understood. Someone who could give her some advice on how to deal with things like this. And as Bella arrived at her feet with another box of unopened raisins in her hand (a fly on the wall would assume she never fed the child), she made a promise to send an email to blogging veteran Tiggy Blenheim that weekend.

'It's not what you know, it's who you know,' she said under her breath, just as a message from Henny pinged on her phone to say they were ready.

Jessica lifted Bella into her buggy and secured the straps in place with a loud snap, and as she pushed her out of the front door and onto the path, Felicity Macdonald, her plum lipstick, and their war of words were already fading from her mind.

5

Followers – 1,022

Dear Bella,

Daddy's first day back at work was just a week after you were born – and I was still a tired, sore, emotional mess. It was a Monday morning and I watched him get ready from our bed, propped up against a mountain of pillows as you fed from me hungrily. We still hadn't got to grips with breastfeeding and I kept having to re-latch you to my boob, gasping with shock at the power of your suck, which felt like you had a hundred little blades planted in your gums to slice into my nipple. Once you got into a rhythm, you sounded like a hungry piglet. As I listened to those grunts and sighs, I watched him button up his shirt, pull on his suit trousers, tie his shoelaces, and fix his tie. I knew he'd be gone in a matter of minutes, and I hadn't worked out how I was even going to have a shower that morning, let alone get through the rest of the day.

When he was dressed and ready, he walked over to the bed and kissed me on the lips. And then he bent down and kissed your head gently, pausing for a moment to breathe in your newborn smell.

And with that, he was gone.

I waited until I heard the door shut behind him downstairs before I allowed myself to dissolve into tears. You had fallen asleep feeding, eventually detaching from my boob and leaning back heavily into my arms with your mouth open and a drop of milk dribbling down your cheek. You looked so peaceful and I stared down at you as I cried. It was just a few tears at first but then I couldn't stop. It was like the floodgates had opened and within seconds, I was howling. Big tears plopped onto your head as you lay there in my arms, rocking you unintentionally as each sob gripped me. A week of emotions was pouring out of me, and I didn't think I'd ever be able to stop.

But eventually, I did. The tears stopped and my sobs eased off. You had stirred, but not woken. I lifted you carefully into your bedside cot, I moved the stash of pillows one by one, before burrowing under the covers and falling quickly into a deep sleep.

I was woken by the doorbell ringing. Once, twice, then again. I glanced over at you quickly in panic, as I always did when I woke in those early days – but your little chest was rising and falling gently as you slept. Satisfied that you were OK, I rolled onto my side and heaved myself out of the bed (my preferred way to get up, given that the stitches still hurt like a bitch), grabbed my dressing gown, and pulled it over myself as I walked down the stairs. 'I'm coming, I'm coming,' I muttered as the doorbell rang out again. Reaching the door, I braced myself for a moment to speak to a stranger. I didn't know if it was the postman, a flower delivery person, or somebody selling double-glazed windows. I just wanted them to go away.

Taking a deep breath, I swung open the door, and standing there on the doorstep were Granny and Grandad. I fell so quickly into Granny's arms that she nearly stumbled off the doorstep. 'Hi Mum,' I muttered as she held me tightly and I breathed in the familiar scent of Cacharel Anais Anais on her cardigan. 'Hi Dad,' I added, as I pulled away and hugged Grandad. For a moment, I felt like a child again – and I knew that I didn't have to worry.

I stood back to let them both into the house, and as they stepped inside, Mum asked, 'Has he gone darling?'

My voice caught with emotion as I replied, 'Yep.'

'Well, we're here now!' she replied. 'Is she asleep? Yes? OK well, we have breakfast. Come on, let's go inside. We come armed with pastries! Do you want a plain croissant or a chocolate croissant? What do you want, Frank? Any coffee on, love? No? I'll make it now. Let me drink a cup and then I'm going straight upstairs to wake that little girl up!'

And that pretty much became the routine, Bella. In those early days on our own. Daddy would leave and an hour or so later, Granny and Grandad would storm through the door with provisions. Auntie Fran popped in a few mornings a week too, when Michael had left for work and Freddie had been dropped at school, usually bringing a stack of Freddie's old Babygros and little cardigans she'd found in the loft.

Oh Bella, I had worried about being on our own in those early days so much, but the truth is that we were never going to be alone with a family like ours. And as I stood there in the kitchen that first morning, with my parents ensuring that life ticked on without Daddy by our side, one hand gripping a chocolate croissant, and the other a cup of coffee, I couldn't have been more thankful about that.

Love from Mummy x

It was 6.05 a.m. on Saturday and Jessica woke to the sound of someone moving around the bedroom. Suddenly he was standing over her, whispering, 'I'm off for a run. See you in a bit.'

'Don't run a marathon,' she mumbled, kissing Chris on the lips. 'And please, please, please don't slam the front door! I will not be happy if you wake up Bella and then disappear for an hour!'

'OK honey', he replied quietly, as he turned to walk out the bedroom. 'I hope she sleeps in for you!'

Jessica held her breath as he closed the front door and when the hum of the baby monitor continued uninterrupted, she exhaled with relief. She stretched out, enjoying the coolness of the new patch of duvet on her skin.

She'd always loved weekends, but they'd taken on a whole new meaning now she was at home with Bella every day. Everything seemed brighter and happier with Chris by her side. She felt far more confident as a mother when she had back-up, and occasionally she even got to have a hot shower in peace or the chance to get to the bottom of a hot cup of coffee.

They didn't have any plans today, which was just the way she liked it. They could go for a stroll to the park, head to their favourite cafés, take turns to cook up some feasts in the kitchen, and hope the weather stayed nice for Bella to toddle around the garden. She might even get to type up her next letter.

With Bella still sleeping peacefully, she rolled over and picked up her phone from her bedside table, clicking straight onto social media to check her stats. When she went to bed last night, she had just over 950 followers on her page – but the number staring back at her now was 1,022.

She blinked a few times to check it was real. She knew that posts going viral could do amazing things for bloggers, but she had never expected it would happen to her. But as delighted as she was about it all, she felt woefully unprepared.

Jessica had started reading parenting blogs in the early

days of her pregnancy, and a few of her favourite bloggers had gigantic followings. She'd seen pictures of those ladies appearing at events, speaking at conferences, and being interviewed on television. They'd been offered book deals, worked with big brands on national advertising campaigns, and been given regular columns in magazines. They were celebrities in their own right and if she'd walked past one of them on the street, she would be just as starstruck as if she'd spotted a Hollywood star.

For a moment, Jessica let her mind wander.

What if her followers kept rising? What if she had so many readers that people started recognising her on the street? What if she was asked to attend an event and hundreds of people bought tickets just to see her? How would it feel to become a household name?

And did she even want that to happen?

She wanted to be successful, of course. She'd love to be known for writing, for connecting with other mums, and for the way she evoked memories and feelings through her words. She'd love these letters from her notebook to be read by thousands and thousands of people. For the first time since starting her blog, she was feeling sparks of ambition.

Inspired, she started scrolling on social media, and one of the first posts that popped up on her phone was by a mummy blogger she followed who lived in Central London. Jessica spent a while studying her photographs and reading her words, quickly coming across a photo of her standing with a number of other bloggers at an event. Amongst them was Tiggy Blenheim.

'Ah, Tiggy.' Jessica said under her breath, pausing for a moment to try and reconcile the down-to-earth Tiggy she remembered from her childhood with the glamorous blogger on the screen.

One click later and she was staring at the feed for 'Tiggy Does Motherhood'. Fran was right; she really did have a lot of children. It was hard to work out exactly how many at first glance, with a gaggle of white-blonde children in beautiful clothes starring in nearly every photo. With some more scrolling, she counted five – from a toddler girl on her hip, to a boy she guessed was around ten years old. Tiggy herself was just as blonde as her children, with the whitest teeth, a supermodel-esque body, and a dark tan that Jessica fully believed came from a sun lounger and not a bottle. Her husband featured in photos occasionally too. He was tall, with a rugby player physique and strawberry blond hair and stubble.

Tiggy's family now lived in the countryside and the photography that accompanied her words was beautiful. There were shots of the family posed against a charming stone farmhouse, of the kids marching through fields in different coloured wellington boots, and impressive picnics spread out on gingham rugs. She'd certainly come a long way from her childhood in a terraced house in South East London. Her life looked picture-perfect and it wasn't surprising that her blog, her photos, and her words had quickly elevated her to being one of the top bloggers in the UK.

Her social stats were definitely impressive. In fact, seeing that she had over 100,000 followers was a bit of a wake-up call for Jessica and she cringed at her own delight at reaching 1,000 just a few minutes before.

Among Tiggy's photos of her children and her home, there were a few adverts scattered into her feed. In one photo, her children sat around a pile of muddy clothes, with a box of washing powder next to them. In another, Tiggy sat at her computer, with a small bottle of smoothie in her hands. Each of these photos was labelled #Ad, but it didn't stop her fans enjoying the pictures. She had over 1,000 likes on each, with dozens of comments stacked up underneath. Jessica scrolled through her feed and studied the photos, imagining for a moment that she might have the chance to do something similar one day.

If she wanted to.

She just wasn't sure.

Noticing it was now 6.30 a.m., she decided to get up. Chris was usually gone for about an hour when he ran at the weekend, and it would be nice to have a pot of coffee brewing before Bella woke up. Climbing out of bed, she pulled the curtains open and stood for a moment in the ray of sunshine now streaming into the bedroom. She wore a T-shirt and knickers in bed, so grabbed a pair of pyjama bottoms from the back of the chair and pulled them on. Catching sight of herself in the full-length mirror, she stopped to stare back at her reflection for a moment. She hadn't made any conscious effort to lose weight (trying to fit the gym or regular classes into her weekly routine without any childcare was nearly impossible) but she had noticed the baby weight slowly starting to fall away. Whether it was because she'd been trying to eat a little more healthily (and she had been trying, although she wasn't always successful) or because she was walking a lot with the buggy now the weather was milder, she didn't know – but for the first time in a long time, she felt a bit more confident about the vision staring back at her.

Her hair, however, desperately needed some attention. Naturally a mousy brown, she liked to add a few blonde highlights to wake up her skin tone, but without time to get to the hairdresser, it had grown back to her natural colour and she looked washed out and tired. She made a mental note to ask her parents whether they could have Bella for a few hours the following week, so she could sort it out.

I bet Tiggy Blenheim has time to get her hair sorted, she thought, as she turned and walked out of the room.

Reaching the door to Bella's nursery, she paused.

Should I just check her quickly? her mind whirred. *No, you'll wake her up! You know you will!*

But what if something is wrong? What if she isn't breathing? her mind taunted.

She'd just sneak inside and have a quick look.

She placed the monitor carefully on the floor and opened the door as slowly and quietly as she could, peeping her head through the crack. Bella was curled in a ball, sleeping on her front. Jessica paused to listen to the sound of breathing, but she wasn't close enough to hear.

She'd just make her way a few steps further in. She

dodged the squeaky floorboards in her path. She hadn't made a noise at all and was feeling quite proud of herself when suddenly, Bella moved her arm and let out a soft groan.

She darted back out the room in panic, pulling the door quickly behind her. Reaching the landing, she stood still and listened behind the door, but she could only hear the sound of her own heart thumping loudly.

Please don't wake up yet, Bella Boo. Just ten more minutes.

Satisfied that she was asleep again, she started to climb down the stairs. Slowly and carefully, so the sound of her footsteps didn't wake her. She had visions of a relaxed coffee downstairs with the sunshine streaming into the lounge and the radio playing quietly in the background. She could see the kitchen now and felt jubilant that she'd made it, gripping the baby monitor in her hand as she stepped towards it.

'MAMAMAMAMAMAMAMAMA!' it suddenly rang out, stopping her in her tracks.

She was awake – and it was all her fault. She sighed loudly and turned back up the stairs.

'Coming Bella', she shouted, as the protests grew noisily. And then louder: 'Mummy's coming! Hang on!'

A few minutes later and they were back downstairs, Bella toddling around in her sleepsuit, while Jessica made her way into the kitchen to fill the kettle. Once she'd put it on to boil, she strolled back into the lounge and pulled open the curtains to the garden. It was a lovely day and the grass was dry, so she decided to open the doors and let Bella have a play on the lawn as she pottered around downstairs.

With newfound freedom, Bella stepped outside and quickly made her way to the toys lying in a pile halfway up the garden. Listening for the bubbles of boiling water from the kitchen, Jessica paused for a moment, watching her daughter. She didn't look like a baby any more, 16 months old now and walking confidently. As she played, she babbled to herself, with the odd intelligible word now making its way into her speech.

Bella had dark hair and big, green eyes, just like Chris, but she had inherited her mother's light skin tone. Her hair was growing quickly now, not long enough to pull into a ponytail or pigtails yet, but it wouldn't be long. She had sweet chubby cheeks and one dimple in the right side. She had always been small for a baby, right on the twenty-fifth percentile line, and that hadn't been surprising, given she was early. Recently though, she'd shot up and they wondered whether she was going to be tall, just like her daddy.

Jessica knew she was biased, but she thought Bella was beautiful. As she stood in the doorway watching her daughter pick up her small plastic spade and march around the garden clutching it delightedly, she felt her heart swell with pride.

But the spell was suddenly broken by a pat on her shoulder.

'Hi honey', Chris said, red in the face and dripping in sweat. She smiled as she turned to him, kissing him quickly on the lips.

Within seconds, Bella had spotted him. 'DADADA

DADADA' she squealed with delight, toddling towards them.

At the sight of his daughter, Chris' face broke into a smile. 'Hi, baby girl!' he said happily, as he scooped her into his arms and lifted her into the air. Bella laughed as she flew, cupping her hands around her daddy's face as he pulled her back to his chest.

Deciding to leave them to it, Jessica stepped back inside the lounge and towards the kitchen to make the coffee. They had a snazzy machine to make single cups, but preferred to work their way through a large cafetière at the weekend. As she poured the water over the ground beans, the scent of rich, nutty coffee quickly filled the kitchen. She inhaled deeply, feeling happy.

'I'm just heading up for a quick shower,' Chris called, as he made his way up the stairs. 'She's happy in the garden.'

'Hang on,' she called back. 'Want to take your coffee up?' But he was already gone, so she carried two mugs out to the garden and placed them on the wooden patio table. Pulling out a chair, she sat down. Cupping her coffee, she watched Bella play on the lawn.

After a few minutes, she pulled her phone from the pocket of her pyjamas and spent a while checking all her latest blog statistics, before finding her way back to Tiggy's blog page and hovering over the 'Send message' button.

She'd just draft something quickly, she thought, clicking on the button and beginning to type:

Hi Tiggy,

I hope you are well! I don't know if you will remember me, but I'm Francesca Colleridge's sister and we were neighbours as children in Mottingham. It's been so lovely to discover your blog and see pictures of your beautiful family! Congratulations on doing so well with the blog! I'm seriously impressed!

I recently started my own blog and if you have time, I'd really appreciate your advice. It's been going much better than I expected and I now have over 1,000 followers. I don't really know whether I am doing everything right and I found my first negative comment quite tough to deal with! Would you have time for a coffee soon? I don't know how easy it is to get to London, but I'm always happy to come to you. Or maybe we could chat by email if that is hard to organise. The link is here if you want to look – www.letterstomydaughter.co.uk. Thank you Tiggy! I hope to chat soon!

Love Jessica

She read back over what she'd written a few times. She just sounded so inexperienced! She mulled over whether to delete it. Her mind continued to taunt her, embarrassed by her obvious naivety, but she knew she needed to send it.

Hearing Chris coming back down the stairs, she thought, *fuck it* and pressed 'Send'. And just like that, her message was hurtling towards the inbox of one of the UK's most successful mummy bloggers.

They spent the rest of Saturday together as a family and it was all pretty idyllic until Bella decided an impromptu brunch at their favourite Greenwich café would be the perfect time for one of her finest tantrums to date. It was so fine that it involved scrambled eggs on the floor (dangerously close to a fellow diner's handbag), a smacked head on a table (not one of Jessica's parenting highlights), and an under-their-breath argument between Jessica and Chris that involved plenty of 'I told you this was a bad idea!' and 'Will you just relax and try to enjoy it?!!' as they shot glares at each other across the table.

So embarrassed by the commotion, Jessica had finished her eggs benedict and cappuccino in a couple of minutes, strapped a rigid Bella into her buggy, red-faced and screaming, and stormed out the café, leaving Chris to finish his breakfast and pay the bill.

Ten minutes later, he had followed them into the park. Jessica tried to swallow her anger and apologise. 'I'm sorry babe,' she said, turning to look at him. 'I find it really hard at the weekend, as we're in such a good routine during the week. I want her to be one of those chilled children that sits nicely in a highchair in a café when we fancy a meal out, but it just never bloody works.'

'Well, it'll never work if we don't try,' Chris said, sipping the remainders of the coffee that he'd asked the waitress to transfer to a takeaway cup.

Jessica shrugged. 'But then on Monday, when I need

her to nap at lunchtime, she'll be out of the routine again. And what's more important? Taking her to a restaurant at the weekend for a screaming match, or me getting through the week without having to resort to a shot of gin at lunchtime?'

'Well, why would you want to stop that now?' he asked with a smile.

'Oi! Things aren't that bad,' Jessica replied. 'Despite Bella's best efforts.'

Throwing his coffee cup in a nearby bin, he took the buggy from Jessica with one hand and found Jessica's hand with the other. For a few minutes, they walked hand-in-hand towards the far gate of the park.

'Why don't you leave us to it one weekend?' Chris asked, as they walked through the large iron gate and onto the pavement. 'I'll stick to the routine at home, and you can get away for a few days and have a break?'

'What do you mean?' Jessica replied. 'Go to Mum and Dad's? I don't think there's actually room for—'

'No, I don't mean your mum and dad's house!' Chris laughed. 'I mean a proper break. I don't know, I mean with a friend. Why don't you head down to Southampton to see Callie for the weekend or something like that?'

Jessica flinched. 'Oh no, I don't think that would work… It would be hard as she works shifts at the hospital and probably wouldn't be around…'

'So what?' Chris said. 'Then go shopping while she's working? Or go to a spa and get a massage? Just do something for yourself! And then you can both catch up properly when she's home.'

'Yep well, we'll see... I'm not sure we're on good enough terms, to be honest,' Jessica said, looking down at her flip-flopped feet as she walked.

'Why? Because she didn't come to Bella's birthday party?' Chris asked.

'Well yes, I'm still a bit upset about that,' Jessica replied. 'She hasn't messaged since then either.'

'I didn't realise that. Was she working that weekend? Did she give you a reason?' Chris asked.

'She didn't reply to the invitation for weeks,' Jessica explained, 'and when I messaged her to ask if she was coming, she said she already had plans to go camping with some friends from work.'

'Well, maybe she did have a plan,' Chris replied. 'But she should probably have said that from the start.'

'Yep...' Jessica said, her tone flat. 'I understand my life is very different now. She's single, doing really well in her career, and has a busy social life. I get that visiting babies isn't high up her priority list, because it wouldn't have been high up mine until a year ago – but I'm still the same person, so why is she letting the friendship fizzle out? We've been friends since we were eleven years old.'

'It's just one of those things, I think,' Chris said. 'It's sometimes the people you least expect to be flaky that disappear from your life when it takes a different turn. I was surprised how few of my mates reached out when Mum died, but that's life. As the years go on, you learn who really values your friendship.'

'Thank God I met the girls,' Jessica replied. 'The weeks would be pretty dull without them.'

'I'll take full credit for that, thanks,' Chris said, winking. 'I knew you should go to that class!'

'Yes, you're just bloody amazing, aren't you babe?' Jessica replied, laughing. 'And a bloody know-it-all too...'

'That's why you love me,' he said, moving his hand to her shoulder with a squeeze. 'But think about it, OK? Head away with Fran for the weekend – or get the girls together for a night away. Me and Bella will be fine on our own!'

'I can't imagine leaving you both,' Jessica replied. 'But I will think about it, thank you.'

They strolled home slowly in the sunshine, with Bella fast asleep in her buggy. The rest of the day was spent lazily at home, watching films, playing in the garden, and reading recipe books on the sofa. Jessica even got the chance to type up her next blog post, watching the likes immediately start rolling in. It was a good day, and as she lay on the sofa with Chris that evening, with a tummy full of Indian food he'd expertly knocked up while she'd put Bella to bed, she felt happily relaxed. She loved her weekends with her little family.

In fact, she was so distracted by the normality of the day that it wasn't until 9 p.m. that she remembered the message she'd sent Tiggy Blenheim that morning. As soon as it crossed her mind, she reached for her phone on the arm of the sofa to see whether she'd had a reply.

Disappointingly, but probably not surprisingly given that Tiggy had five children, she hadn't written back – but Jessica could see she had read it, with the words 'Seen at 10.02 a.m.' written underneath the message. Knowing she'd seen it made Jessica's stomach plunge with nerves. She sat for a moment, imagining the moment Tiggy had seen the message pop up on her phone in her country farmhouse.

She felt silly for even sending it now. Why would the creator of 'Tiggy Does Motherhood' want to have a coffee with her? Thinking about it, she sighed loudly, which prompted Chris to turn his attention from the TV to ask: 'You OK, what's wrong?'

'Yep,' she replied, knowing he would think she was overreacting when she explained. 'It's just that I sent a message to the blogger this morning, the one that Fran suggested, and she hasn't replied.'

'You sent it this morning?' he asked, with a raised eyebrow.

'Yep.'

'Give her a chance, honey. She probably gets a hundred messages every day,' he said.

'You think? A hundred?'

'Probably!' Chris said. 'I don't know!'

Jessica shrugged. 'Wow.'

'Have you had any messages from your readers yet?' he asked.

'Well, kind of,' she replied. 'I had a few messages on social media commenting on various blog posts. Not many, but a few.'

'And what about emails?' he asked.

'Emails? I don't think I have an email address for the blog?' she said, suddenly not feeling entirely sure herself.

'Of course you do, Jess – it's written in your "Contact

Me" section. Do you know how to get onto your inbox? Did Becca set it up?' he asked.

Jessica didn't reply, but instead clicked onto her blog on her phone and found the 'Contact Me' section.

Chris was right; there it was in black and white.

Want to get in touch? Send me an email at jessica@letterstomydaughter.co.uk

I'll get back to you as soon as I can!

'Shit. You're right' she finally said. 'I've no idea how I'm supposed to check them…'

Leaving the warmth of the sofa, she made her way to the dining table to grab her laptop. After a few minutes scrolling through the documents Becca had sent her weeks ago with instructions on how to work her blog, she found the details for cracking into her emails. And just a few scrolls, clicks, and taps later, she was staring at an inbox.

'Oh my God,' she finally managed to splutter, as her eyes darted up and down the screen.

'Are you in? Anything exciting?' Chris asked, turning to her from the sofa.

'Yep I'm in,' she replied. 'And I have 106 unread messages.'

'Really?' Chris asked, raising his eyebrows in surprise. 'Anything interesting?'

'It's going to take me all night to go through them,' she replied, scrolling and reading as she spoke. 'But bloody hell, look at this one…'

'What does it say?' Chris asked, as Jessica's eyes scanned down the email.

'Well,' she said, looking up with wide eyes. 'I've been invited to an event!'

6

Followers – 1,850
Emails in inbox – 106
Event invitations – 1

Dear Bella,

You were three weeks old when we finally decided on your name. We knew that 'Baby Girl', 'Piglet' and 'Sleep Thief' wouldn't cut it in the real world, so one evening, Daddy and I sat down together on the sofa and vowed that we wouldn't get up again until we'd decided. We had to back down on that promise when midway through discussions we heard you explode into your nappy while lying asleep in your basket on the living room floor. The noise was quite frankly astonishing, and we quickly discovered that you needed an entire head-to-foot change, as did the sheet you were lying on.

When we got back to the nitty gritty of name choosing (and believe me Bella, it took a while), Daddy had a couple of favourites, as did I. My argument was that having grown you and pushed you out, I should get the final say on the matter – but he just didn't think you suited anything I suggested, so we had reached a stalemate.

I had a big book of baby names that Granny had bought us in the hope that we might open a page and pick something eventually. Occasionally I'd flick through it in desperation and shout out a suggestion. 'Minnie?' I offered, trying it out for size. We both looked down at you in your basket to see whether it worked. 'No,' Daddy said, 'it doesn't suit her.' 'How about Ada?' I asked. 'No', Daddy quipped back quickly, 'I like it, but my school dinner lady was called Ada and I'm not sure if I could....' 'Elizabeth?' he asked, looking at me hopefully. 'No, too regal for our Piglet,' I shot back, without taking my eyes off you. 'Isabella?' he asked again, as you flinched suddenly in shock. 'I don't know,' I replied, 'Isabella. Isabella. Isabella.' I tried it out a few more times, seeing whether it rolled off the tongue. 'I don't hate it, but I'm not sure. It's just not quite right.' We both sat in silence for a few minutes, before it seemed to dawn on us at exactly the same moment that we'd stumbled on the perfect name. 'BELLA!' I said, jiggling with excitement on the spot. 'Just Bella! She's BELLA! I love it!' I was so excited that I hadn't even glanced at Daddy but when I finally stopped dancing and looked over, I discovered that he was smiling widely. 'It suits her,' he said, reaching down to lift you out of your basket. 'How about Bella Evelyn, after my mum?' he said, kissing you gently on the forehead as you yawned widely. 'Perfect,' I replied. 'Just perfect.'

Sorry it took so long, Bella.

But I think it was worth the wait.

Love from Mummy x

'Can you read the email out loud?' Fran asked, curled on the sofa next to Jessica at their parents' home, warming her hands on her mug of coffee. It was raining again and as they chatted, drops drummed noisily on the windows.

Jessica noticed her mother standing in the doorway. She was wearing an apron over her dress, which had grease splatters on it already. The scent coming from the kitchen was delicious, as a joint of beef sizzled away in the oven, surrounded by the crispiest roast potatoes and a huge dish of bubbling cauliflower cheese. Chris and her dad were chatting in the kitchen, Freddie was lounging in an armchair watching videos on his iPad, and Bella was happily unpacking a giant box of vintage toys from the 1980s, which had been rescued from the attic when she was born.

Jessica pulled out her phone at Fran's request and spent some time clicking and scrolling until she found the email. She cleared her throat with a quick cough and continued:

Dear Jessica,

We've been keeping up to date with your blog for a few weeks now at Jumbled Agency and we are big fans of the way you write and how naturally you interact with your readers! We think <Letters To My Daughter> would be a great fit for a new baby food product we are launching — and we wondered if you would like to come to the launch in a few weeks' time? All the details are below — if you'd like to come, please send me a quick RSVP!

Yours Sincerely,

Victoria Demblebury
Account Executive
Jumbled Agency

* * *

YOU ARE INVITED TO THE LAUNCH OF 'SQUEEZE & GURGLE' ORGANIC BABY FOOD POUCHES!

Please join us on Friday 20th July 2018 at Munch! in Borough Market, from 10 a.m. to 5 p.m.!
Drop in whenever you like for bites to eat, mini manicures, face painting for little ones, and the chance to check out the exciting new Squeeze & Gurgle range!
Make sure you RSVP, as we have a generous shopping voucher for every attendee!

As she finished reading, Fran raised her eyebrows and smiled. 'Wow,' she said. 'Do you think you'll go?'

'Generous shopping voucher?' her mother interrupted loudly from the doorway. 'Of course, she's going to go! I wonder how much it'll be.'

'Alright Mum,' Jessica interrupted. 'I'm pretty sure that whatever the value of the shopping voucher, it isn't going to be worth dragging Bella into Central London for the day.'

'Well, drop her here first then! Go on your own!' her mother replied, quickly followed by a yell to the kitchen: 'Frank! Can you check on the beef? It's not burning, is it?'

Satisfied that the lunch wasn't on fire, the conversation continued. 'Thanks Mum, but if I decide to go, I'll take Bella with me. I don't want to be the only one that turns up childless to an event selling baby food!'

Her mother nodded and turned back to the kitchen, giving Fran and Jessica the chance to chat. 'It is amazing though, isn't it, Jessy? You hadn't even written a blog post until a few months ago and now you're being invited to posh launches! Did you get anything else interesting in that inbox?'

Jessica shrugged. 'Not really. A few companies emailing me to tell me about kids' clothes or kids-eat-for-free deals at pizza restaurants. A few lovely emails from readers, commenting on blog posts. And an email from Mr J. Adajowbi in Nigeria telling me I was the lucky winner of one and a half million pounds...'

Fran laughed, distracting Bella from shooting cars down the ramp of her toy garage for a moment. Fran and Jessica's parents had lived in the same house for forty-four years, bringing both their daughters into the world and raising them within its grey, pebble-dash walls. The house was a modest semi-detached on a quiet street, with three bedrooms and a bathroom upstairs and a lounge, kitchen, and small office downstairs. They had paid the mortgage off twenty years ago, but it hadn't even crossed their minds to move.

'Why on earth would we do that?' her mother would say with a shocked expression if anyone enquired. 'This is our home!'

And most Sundays had panned out like this for as long as Jessica could remember. Throughout her childhood, after the birth of Freddie, during the collapse of Fran's first marriage, on visits home from university, in the whirlwind early days of her own relationship, for the first kicks and then shocking wallops of a baby growing in her tummy, in the days since Bella had been born, and the dark days after Fran and Freddie returned home. All the family gathered together, chatting, eating giant plates of food, and heading home when her parents insisted on retiring to the lounge for their weekly fix of *Antiques Roadshow*. It was Jessica's happy place. It was her safe place. And she knew that as Bella grew up, she'd feel exactly the same.

Jessica wasn't sure whether Fran and Freddie would ever move back to their old neighbourhood of Dulwich. She knew her mum and dad loved having them close, never happier than when their house was filled with bustle, noise and family.

Freddie was a quiet child, but he seemed happy. He had joined a school close to his grandparents' house shortly after they had moved and had quickly found a group of friends to kick a ball around with after school. That led to an invite to the local football club – and with weekends spent playing matches, watching matches, or eating his grandmother's gigantic roasts, he was a happy, carefree thirteen-year-old boy. Jessica couldn't feel prouder of him, as she watched him glued to clips of *Extreme Soccer Skills* on his tablet.

The spell was broken by a yell from the kitchen: 'It's ready! Come through!'

And the whole family was soon sitting around the kitchen table, tucking into slices of perfectly-cooked beef (brown on the edges, pink on the inside), scoops of gooey cauliflower cheese, spoonfuls of runner beans, piles of peas, and generous helpings of roast potatoes.

As the boys at the table started chatting about last season's league positions (Chris entirely motivated by the fantasy football league he was planning to join in with again at work) and her mother busied herself passing dishes around the table, Jessica and Fran had a moment to talk.

'So, Jessy, do you think you'll go to the big baby food launch? You probably should... You can't really turn these things down if you want to be a serious blogger,' Fran prodded again.

As she finished chewing her mouthful of roast potato, Jessica paused for a moment to think. 'I probably will. I guess I'm lucky to be invited. I just hate going to things where I don't know anybody.'

Fran thought for a moment. 'What about Tiggy? Maybe you could ask if she fancies going together?'

'Well, no,' Jessica said, feeling her cheeks blush. 'She still hasn't replied. She's probably busy. Or maybe she doesn't remember me after all...'

Fran stopped cutting into her slice of beef and looked up at Jessica. 'Really?' she said. 'I know it's been a long time, but I'm sure she'll get back to you.'

'Yes, I mean, I only sent the message yesterday. She's just busy. She's probably read it and completely forgotten about it...'

But their conversation was interrupted by a flying pea, which landed in the middle of the table, bounced, and landed with a plop in Jessica's gravy, splashing her perfectly in the eye. The whole family turned to look at Bella, who let out a squeal of delight.

'Nobody laugh,' Jessica cut through the silence. 'Nobody *bloody* laugh!'

But as Freddie exhaled, squeaked, and then dissolved into a fit of giggles, Bella grabbed a fistful of the peas remaining on her tray and launched them across the table. With a bounce, a plop, another bounce, another plop, and plenty of rolls, the entire family were covered in pea confetti.

Chris' chair scraped backwards. 'No, Bella!' he said, trying his hardest not to laugh as he piled what was left on her plate into his hand to prevent further assaults. Bella, meanwhile, was waving her spoon in the air with delight and squealing happily. Her grandmother was trying to stifle her laughter, getting up from the table to grab a cloth from the kitchen sink while Grandad's shoulders were shaking silently as he tried to hide his giggles. Fran was smiling proudly at her niece. Finally, Jessica and Chris allowed themselves to laugh along too, half-outraged and half-proud of their frustratingly vivacious daughter.

It was 5 p.m. when they finally made their way home, with tummies full of roast dinner and a Tupperware pot containing leftover apple crumble for Bella to tuck into the next day. With Chris agreeing to be the designated driver, Jessica had allowed herself a couple of glasses of red wine with lunch too, but now the bedtime routine was stretching ominously ahead of her, she was feeling sleepy and regretting the second glass.

'You fancy putting Bella Boo to bed tonight,' she said to Chris, as he pulled out of her parents' drive and into the street.

He glanced at her and smiled. 'Yep, why don't you start typing up the next letter and check that email account for any new exciting event invites? I like doing bedtime at the weekend anyway.'

She smiled at her husband, placing her hand on his thigh as he drove. And as she watched the same familiar route flash past the window, she thought about publishing the next post and watching the comments pop up – and despite knowing it was silly, she felt tugs of worry about whether she might be on the receiving end of more negativity.

Deep in thought, the journey was quick for Jessica. They were soon pulling up alongside their house, Chris parallel parking on the street opposite. As Bella yawned sleepily, Jessica pulled her from her car seat and walked across the road to their blue front door.

Making the decision to accelerate bedtime, Chris had her bath running upstairs moments later and Jessica settled down at the dining table and opened her laptop. She started by logging into her email. She knew she should go to this baby food launch, and while she was in this mindset, she was going to send a reply to the PR to say she'd be there.

But as she opened her inbox, she was met with the sight of a new message highlighted in bold at the top.

Maria Davies: Collaboration with Mama & Me Designs?

'Collaboration?' Jessica said out loud, her fingers moving quickly to open the message.

And there it was.

Hi Jessica!

I hope you don't mind me emailing out of the blue! My name is Maria and I am the head of digital marketing for Mama & Me Designs. We make a range of stylish, organic clothing for women and their children, and for the last three years, we've worked with a team of mummy bloggers to showcase our range through their posts and social media feeds.

This year, we'd like to mix things up a bit and add some new members to our team – and your blog has caught our attention. We love the way you write and illustrate your posts, and it would be great to be one of the first brands that you collaborate with. This would be a paid campaign, so there would be a fee and you'd get to keep the clothes that you both model too.

Perhaps we could have a quick chat on Monday and I can explain more?

Kindest,

Maria Davies

'Me?' Jessica repeated out loud.

And as she re-read the email from beginning to end for a second, and then a third, and then a fourth time, her mouth fell open in shock.

7

Followers – 2,770
Emails in inbox – 23
Event invitations – 1
Paid collaborations – 1

Dear Bella,

I was scared to take you out on my own at the beginning.
Really scared. You didn't cry very often but when you
did, you demanded milk that very second. The thought
of us being in the middle of a park or wandering down a
street when you started screaming, filled me with dread.
So, we stayed at home for the first few weeks, comforted
by the proximity of the sofa, my giant breastfeeding
cushion, and a vast supply of spare Babygros folded
neatly in a drawer. I lived in my maternity pyjama
bottoms and baggy T-shirts that skimmed my still-
deflating tummy. I was mostly covered in baby sick and
usually walked around with a soggy muslin over my

shoulder, which meant that I exuded a strong whiff of vomit too. In hindsight, I know my unkempt appearance, baggy clothes, and suspicious aroma was totally normal for the early days of motherhood, but I felt like a mess. Looking back now, I realise my confidence was at an all-time low.

So, we only ventured outside our front door in the early weeks when I had back-up in the form of Daddy or your grandparents – and even then, I made every effort to persuade them that staying at home was a better option. Sometimes visions of the pre-baby me crossed my mind, kissing Daddy at the station in the morning, skipping down the high street to get a coffee, and catching the reflection of my growing baby bump in shop windows as I strolled past. How could so much have changed in so little time? Why was I suddenly so scared to leave the safety of our little world at home?

Everybody encouraged me to put you in your pram and go for a little stroll, even if it was just to the end of our road and back, but the more they pushed, the more I feared doing it.

'It'll clear your head,' Granny said, as she stood over me while I was feeding you on the sofa.

'Come on, Jess, you can't stay at home forever', Grandad said, as he watched me make myself another coffee in the kitchen.

'You'll feel so much better for it,' Daddy said on loudspeaker, as I changed yet another nappy and shook my head silently in reply.

He didn't understand. None of them did.

But in the end, I didn't have any choice. It was a Wednesday afternoon when my phone rang, and Auntie Fran was on the other end. 'Can you pick up Freddie?' she asked breathlessly – and I felt my breath catch in my throat.

'Pick him up?' I finally managed to get out, stuttering as I spoke.

'Yep, please, Jessy. He's in Greenwich Park with his football team and my client was running late so I lost track of time. Can you grab him and I'll pick him up from yours? I've left it too late now. I'm panicking.'

'Can't Mum or Dad do it?' I shot back. 'I mean Fran, I'm really busy. Bella is due a feed soon. I'm not sure… I don't know…'

'I can't get through to Mum and Dad – and I'm not going to make it in time now.' She paused for a second, leaving me to desperately try and think up a better excuse, before adding: 'He'll be on his own, Jess… Please.'

I couldn't leave your big cousin in the park on his own. A few seconds later, a message arrived with a pin to his location. I felt beyond panicked. In fact, I felt so dizzy with adrenaline that I stumbled a bit as I lowered you into your pram basket fast asleep, angry with myself that I could have woken you. You didn't stir, so I bundled a couple of blankets on top of you and tried to gather my thoughts for a moment, making a mental checklist of what I might need over the next hour or so. Throwing a nappy, big muslin blanket, and some baby wipes under the pram, I took a deep breath and opened the door. A gust of wind hit me in the face as I negotiated our way down the path.

And just like that, we had left the house.

Together.

Just you and me, Bella.

For the very first time.

And do you know what?

It wasn't nearly as bad as I feared.

Love from Mummy x

'The thing is,' Maria explained, as Jessica held the phone to her ear, 'Mama & Me is a young, fashionable brand – and for that to be communicated, we need a few new faces on the campaign.'

'OK,' Jessica replied, trying to sound professional as Bella and Tallulah scattered building blocks around her feet.

'One of the girls in the office is an avid reader of your blog, so passed on your details,' Maria continued, 'and I really, really like it. And I think it's amazing how quickly your following has grown!'

'Oh, thank you', Jessica said, following with a nervous laugh.

'It's impressive! And this is totally off the record,' Maria continued, dropping the volume of her voice, 'but we would like to make our campaign a bit younger and fresher this year, with younger mums and younger babies!'

Jessica laughed again, wondering just how young Maria thought she was.

'So now the big question!' Maria said, raising her voice to its regular volume again. 'Would you like to be on our team?'

'Oh, well yes, I think, I'd love to be. What would it involve?' Jessica asked, reaching down to pick up a brick from behind her heel and realising her hand was shaking with nerves.

'That is brilliant news!' Maria replied. 'We are so pleased to have you on board! So we'll start with a post today on our social feeds announcing the new team, and then we'll send you over the details for the shoot, which will be towards the end of August at our head office.'

'Wow, OK,' Jessica said, swallowing with nerves and excitement.

'And then when those pictures are ready, we'll just ask you to share one or two on your social feed. We'll pay your invoice within thirty days,' Maria added cheerfully.

So it was official: Jess was joining the Mama & Me blogger team. As she walked back to the kitchen, where Henny was busying herself washing up coffee mugs, she couldn't help smiling.

'All go OK, babe?' Henny asked, as she turned off the tap and looked up at her friend.

'Yes,' Jessica replied. 'Oh, you didn't have to wash up Hen, I was going to do that later.'

'Oh, it's no bother! So what did she say?' Henny asked, as she scooped Tallulah into her arms.

'Well, I think it's all sorted,' Jessica replied, glancing back into the lounge to check that Bella was still playing happily. 'I'm going to be on the new team and they're going to announce it later today. Everyone is going to be like "Who the hell is that?!"'

'I think you'll be surprised,' Henny replied. 'All the mums at school are reading now and were quite starstruck when they found out we were friends!'

'Really?' Jessica asked, taken aback. 'I can't quite get my head around that.'

'Get used to it, babe,' Henny said. 'You'll probably start being recognised on the street after doing this campaign!'

'Oh, I doubt it,' Jessica replied, laughing. 'But guess what, Hen? I'm getting paid too.'

'No way!' Henny said, smiling at her friend proudly. 'How much are we talking? Do you mind me asking, babe? Or is that rude?'

'No, don't be silly! It's going to be £200 for each of the posts. Do you think that's good?' Jessica asked.

'£200 for posting a picture?' Henny asked. 'I think that's bloody amazing babe!'

'Probably a lot less than other bloggers get offered, but it'll be nice to have a bit of my own money again,' Jessica replied.

'How much do you think they charge, then?' Henny asked, as Tallulah struggled to get back down again. 'I know it's really uncouth to talk about money, but I'm really interested in it all.'

'Oh God I don't know? Hundreds more? Thousands more?' Jessica said. 'I really don't know.'

'Wow, fair play to them. Did you hear back from the blogger lady you contacted, by the way? The one you knew when you were growing up?' Henny asked.

'Tiggy?' Jessica asked, pretending she wasn't painfully embarrassed by the lack of reply. 'Oh no... I'm sure she's got enough on her plate with the blog and her kids...'

'Oh yeah, probably, I'm sure you'll hear back soon.' Henny replied, with a kind smile.

And Henny was right – but it didn't happen for another three weeks. The message finally came on a Friday night while Jessica was bathing Bella and sending a silent prayer that her husband might be joining her at some point on the sofa. In fact, when her phone had pinged, she had fully expected it to be a stream of excuses about why he was still at his desk – so seeing it was a message from Tiggy had been a relief of sorts.

Until she read it, that was.

Because even though Tiggy hadn't been rude or deliberately unkind, Jessica knew it was a snub. She didn't want to have coffee with her, or chat to her, or give her any advice. And right from the moment she read the words on the screen, she wished she could backtrack and un-send her message. She was painfully embarrassed.

That Sunday, while surrounded by her three best friends and their families at a barbecue hosted by Mel, she confided in the girls.

'So, what did the message say?' Mel asked, as they all stood around her in the kitchen.

Jessica pulled her phone from the pocket of her jeans and scrolled to the message.

Jessica

I'll check out the blog if I find the time.

Best of luck with it all.

'And that's it?' asked Deena.

'Yep, that's it.' Jessica replied.

'And you reminded her about growing up on the same road? And asked if she fancied meeting for a coffee, so you could chat?' Henny asked.

Jessica nodded.

The four friends were silent for a moment, replaying the message in their minds.

'Well, I guess it's better than nothing,' Deena said, finally. 'She does have five kids...'

'I know,' Jessica began. 'To be honest, I didn't expect to get a reply at all...'

'What, because she's got a billion followers on social media?' interrupted Mel, as she dropped a slice of lemon into each glass. 'Oh, come on, Jess! You know her from childhood! Surely she owed you more than a quick "Sorry I'm busy, see ya!"'

Jessica nibbled a fingernail.

'You know what?' Henny said. 'She could just be busy! She might send another message when she has time. I mean that could happen? Give her the benefit of the doubt.'

Jessica nodded.

'Do you know what, though?' Mel said, unscrewing the lid from a bottle of gin. 'I don't even think you need her help any more. You're doing pretty well on your own, aren't you? Event invitations, paid jobs, loads of followers! You only started your blog a few months ago and look where you are already! Forget her! You can sound things out with us if you aren't sure about something.'

'For sure,' added Deena, watching Mel pour generous measures of gin into the bottom of each glass.

'Let's just forget it,' Jessica said quickly. 'It's really not the end of the world that she doesn't want to go for a bloody coffee with me!'

'We'll always be here for coffee, anyway,' Henny said, squeezing her arm and smiling.

'Or a massive gin,' Mel added, bending down to

check each glass had the same measure – until she was interrupted by the sound of screaming.

'Oh shit, that's Lara,' Mel said, quickly dashing out the wide kitchen doors and into the garden. But Henny's husband Dan had got there first and was consoling Lara, as Tallulah marched away from the scene with a doll in a buggy.

'She OK?' Mel called from the doorway.

'Fine,' Dan called back. 'Tallulah's just not very keen on sharing!'

'Where's Steven?' Mel asked, searching the garden for her husband.

'Just getting the charcoal to light the barbecue,' Dan replied.

'Ah. Well just shout if you need me', she called back, as she turned back to the kitchen.

'Do you think she'll be at that baby food launch thing you're going to?' Henny asked, as Mel started topping up each glass with tonic water.

'Oh, bloody hell, I forgot about that. When is the big launch?' asked Mel.

'Next Thursday,' Jessica replied. 'But I'm sure she won't be there.'

Mel finished the drinks by scooping a couple of ice cubes into each glass and then handed one to each of the girls. They each took a sip, pausing for a second to enjoy the bubbles on their lips.

'Oh, that's good!' Deena said, smacking her lips.

'Shall we hand the others to the men? Or shall we just hang out in the kitchen and drink the lot?' Henny asked, followed by her characteristic giggle.

'Plenty more where that came from,' Mel said, picking up two glasses. 'I ask Steven to buy a bottle of something whenever he passes through duty-free – and believe me girls, we're building up quite a stock... Now grab an extra glass each and let's head outside. I need to make sure he's lit the bloody barbecue or we'll still be on G&Ts at sunset.'

Each of the girls picked up an extra glass and followed Mel through the doors to the garden, enjoying the feeling of the mid-July sunshine on their skin. As the toddlers played on the lawn, taking it in turns to drive a big plastic car, push the doll buggy, and jump into a big paddling pool turned into a ball pit (or trying their best to take turns, at least), Henny's husband, Dan and Deena's partner, Ian stood alongside them kicking a ball with five-year-old Thomas. Steven and Chris were down on the patio working on lighting the barbecue. After checking that Bella was behaving herself, Jessica strolled towards them.

'Thanks, honey,' Chris said, taking his glass.

'So how's work going?' Steven asked, as he struck a long match.

'Oh, the usual,' Chris replied, turning back to Steven. 'You know, generally trying to deal with a company that thinks there are forty-eight hours in the day and attempting to escape my desk at a decent time every evening before the wife divorces me!'

'Well, silly me for thinking it was because you actually wanted to see us,' Jessica laughed, rolling her eyes. 'I'll leave you two to it.'

Heading back to sit with her friends at the table and watch the children, she spent a happy hour or so in the sunshine. As the scent of barbecuing meat started to fill the air and glasses were topped up, they took it in turns to leap up to diffuse toy tugs-of-war or pick toppled toddlers from the floor and send them on their way again.

After some teamwork in the kitchen pre-lunch, preparing a colourful spread of salads, buttering bread rolls, and grabbing bottles of sauce from the fridge, they were soon sitting together at the big wooden table in the garden, working their way through plates of food and batting wasps away as they chatted. Toddlers sat on laps and the sunshine was still (quite remarkably for London) shining brightly.

'So, Jessica, Hen tells me you've started a blog,' Dan boomed over the table in his strong Welsh accent. 'What's it about?'

Jessica felt her cheeks blush as she cut into her lamb chop. 'Oh, it's a series of letters I've been writing to Bella since she was tiny. It's just about being a mum really...' She glanced at Bella sat on Chris' lap and added, 'I guess it's about Bella. And me. But mainly Bella.'

'Ah, that's great,' Dan replied, smiling at her. 'Well done you!'

'I wouldn't want Mel to write about Lara on the Internet,' Steven suddenly called from further down the table, without looking up from his plate. 'I just don't think it's right.'

Mel shifted in her seat uncomfortably, as Jessica opened her mouth to speak – but Chris cut in first. 'Really mate?

She's very much part of Jessica's story, so it would be quite strange to leave Bella out.'

'I just don't think it's right,' Steven repeated, as he put a bit of sausage in his mouth and chewed. 'I don't really see the point of those mummy blogs at all, to be honest. Our parents got by without them, didn't they? They didn't need someone to tell them how to put a nappy on a bloody baby!' Steven laughed, while Jessica tried to cover her embarrassment by laughing along too.

'Each to their own mate,' Chris replied, taking a sip of his beer. 'I respect your opinion, but it's not how I look at it. I think it's important that there's help out there for mums. It's not something I could do every day. Hardest job in the world!' Under the table, Chris squeezed Jessica's leg in solidarity.

'You don't put pictures on the Internet of her, do you Jessica?' Steven boomed down the table, choosing to ignore Chris.

'Well,' Jessica stuttered, pushing her potato salad around her plate with her fork. 'Just the odd one...'

'I don't think it would work if she didn't include Bella,' Mel said, sticking up for her friend. 'I mean, you've got to invite people into your world for them to trust you and want to follow you. Every job demands you make big choices and take risks, and I don't think blogging is any different.'

Jessica smiled at her friend and nodded. 'Yeah that's kind of what—'

'What the fuck do you know about mummy blogging?' Steven cut her off loudly, howling with laughter. Without even looking up from his plate, he added: 'Anyway, shall we top up the ladies, darling? They're getting a bit low? The chilled Sauvignon? Do you mind? Let's keep them topped up! Thanks, darling.'

Henny, Deena and Jessica turned in shock, whilst their confident, spunky friend visibly flinched, pushed her chair back, and stood up, placing Lara down in her seat to continue eating as she made her way to the kitchen to get the next bottle of wine that was chilling in the fridge.

For a moment, the adults all ate in silence, while the toddlers babbled and threw food on the floor as a welcome distraction.

'Hey, Dan, you joining any fantasy football leagues next season?' Chris finally asked breaking the tension. 'You're welcome to join in with mine at work?'

And as they chatted about players, and goals and league tables, Deena, Henny and Jessica's eyes met across the table.

The sun eventually began to cool and drop lower in the sky, and the families all started to say goodbye and walk towards their respective homes. Jessica and Henny walked back to their neighbourhood together, falling back as the men walked ahead with the children.

'Have you ever seen him talk to her like that before?' Jessica asked quietly.

'No,' Henny replied. 'I've never seen anyone talk to Mel like that before. She's a lawyer! She can hold her own!'

'I find him pretty intimidating at the best of times, but I kind of wish one of us had stood up for her,' Jessica added, chewing her lip.

'Ah no, babe. We couldn't have done anything about that. It just isn't our place. He was equally spiteful to you, anyway.' And for a while neither of them said anything, feeling the chill of the evening as the sun dipped towards the horizon.

'It would be nice to have a proper catch-up soon, without the kids around. You wouldn't be able to pop over tomorrow evening, would you?' Henny asked, her voice upbeat.

'I should be able to,' Jessica replied. 'What are you thinking?'

'Well, Dan is out at a work thing. We could open a bottle and have a proper chat without the small people around? I'll ask Mel and Deena too?'

'God yes!' Jessica said. 'I'd love that.'

'Fab, see you tomorrow then, babe,' Henny said, pulling Jessica into a hug as they reached the end of her road.

'See you, Hen,' Jessica replied, kissing her on the cheek and turning to Dan and Tallulah to say goodbye.

As they walked the last few steps towards home, Jessica linked arms with Chris and peered over the top of the buggy to check Bella was still awake. Right on cue, she yawned widely.

Once they'd reached home and shut the world out for the evening, Jessica spent a moment unpacking her bag, and within seconds, her phone beeped in her hand.

Fran: Call me please, sister. Mega important.

Messages from Fran always worried her, so she clicked

on her number within seconds and pulled the phone to her ear.

'Hey,' Fran said breathlessly, as she picked up the phone.

'You OK?' Jessica asked.

'Yes, sorry, I ran for the phone,' Fran replied.

'No, I mean the message? Why did you want me to call you?' Jessica asked.

'Well. You aren't going to bloody believe this, Jessy. Are you ready?' Fran said.

'YES!' Jessica said impatiently, laughing with frustration. 'SPIT. IT. OUT.'

'OK, OK. Guess who's been nominated for one of the UK's biggest blogging awards?'

'I don't know,' Jessica said, bristling at the mention of blogging. 'Probably bloody Tiggy? And before you ask, no, I haven't replied to her message and I'm not going to either...'

'Well, yes, Tiggy has been nominated,' Fran cut in.

'And why did you ring to tell me this?' Jessica asked.

'Because somebody else has been nominated too,' Fran replied, enjoying teasing her sister.

The penny dropped.

'... No way,' she managed finally.

'Yes way,' Fran continued, clearing her throat as she prepared to read the news. She carried on in her best version of a cut-glass English accent: 'The following blogs have been nominated in the "Best Parenting Blog of 2018" category of the "Blog Network Awards 2018" ... Including – drumroll please – JESSICA HOLMES OF LETTERS TO MY DAUGHTER! We now invite votes in all the categories, before the four finalists for each award are revealed on Tuesday 7th August 2018 and invited to a glittering awards ceremony at Old Billingsgate on Saturday 1st September 2018. Congratulations to all the nominees – and good luck!'

'Oh my God. Are you sure? It doesn't make any sense,' Jessica said, as she let the news sink in.

'Absolutely sure. It's written in front of me, clear as day,' Fran replied.

'And how the hell do you know this? What are you reading?' Jessica asked.

'Well, I followed Tiggy's blog after we chatted about it in the park, and I saw her gloating about being nominated about half an hour ago, so I clicked on the link and discovered your name up there too,' Fran explained.

'I don't know what to say,' Jessica said, stuttering. 'This is… this is insane.'

'I know. It's insane, but it's deserved Jessy. And if you make it through to that swanky do – which obviously you will – I've already got my dress ready to be your Plus One,' Fran said.

'You'll have to kill Chris first,' Jessica replied, laughing.

'I think I can bring him down,' Fran shot back – and she was only half-joking.

8

Followers – 3,588
Emails in inbox – 289
Event invitations – 1
Paid collaborations – 1
Award nominations – 1

Dear Bella,

Back when I was pregnant with you, just about the stage where my bump started to pop and I felt a bit more confident that passers-by knew I was about to have a baby and not a big poo, I dragged your daddy to a free class about breastfeeding at the health clinic. 'Do I really have to go?' he'd asked me, as we got ready that morning. 'It's not me that is going to be breastfeeding the baby!' I was well aware that visions of a lazy afternoon on the sofa were crossing his mind. 'It says on the leaflet that both parents should attend if possible,' I replied, feeling daunted about walking into a room full of strangers to talk about my nipples. 'Please come. I don't really want to do it on my own.'

I looked at him with big, pleading eyes and rubbed my swollen belly, and after a brisk five-minute walk from our house in what felt like sub-zero temperatures, we were both strolling through the doors of the clinic. It was a two-hour session that involved holding dolls in various positions and an expert at the front demonstrating compressions with a neon pink crocheted boob. It was surreal and I had to stifle giggles on more than one occasion, but when we walked out, I felt so well educated on all things lactation that I didn't have a doubt we would make it work. I was all set to be an Earth Mother, going about my daily business with a baby attached to my boob.

But when you arrived Bella, I realised that real nipples were completely different from neon pink crocheted ones. And the baby? Well, let's just say that you were harder to manipulate into all those positions than a plastic doll weighing less than a bag of sugar. I found the whole thing desperately and shockingly hard.

Why did nobody tell me that it would be so difficult? Why didn't that woman standing at the front say: 'Now listen, ladies! You are going to find this really fucking difficult – but keep going! It will get better! Remember these words when you are sat on your sofas with newborns in your arms! It WILL work eventually and I promise it will be worth it!' Because that would have been a bit more help than harping on about the best ways to store breastmilk in the fridge or sharing her personal recommendation for nipple pads that wouldn't chafe.

In those early days, I was so angry with that woman and her neon pink boob. In fact, in a couple of particularly fraught moments when you weren't latching and I thought you were going to starve, I asked your daddy to track her down and kill her (and believe me Bella, I wasn't entirely joking). It was frustrating, it was painful, and it was worrying. And to be honest Bella, I didn't enjoy those early few weeks of breastfeeding at all.

But we kept going. And as the weeks ticked on and we got into more of a routine (along with a perfectly timed visit from our health visitor, where my boobs were squeezed way more times than felt appropriate), it suddenly seemed to get easier. We were finding a routine and getting used to feeding positions, and we were getting better as each day passed.

In fact, I was happily scrolling through social media on my phone during a feed when you were about three weeks old when it suddenly struck me like a lightning bolt. THE LATCH HADN'T HURT! In fact, I barely remembered placing you on my boob – it had just kind of happened. And with that moment of realisation, I put down my phone and stared at you feeding, chomping away like a little snorting piglet.

I wasn't an Earth Mother, Bella. I never mastered the

art of walking around feeding you, I didn't pose for empowering photos with my boob out, and choosing what to wear that allowed easy access to my nipples every morning was always one of the hardest decisions of my day.

But it was finally working.

And I felt so bloody proud of myself for carrying on.

Love from Mummy x

Jessica re-read the email.

Dear Jessica,

Firstly, I'd like to personally congratulate you on the success of your blog since you launched it back in May. Here at the 'Blog Network Awards', we nominate one up-and-coming blog every year in each category. We understand it's a hard industry to break into and want to recognise those bloggers that have managed it quickly and admirably. And on that note, we are delighted to inform you that a judging panel has chosen 'Letters to My Daughter' as the newcomer in the 'Parenting Blogger' category for 2018!

'Letters to My Daughter' has been listed alongside seven of the top Parenting Blogs in the UK and will now be open to votes until the shortlist is announced in early August. We wish you the very best of luck with both the awards and the future of your blog. If you have any questions regarding the process, please don't hesitate to reach out to me. I do hope to meet you personally on Saturday 1st September.

Kindest Regards,

Bob Thomas, Chief Executive of the Blog Network Awards

It was Monday evening – and a day had passed since Fran had delivered the news, since Jessica had logged onto her emails with hands shaking and heart racing and since she'd told Chris and stared at him with an open mouth, barely able to string a sentence together in shock. But as the email re-played in her mind, she still found it hard to believe it.

She'd been nominated for the biggest and best respected parenting blogger award in the country. The one everyone wanted to win. For a moment, she let herself imagine walking into that awards ceremony clinging to Chris' arm. She let herself hear 'Jessica Holmes of Letters to My Daughter' being called out in a packed ballroom. It all seemed like a bit of a dream – and if she didn't get enough votes to make it through to the shortlist, it would remain just that.

Hearing Chris' key turning in the front door, she quickly snapped back to reality. And with a pass of the baby monitor into his palm, Jessica ran out the door as soon as he came through it.

'Just in time,' she whispered as she made her way out of the door, adding over her shoulder: 'Don't forget to check her, OK? I won't be late.'

'Wait, honey!' he called back. 'You forgot this!'

She stopped by their front gate and glanced back at him, noticing for the first time that there was a bottle of champagne in his hands. Jessica broke into a smile and walked back to take it from him.

'You deserve it,' he said, handing it over. 'I'm so bloody proud. Have a great night!'

Jessica kissed him and smiled, retracing her steps out of their front gate as she said goodbye. The walk to Henny's house was only a few minutes and her hand slowly grew more and more numb against the coldness of the bottle as she walked. Henny had sent her a text a few minutes earlier.

Door is on the latch! Let yourself in when you arrive and pour yourself a glass from the fridge. I'll be downstairs as soon as I can.

Reaching the front door, Jessica quietly pushed it open and stepped inside. She could hear voices and the sound of water rushing down a plughole upstairs, so walked quietly through to the kitchen to put the champagne in the fridge. The kitchen was small and cluttered, with a baking tray still sitting on the side covered in crumbs and the sink full of dirty dishes from teatime. The fridge and walls were covered in colourful pieces of Thomas' artwork, while the kitchen worktop still bore the sticky remnants of a couple of superhero stickers that Henny had obviously attempted to remove.

As she wandered into the lounge next door, her foot slipped on a small toy car on the carpet and she nearly went flying across the room. Steadying herself, she bent down to pick it up, stashing it in a toy box with an audible clunk. She had to move a big pile of washing from the sofa before she could sit down, feeling awkward when her fingers brushed a pair of Dan's boxer shorts on the top of the pile.

It might not be show-home-perfect, but Jessica loved being at Henny's house. It was warm and homely, very much like her lovely friend who owned it.

'Hi, babe!' Henny called, as she made her way down the stairs (at least a couple of octaves quieter than her usual voice). 'Did you get a glass of wine?'

'No, Chris sent me with champagne!' Jessica said, as she walked out the lounge to meet her.

'Oh, bloody hell!' Henny hollered, forgetting to quieten her voice in her excitement. She paused for a second, turning towards the stairs, and when silence resumed, she continued in a loud whisper: 'He's a keeper! Ah I wish Mel and Deena were coming so we could all celebrate together.'

'Deena can't make it?' Jessica asked. 'I knew Mel couldn't make it as Steven is away again, but I was hoping Deena would come.'

'She's got to work, babe, somebody called in sick,' Henny said, picking up a small robot from underneath her foot and throwing it into the toy box behind her. 'It's crap, I know. I was so excited for us all to all be together! But never mind, we'll still have a great night! Come on, let's open the champers in the garden!'

They walked into the kitchen together, with Henny swooping down to grab the champagne from the fridge as she passed. 'Can you grab two glasses from above the sink, babe?' Henny asked, as she unlocked the door to the garden and stepped outside. Jessica reached up to discover a row of champagne glasses with the words 'BEST MUMMY' emblazoned across them in pink glitter. Grabbing two, she followed Henny outside and watched as her friend twisted the cork and effortlessly popped it.

It was still bright and sunny at 7.20 p.m. and the sound of birdsong and a distant lawn mower filled the air as they clinked their glasses together. 'Well done on the award nomination, babe,' Henny said warmly. 'It's amazing really. I'm totally made up for you.'

Jessica smiled, and they both took their first sip.

'Oh wow, it's a good one!' Henny said, as the bubbles filled her mouth. 'He must be very proud of you! He doesn't even get to drink it himself!'

'There's a first for everything,' Jessica laughed. 'He's probably hoping we'll save him a glass.'

'No bloody chance,' Henny said, giggling. 'Come on, let's go back inside in case the kids cause trouble.'

When they got back into the lounge, Henny put down her glass and whizzed around the room picking up toys and throwing cushions back on the sofa.

'You don't need to do that!' Jessica protested.

'Well, this is the time I usually do it, babe! My two

become feral before bed,' she said, picking up the pile of washing from the floor and moving it into the hallway. 'Now that's done, let's drink!'

'Cheers to that,' said Jessica, as they both took a sip.

'So you got nominated as the best newbie blogger then?' Henny asked. 'How many others are on the list? I'm intrigued!'

'There's eight in total,' said Jessica, picking up her phone to look at the list she had taken a screenshot of earlier. 'The others have all been around for a while, so I'm pretty sure this is the furthest I'll get, but it's very cool to be included. It actually makes me feel like a real blogger!'

'You *are* a real blogger!' Henny protested, shaking her head and laughing.

Jessica smiled at her friend. 'Want me to read out the other names?'

When Henny nodded enthusiastically, Jessica cleared her throat and made her way down the list:

- Tiggy Blenheim – Tiggy Does Motherhood
- Graeme Henley – Papa Won't Preach
- Lucy Wilde – Wilde About The Girls
- Jessica Holmes – Letters To My Daughter
- Amaya Abbas – Quiet Kids, I'm Blogging
- Jackson Freeman – And Then Came The Kids
- Wendy Felicia Cooper – Hiding in the Bathroom
- Anwen Michaels – This Is Where The Wild Things Are

'I haven't even heard of half of them, so I think you

stand a brilliant chance! And how many get through to the big glitzy ceremony?' Henny asked.

'Four. So half won't make the cut,' Jessica explained.

'Jesus, it's like *Big Brother*,' Henny said, giggling. 'So how do you get through to the next bit?'

Jessica paused, letting the bubbles pop in her mouth before she swallowed. 'I'm supposed to ask my readers to vote for me. It just feels a bit cringe! I'm not sure I'm going...'

'No!' Henny interrupted loudly, taking Jessica by surprise. 'Of course you have to! Right, let's do it now.'

'Ah no,' Jessica said, shifting in her seat. 'I'll do it tomorrow or something, I've no idea what I'm going to say.'

'Don't be silly, babe. You're great with words. Let's write it together,' Henny said, standing up and grabbing a pen and piece of paper from the cabinet in the hallway.

'Uh right, well OK,' Jessica replied hesitantly.

'Hang on, we need a photo of you to go with it,' Henny said, sitting back down on the sofa. She paused for a moment and looked at Jessica to think. As Jessica lifted her glass to her mouth, Henny suddenly jumped up. 'I've got it! The champagne glass!'

Jessica looked down at the glass. 'BEST MUMMY' it read in pink glitter. She supposed it worked quite well with her holding up a champagne glass to celebrate her nomination. But if the picture was going to be light-hearted and cheery, she already knew the words alongside it needed to be from the heart.

'OK, write this down,' Jessica said, sitting forward.

Henny nodded, poised with pen and paper, and the pair of them got to work. Finally, when they finished, Jessica picked up the piece of paper with pride.

Dear readers,

I usually write my letters to Bella, but tonight, I think it is time that I write to you. Because I need to say thank you for following my blog for the past couple of months. Thank you for your comments, for liking my posts, for sharing them with your friends, and for taking the time to read my many mumbles about motherhood. I have always wanted to be a writer and penning these letters to my daughter has given me an outlet to do it.

But it's more than that. It's about revisiting those early days as a mother when I sit down at my laptop. It's about feeling supported by a wonderful tribe of ladies who understand exactly how I feel. And it's about creating a document for Bella in the future, so that she can look back and understand that it might not have always been easy, but that she was always my priority.

But now, my lovely readers, I need a favour. For some inexplicable reason, these letters to my daughter have been nominated in the 'Blog Network Awards' in the 'Best Parenting Blog' category. One very new blogger is nominated every year in each category, and for the parenting award, that happens to be me. Once I'd picked my jaw up from the floor after hearing this news, a mere two months after I first published a blog post, I discovered that I would need to ask my readers to vote for me. And if enough of you lovely lot are kind enough to click on the link I'm going to pop below, I may get the chance to wear a pretty dress and head to a glitzy awards ceremony in September. So I am asking if you'd mind giving it a quick click? I quite like wearing frocks and drinking champagne – but mainly, it would mean an awful lot to be recognised as an actual writer and to know that you all enjoy these letters as much as I have enjoyed writing them for my daughter.

Thank you, thank you, thank you – from Bella, from my husband, but mostly from me xx

'Bloody hell, you're good with words, babe,' Henny said. 'It's perfect.'

Jessica smiled at her friend. 'Right, I'm going to type it on my phone and then, when I've had a few more glasses of the strong stuff, I'm going to post it.'

'Hang on, babe, we need the picture!' Henny said, grabbing her phone. 'Now stand against this wall and raise your glass.' Henny pointed at a space of plain white wall to the left of the TV and Jessica dutifully nodded and moved to it.

'How shall I pose? I'm not good at this...' Jessica asked, suddenly feeling very awkward and taking a sip for courage.

'Jess, stop drinking! The glass needs to be full!' Henny laughed. 'Now, raise the glass to the camera.'

Jessica did as she was told, smiling into the camera as if to say 'cheers' to her readers. After taking about twenty photos, Henny flicked back through her camera roll and passed it over to Jessica to have a scroll.

'Oh God, they're awful,' she said as she flicked through the photos, the same response she always gave when she saw a photo of herself.

'No! You look beautiful, babe. Look at the second one, it's gorgeous,' Henny said, grabbing her phone back and flicking to the photo to show her.

Jessica stared at the photo of herself. She looked tired, with dark circles underneath her eyes. A couple of hormonal blemishes on her chin needed a bit of concealer. Her hair could probably do with a brush. And while she was pleased she'd bothered painting on some lipstick before she left the house, she could see a smudge on her tooth in the photo. But despite all this, she knew she was her own worst critic and that blogging was all about revealing her true self.

'Oh, fuck it. It'll do,' Jessica said, passing the phone back to Henny. 'Can you send it to me? I'll type out the message and then I can attach it.'

The girls sat together as Jessica typed out the message and Henny drank her champagne. A cry from Tallulah resulted in a dash up the stairs, with her mother ranting about the 'bloody pointlessness of dummies' when she came back down and joined Jessica on the sofa. When Jessica had finished typing, she passed her phone to Henny to read through. 'Can you double-check it? This champagne is going to my head!' she said, her cheeks starting to flush.

Henny laughed and took the phone. 'You and me both, babe, but I'll do my best.'

She read and scrolled, pointing out a couple of typos, and when she was sure everything was OK, she passed it back. 'Right, I think we're good to go. Ready to post it?'

'Do you think I should wait until the morning? Maybe I need to sleep on it…' Jessica said.

'No!' Henny squealed. 'Just post it. I'm off to get the bottle, because this stuff is too good to leave in the fridge.'

While Henny was grabbing the bottle, Jessica took a deep breath and pressed 'POST'.

'OK it's done,' she said under her breath. 'Now let's just see what happens.'

It wasn't long before they both forgot about the post, polishing off the champagne, then opening the bottle of white wine that was waiting in the fridge.

'Oh, I wish the girls were here with us,' Henny said, as she poured the first glasses, splashing wine onto the coffee table as it glugged out of the bottle.

'Me, too, it's been ages since we've got together without the children,' Jessica replied, taking her glass from Henny.

'Do you think Mel's OK?' Henny asked, her voice suddenly quiet and concerned.

'I don't know. I've been thinking about the way Steven spoke to her a lot since yesterday,' Jessica replied.

'I mean, what he said wasn't that bad. But if he talks to her like that in front of us lot, what is he like behind closed doors?' Henny added, curling her legs underneath her on the sofa as she spoke.

'Well, it sounds like he isn't around a lot at the moment. And maybe that's a good thing…' Jessica shrugged and sighed.

'He's always on work trips, isn't he?' Henny asked. 'I know they have an insane house and tons of money, but how are you supposed to enjoy it if you're never together?

'I think it's a mixture. Sometimes work trips and sometimes visiting his other kids in Sweden,' Jessica said. 'I always forget about the older kids being over there.'

'Me too… Mel hardly talks about it. And I don't think his ex-wife has brought those kids back to London a single time since she moved, so Steven has to fly out or he doesn't see them,' Henny added. 'It must be hard for him, I guess. Can you imagine if Chris couldn't see Bella? I mean, that must be tough.' Henny shook her head. 'But that still doesn't give him the right to talk to her like that. It scares me.'

'Me too,' Jessica replied, remembering the moment Mel flinched at his words.

'I hope she's OK. I mean, I selfishly don't really want her to go back to work, because it means our Tuesday coffee dates will be over, but I know she'll be happier when she's back at her desk and feeling like herself again.'

'So why doesn't she go back? What's the hold up?' Jessica asked.

'Steven doesn't want her to,' Henny explained. 'He didn't have a nanny for his son or daughter from his first marriage and he doesn't want Lara to be bought up by one either. They've argued a lot about it.'

'But he knew she was a lawyer when he met her! That's hardly fair!' Jessica said, shaking her head.

'Well, exactly babe…' Henny said. 'But I hope they work it out. I know she wants it to work. She bloody loves that man. We'll just have to keep an eye on her.'

Jessica nodded, and Henny smiled in reply.

'Now, are you ready for a funny story?' Jessica asked.

'Go on,' Henny said, sitting forward to listen.

'I spent most of this morning with my child's poo smeared on my forehead.'

Having just taken a sip of wine, Henny nearly spat it out all over the sofa. 'Whaaaaaat?' she asked, her eyes wide with shock.

'Yep, you heard me right,' Jessica replied. 'I had to change the most horrendous nappy first thing this morning. You know the kind that goes right up their back and you have to chuck them in the bath and do an entire head-to-foot change? It was one of those. Typical that she stored it all weekend when her dad was around and left it for me on a Monday morning. But anyway, I had to sort it out. And God knows how, but I managed to smear some on my forehead as I was cleaning her up. Just above my right eyebrow. I didn't even notice until past lunchtime.'

'Oh shit!' Henny said, howling with laughter. 'I mean literally! Shit!'

'And do you want to know the worst bit?' Jessica asked, struggling to stifle the giggles.

'I don't know if I can take it...' Henny gasped.

'I went to Tesco this morning. I went to bloody Tesco!' Jessica replied, which sent Henny over the edge.

'Stop! Stop babe! I'm going to wee myself! My pelvic floor can't take it!' she howled, before Jessica snorted and the cycle started all over again.

They were laughing so loudly that they didn't even hear the front door opening so they jumped out of their skin when Dan walked in and suddenly piped up: 'Oh bloody hell! What do we have here?' at the sight before him. 'Hello, Jessica,' he added. 'And I believe, congratulations are in order too!'

Jessica blushed as she stumbled to her feet and walked over to kiss him on the cheek. 'Oh, thanks Dan, so embarrassing. How do you know?'

'I saw it just now on your page! I was looking on the train. Stood against that wall right there, with a champagne glass in your hand, you were. You've got a lot of likes and comments already. I bet you're cleaning up on the votes too!' he said, stroking his beard.

'Have I?' Jessica replied, trying to find her phone to have a quick scroll. 'Oh crap, I can't find my phone now. Hen, do you have my phone?'

'No, let me help you look. We need to look at that post and see how it's doing,' Henny replied, starting to pull out the sofa cushions next to Jessica to hunt for the phone.

Dan started guffawing with laughter, his belly shaking from underneath his slightly-too-tight shirt as he howled. 'It's right next to you, Jessica! On the arm of the sofa! How much have you both had?'

Henny joined in with the laughter, quickly followed by Jessica. Before long, they were both on their knees laughing, with Henny squealing, 'I can't laugh like this! I've had two babies! I need a wee!' which set Jessica off all over again.

'I think it's time to go home,' Jessica said finally, with tears streaming down her face. 'Thank you for an amazing evening, Henny! I really, really needed this!'

She stood up and kissed Henny goodbye, stumbling a little as she walked across the lounge. Glancing down at her phone in her hand, she noticed the time.

00:21

'Oh shit, Chris will be sending out a search party,' she said. 'Really need to go home!'

Dan walked her to the door. 'See you soon, Jessica,' he said. 'Enjoy the headache in the morning!'

Walking out their front door and down their path, Jessica turned and blew a kiss back to Dan and Henny standing in the hallway.

And with that, she hiccupped towards home.

9

Followers – 5,201
Emails in inbox – 51
Event invitations – 7
Paid collaborations – 1
Award nominations – 1

Dear Bella,

It was a warm day in the middle of May, and you were just nine weeks old, sleeping in my arms after a feed. I was zoned out watching some nonsense on the TV, with the doors open to the garden and a lovely breeze wafting into the lounge to cool us. Suddenly my phone started ringing next to me, jumping and buzzing as it rang, threatening to fly off the sofa. I was annoyed with that phone call at first, fearing it would wake you, and I considered stuffing the phone down the side of the sofa and ignoring it. But instead I sighed, picked it up, and answered it.

And that phone call turned out to be the worst phone call of my life.

'Is that you, Jess?' Granny asked, as I answered. 'Yes, Mum, of course it's me, are you OK?' It didn't sound like Granny. Her voice was high and nasal and my first thought was that she had a really heavy cold. When my question was met with silence, I added: 'Are you sick?' When that was met with silence too, apart from a couple of sniffs, it suddenly dawned on me that something was wrong. My body froze and my blood turned completely cold. I held my breath and waited, with every muscle tensed to try and protect myself against what was about to come.

'Mum? PLEASE TALK TO ME!' I was shouting now; confused and panicked. In my arms, your eyes opened. You stared up at me and then shut them again, completely oblivious to the horror that was unfolding.

Suddenly Grandad's voice was on the end of the phone. 'Jessica?' he said.

'Yes, Dad!' I said, relieved to hear his voice. 'What's going on?'

'It's Michael,' he replied.

'Michael? What's wrong? He's had an accident?'

'No, Jess, he's dead.'

And then silence.

Grandad went on to tell me about how Uncle Michael had been on a business trip to Paris and hadn't turned up to his meeting that morning. A chambermaid had found him in bed in his room later that morning, unresponsive. An ambulance was called and he was taken to hospital, but he'd already been declared dead right there on the hotel bed, with a view of the Eiffel Tower from his window.

As he spoke, I could hear the sound of sobbing in the background.

'Where's Fran?' I interrupted.

'She's here. I'm leaving to get Freddie from school now. I've no idea how to tell him, Jess. I don't know what we'll say...'

'How is she?' I asked, unable to concentrate on anything but the sound of her sobs.

Grandad paused and sighed. 'Well...' he began, but his voice broke. And I didn't need to hear any more.

Life changed when we got that phone call, Bella.

For Auntie Fran, who has missed Michael every second of every day since.

For Freddie, who lost the man he'd always considered a father.

For Granny and Grandad, who gave up their home without hesitation and stumbled, unprepared, into grief.

For Daddy, who lost one of his closest friends.

For me, because I watched people I loved so dearly fall apart.

And for you, Bella – because you never got to know an amazing man who loved you. Who held you in the biggest cuddles, rocking you gently until you slept. Who was always smiling, bringing warmth to a room as soon as he walked into it. Who made your Auntie Fran so happy, so complete, and so loved. I have no doubt that he would have been such an important and appreciated influence in your life as you grew up. But suddenly, it was all taken away.

That phone call changed everything Bella, but it taught me something too. It taught me that life can take a different turn at any second.

And, from that day onwards, our cuddles were always a little tighter.

And we held onto each other, hoping that life would once again seem a little brighter.

Love from Mummy x

Jessica made it home from Henny's five minutes later, stumbling in the dark to fit her key in the lock and open the door as quietly as she could. As she walked into the hallway, she could see the light in the lounge was off, which meant Chris had already gone to bed. She picked up a foot to take off her shoe but swayed into the wall and giggled. Realising sitting down was a better tactic, she slid down the wall to the floor – and that was when she noticed a note scrawled on a piece of paper at the bottom of the stairs.

SURPRISE! I'VE GOT THE DAY OFF WORK TOMORROW!
I took the day-in-lieu I was owed, so we could all spend the day together.
I'm in the spare room so Bella and I don't disturb you in the morning.
HAVE A LIE IN – WE ARE SO PROUD OF YOU!
xxx

'Jesus,' she said out loud, letting the words sink in. 'But I have music class! I'll still have to go to music class! He's forgotten, but we can't miss that.'

But when the hallway started to spin around the note, she decided it was time for bed. She poured herself a large glass of water in the kitchen and climbed the stairs slowly, determined not to trip and wake Bella. And after throwing her clothes into a heap on the floor and climbing under the duvet, she fell into a deep sleep in seconds, with her lashes still coated in mascara, the curtains still wide open, and the light still shining brightly on the ceiling.

She didn't open her eyes again until 7 a.m. the next morning, and she immediately regretted it. 'Oh fuck!' she groaned, as light streamed through the open curtains and burnt her eyeballs. 'That second bottle was *such* a bad idea.' She lay still for a while, expecting to feel a rush of nausea or pain flood to her head. When it didn't come, she decided to stay that way for a few minutes, lying as still as possible and hoping to fall back to sleep. But after hearing Bella chatting in her cot in the room next door, there was no way she was going to be able to drift off.

Bella's chattering quickly turned to loud protests and she eventually heard Chris' footsteps across the hallway to collect her, saying 'Shh, don't wake Mummy,' as they made their way down the stairs.

Giving up on sleep, she opened her eyes slowly, letting them get used to the light. Heaving herself out of bed, she pulled the curtains shut and turned off the light above her head quickly, exhaling with the relief that came with darkness. Once back in bed, she picked up her phone from her bedside table and clicked onto social media. And there was the post, complete with a cheesy grin and flushed cheeks from a bit too much champagne.

Jessica cringed as she studied the picture and read the accompanying words. 'Why didn't I wait until I was sober?' she thought, continuing to scroll down the page. But her embarrassment turned to shock as she clapped eyes on '1.5K Likes' written underneath the post.

'OH. MY. GOD!' she said out loud, scanning her eyes on the hundreds of comments underneath:

Katie Feltmore: I don't think it's any exaggeration to say that I have fallen in love with your blog posts, Jessica. I have a five-month old baby and hearing your story through these beautiful letters to Bella has made it all seem a bit less scary.

Rosie Baker: VOTED! Best blog ever and very well deserved! So happy to hear they chose you as the newcomer – and I hope you go on to win it!

Janice Brown-Turner: This is the best news! I love your blog and you have my vote! Good luck!

Wendy Pullen: I have just voted for you dear. I am a grandmother now to three little pickles and your letters to Bella have brought everything back.

Caroline Louise Taylor: I never write comments on here but I had to write to say congratulations and that I've already clicked through to vote. I have just had my second baby and reading your letters to your daughter over the past few weeks have become the highlight of my day. Keep going and well done!

Jessica read every comment, sprawled out in bed like a starfish. Self-promotion didn't come easily to her, and as she read, she swung between blushing and smiling. *Have they all clicked through to vote for me?* she wondered, as her mind turned for a moment to the possibility of being invited to the awards ceremony. But as quickly as she thought about it, she forced herself to stop. She knew she had very little chance of beating the likes of Tiggy and her equally-popular fellow nominees.

Oh, Tiggy Blenheim. As much as she tried not to think about her, she found it impossible – and as soon as she popped into Jessica's mind, her fingers worked on autopilot to click through to the other blogger's social media page and see how her own 'VOTE FOR ME!' post was doing.

And there it was, pinned to the top of her page. A photo of Tiggy and her kids sitting on a white sofa, with a bottle of champagne in one hand and in the other, a sign written by a child that read: PLEASE VOTE FOR MUMMY!

Jessica continued scrolling, with the words underneath the photograph reading:

We're celebrating in the Blenheim house today! 'Tiggy Does Motherhood' has been nominated to be the 'Best Parenting Blog' in the 'Blog Network Awards' for the third year in a row! And this year, we're hoping Mummy will take the crown! We'd love your vote at this link: http://www.blognetworkawards.com.

Should I congratulate her? Jessica thought, as she read to the end of the post. It seemed unfair to carry on scrolling without saying something. Tiggy had done well to be nominated three years in a row, and Jessica could only imagine how demoralising it was to walk away without winning it.

She made a snap decision and started typing in the comment box underneath Tiggy's post.

Congratulations Tiggy! So well-deserved and best of luck with the shortlist. Jessica (Letters to my Daughter) xx

Reading her comment back and then posting it, she threw her phone down next to her on the pillow and sighed. Her head was starting to pound, but she knew she needed to ward off the hangover by eating some breakfast. Taking a deep breath, she heaved herself out of bed, grabbed her pyjama bottoms from the back of the chair, and made her way downstairs.

'Anyone home?' she called, as she got to the bottom of the stairs.

'MAMAMAMAMAMAMAMA' came a little voice, as Bella toddled towards her and threw herself with force at Jessica's legs. She picked her up and cuddled her close, kissing hair that smelt like baby shampoo.

Chris quickly appeared from the kitchen. 'You're supposed to be in bed! How's the head?'

'Umm, not sure yet,' Jessica said, as Bella writhed in her arms to get down. Allowing her to toddle off, she walked towards Chris and kissed him on the lips. 'This was a nice surprise, thank you babe!'

Chris smiled, as Jessica leaned into him for a cuddle. 'Nothing I'd rather do than spend the day with my girls,' he said. 'And Bella has been teaching me all about *Teletubbies* this morning. It's been fun.'

'Oh, lucky you,' Jessica laughed, enjoying the feeling of being in his arms. 'You know I'm supposed to be at class with the girls today, don't you?'

'Oh shit,' Chris said, pulling away and looking at her. 'Do you want to go? We can always just hang out as a family this afternoon.'

'No, I think I'll wallow here in my pyjamas instead. I'll message the girls and say I'm out today,' Jessica replied. 'Is there anything for breakfast?'

'You're in luck,' Chris said, smiling. 'Bella has just enjoyed the finest scrambled eggs and bacon – and there's a portion left for you.'

'My bacon is going into a sandwich,' Jessica said cheerily, strolling into the kitchen to get started.

'OK, honey,' Chris said, walking into the lounge to find Bella. 'And no need to hurry, because Bella and I are planning to head to the park soon and leave you in peace to shower and type the next award-winning blog post. So if you are sure about skipping class, you can just hang out on the sofa.'

He kept his promise, and twenty minutes later, with the crumbs from one demolished sandwich on her plate, they had left. Jessica wasn't sure he'd taken anything for Bella to eat or drink, or wipes and nappies, but she hadn't had the energy to get involved in the getting-ready process, soaking up the rare opportunity to relax on the sofa and watch Bella play as her daddy did all the running around.

And now it was quiet. Jessica couldn't remember the

last time she'd been left alone at home. The silence roared in her ears as she sat on the sofa and tried to muster up the enthusiasm to head upstairs to shower. When she finally managed it, she climbed the stairs slowly and grabbed her phone from the bed to check for messages.

Two stared at her from the home screen:

Fran: UMMM HELLO! 1.6K LIKES! You are so winning that award Jessy! Talk later?

Henny: How's the head, babe? Can't say mine feels great. School run wasn't fun this morning! See you at class. May vomit. xx

She typed back quickly:

Hey sister. Head thumping from too much champagne last night. STOP TALKING ABOUT THE AWARD. I AM NOT GOING TO WIN. Need to chat to you about something shortly. I'll call when I'm out the shower.

Hey Henny. Don't hate me but I got home to discover a note from Chris saying he was taking the day off and am now home alone… I'm skipping class today and spending the day on the sofa. Say hi to the girls from me and sorry we won't be there xx

Once she was back downstairs, showered and feeling much more human (with a hot coffee in her hand that she'd actually get to drink), she picked up her phone. Fran answered after two rings.

'Hello, this is Fran speaking. Any top mummy bloggers on the other line?'

'Ha, ha,' Jessica said. 'Enough of that. Although it's kind of why I'm calling.'

'Why, what's up?' Fran asked.

'I've written a blog post about Michael,' Jessica said, hearing Fran swallow loudly on the other end of the phone. 'It's a really important part of Bella's story, but I need to make sure you're happy with me posting it.'

'OK,' Fran said quietly. 'Send it to me.'

'Are you angry?' Jessica asked, aware of the change in tone.

'No, I'm touched, Jessy. Really touched.' Fran replied.

Jessica paused. 'I'm going to email it to you now. Let me know, OK?'

'I'll pour myself a large whisky and read it,' Fran said, laughing.

'Make it a large coffee. And if you want me to change anything, let me know. I'll change anything you want.'

'Deal. Speak soon. And Jessy?'

'Yep?' she answered.

'Thank you. For remembering him.'

'How could I ever forget?' Jessica replied, with a lump in her throat. 'Speak later. Love you.'

'Love you, too,' Fran said, hanging up.

Jessica grabbed her laptop and emailed the blog post to Fran. She was worried that it would stir up feelings that Fran didn't want to revisit, but she knew she couldn't write the story of Bella's first year without it.

It had been the morning of Tuesday 16th May 2017 when life had changed forever. Fran had just dropped twelve-year-old Freddie at school and was busying herself in the kitchen before her first client arrived (Rebecca Stirling, 10 a.m., Bikini Wax; details she'd never been able to scratch from her mind). As the kettle boiled, she had heard a knock at the front door and assumed she'd arrived early, but when she swung it open, two female police officers had been standing the other side.

'Mrs Henderson?' the police officer on the left had asked.

Fran would never forget the sympathy in her eyes as she searched them for clues.

She nodded, her tongue suddenly unable to move.

'I'm sorry, but I have some bad news for you. Is anybody with you at home?'

Fran stopped breathing right there on the doorstep, as every member of her family flashed through her mind in quick succession and nausea rose quickly from the pit of her stomach into her mouth.

'Can I come inside?' the police officer had asked, taking her hand.

Fran must have nodded again, as the police officers lead her to a sofa and asked her to sit down. She didn't know how she heard any more of the conversation, because blood roared loudly in her ears.

But she did hear it.

'I'm so sorry to tell you that your husband, Mr Michael Henderson, was found today in his hotel room in Paris. I'm very sorry Mrs Henderson, but he didn't have a pulse and was pronounced dead at hospital shortly afterwards. He had a heart attack. Is there anybody we can call for you? We really are very, very sorry.'

Fran couldn't remember much more about that afternoon, but Jessica knew that she hastily packed a suitcase of clothes for herself and Freddie that same afternoon and moved back to her parents' home, sharing a bed with Freddie until her dad cleared out his office to create a room for him a few weeks into their stay.

They hadn't been back to that home in Dulwich ever since – so on that fateful morning, Fran had lost her partner, her home, and her business in one fell swoop. Michael was gone forever, which was catastrophic. But Jessica couldn't help feeling that Fran was lost that morning too.

Jessica allowed her mind to wander back to the man that Michael had been before that morning, flicking through photographs on her laptop to illustrate the blog post. And after half an hour of reminiscing, she found the perfect shot.

In the photo, Michael sat on the very same sofa she was sitting on now, holding a tiny Bella when she was only a few days old. He was smiling down at her, with Fran beside him, beaming into the camera. As Jessica studied that photo, her heart pricked and ached. The size of Bella in his arms, the look of adoration on his face, and the happiness of Fran's smile. At the time, it was just another photo of Bella being held by a family member in a long stream of first-meetings – but in the space of one two-minute phone call, it had become so much more.

Michael had been a big man. Not chubby, but big. He was very tactile and would wrap you in the biggest bear hugs with giant arms that seemed to envelop your whole body. You could get lost in those hugs. Jessica could still shut her eyes and remember exactly how they felt. But despite his size, he was not imposing. He was warm, caring, and softly-spoken, and children especially seemed to love him.

Fran had met Michael when Freddie was only two years old, shortly after his biological father had upped and left them. And while the whole family had been shocked at first when this giant man had arrived with Fran and Freddie to join them for a roast dinner (after all, her first husband had been partial to designer stubble, skinny jeans, and leather jackets), they all very quickly realised this was the man that they both needed. Older than Fran by fifteen years, complete with a divorce and two grown-up daughters, he wasn't the person Jessica had expected to sweep her sister off her feet – but everybody could see that he was the right one.

Within months of their meeting, it was as if he'd always been part of the family. And that's where everyone expected him to stay.

Lost in thought, Jessica jumped when the door knocked. 'Are you two back already?' she called, as she strolled through the hallway.

But when she pulled the door open, it wasn't Chris and Bella standing on the doorstep.

'Fran!' Jessica said in shock, realising instantly that her sister had been crying. Her mascara was smudged under her eyes, while her skin was covered in telltale red blotches (neither of them had been able to hide when they were feeling emotional throughout their childhood and teenage years thanks to the affliction of those red blotches). 'Oh Jesus, are you OK?'

Jessica expected her to fall into her arms and start crying, as had been so often the case over the past year, but it was different today.

'I'm fine,' Fran said, with a quick smile. 'Are you going to invite me in?'

Jessica took a step backwards and ushered her sister towards the lounge. Fran stepped inside, dropping her bag onto the floor in the hallway with a thud and heading straight for the sofa.

Jessica sat down next to her. 'I'm sorry. I'm an idiot. I should never have assumed it was OK to share that letter…'

'It's perfect,' Fran interrupted.

Jessica stopped.

'It's really perfect,' Fran continued. 'And that's why I cried like an idiot, because it just sums everything up so perfectly.'

Jessica swallowed. 'Are you sure? I really didn't want to upset you. But I couldn't have left it out…'

Fran grabbed her sister's hand and squeezed it. 'Thank you, Jessy. The thing that I've worried most about over the past year, more than anything else in the world, is the thought that he'll be forgotten. That people will stop talking about him, because it's all a bit awkward. And the thought that Bella will never remember him…' She stopped, tears flooding her eyes. 'I want her to know about him when she's older.'

Jessica smiled, glancing quickly up at the ceiling to force her own tears back down. 'So, I'll publish it? Are you sure?' she asked.

Fran nodded. 'Totally sure. And you'd better have the sweetest photo of the two of them lined up to go with it!'

So, Jessica published it. And then the two of them sat together and admired the way it looked, with Michael smiling back at them from the laptop screen.

Jessica usually preferred to close her laptop as soon as she published a post and distract herself by playing with Bella or getting out of the house – but today, she sat with Fran on the sofa and, together, they watched as the traffic, likes, and comments rolled in.

And the blog post did well. Very well. Jessica had worried that it would be the first post that people struggled to empathise with, but she had clearly underestimated how many people had lived through the loss of somebody they loved. And as each comment appeared, Fran read it out loud to her sister:

Allegra Simpson: I'm typing this through tears. I got a phone call like that when I was twenty-five and the way you described the sense of dread was spot on. You've taken me straight back. Thoughts with your family.

Penny Turner: I've been reading your letters to Bella for weeks now and I wasn't expecting this at all. I am so sorry to hear about Michael, it sounds like he was an amazing man.

Louisa Jane Carter: I just love your blog. I'm so sorry to read this.

Olivia Lee: With a mummy that tells stories like this, Bella will always remember him. xxx

Claire Davey: So beautifully written. I lost my mum last year and found out in a phone call. Thank you so much for writing this post!

Before long, there were so many comments under the post that they couldn't keep up. The likes were rolling in quickly. And the numbers of followers and subscribers were rising too.

'It's quite addictive watching what happens when I post,' Jessica said, as they scrolled down the page together. 'At least we haven't got any shitty comments this time. I don't think I could stay calm if it was on this post.'

'Have you had any more hate since that comment I spotted?' Fran asked.

'The odd comment,' Jessica replied. 'But I'm learning to ignore them.'

'Well, I'm not surprised this post is so popular,' Fran said. 'You write beautifully, little sister.'

And for the next twenty minutes, the sisters stayed

that way together on the sofa, clicking and scrolling and reading. And it wasn't until they heard the key turn in the lock, saw the front door fly open, and were jumped on by an overexcited toddler that they were able to tear their eyes away from the screen. And they suddenly became Mummy and Auntie Fran again, playing tunes on a rainbow xylophone on the living room rug, chopping cheese and cucumber in the kitchen for her lunch, and handing out cuddles before Bella went upstairs for her lunchtime nap.

That little girl might never know her Uncle Michael, but they were both determined to ensure that she would grow up aware of his love.

And that blog post was just the start.

Followers – 7,501
Emails in inbox – 20
Event invitations – 11
Paid collaborations – 1
Award nominations – 1

Dear Bella,

The next few weeks passed in a blur. There were lots of tears, plenty of hugs, shopping trips to buy black dresses, online searches for readings and hymns, and messages back and forth at 3 a.m. when Auntie Fran knew I was the only other one awake. It was the hardest time in my life – but with you still so very small and perfect, also one of the best. And even now, a year down the line, I struggle with that. The memories fused together forever in my mind; the very worst and the very best. There were times when I felt guilty for being happy, when my sister and nephew's world was in ruins. But when you lay in my arms (or in fact, any of our arms during that time), I was so thankful for you. You were a constant reminder to everyone that life may be cruel, but it can also be beautiful. That life continued. And that we needed to be strong and keep going; for Auntie Fran, for Freddie, and also for you.

But the time passed quickly and before long, you were three months old. I'd barely even had the chance to process everything, but suddenly you were cooing at us, smiling broadly, and objecting to being cuddled for too long. You were wide awake now, starting to reach for the toys dangling in your face in your baby gym and trying your best to learn how to roll. I was so busy that I didn't have time to reflect on how fast it was going. Until one day when I was standing in a supermarket queue, that is.

I was waiting to pay for a basket of shopping, while you were sleeping in your buggy, when suddenly a newborn baby caught my attention further ahead in the queue. And it was then that I realised, with a sudden pang, how big you'd got. But that wasn't all... As I stared at that tiny newborn, somebody dropped their basket with a clunk on the floor close by, and that tiny baby jumped with a jolt. 'Oh, I love it when newborns do that!' I thought, turning my attention to you in your buggy and smiling affectionately. And that's when I realised. You'd stopped doing it. I couldn't even remember the last time I'd seen you do it. Those days were gone.

Saying that motherhood passes quickly is such a cliché but it was that moment that I realised it was true. Right there in a supermarket queue. Three months had whizzed past, with some amazing highs and some dreadful lows, and while it was all happening, you had been changing. Uncurling. Waking up. Focusing. Growing up. And I'd barely even noticed.

As I unloaded my items onto the checkout belt to be scanned, my heart physically ached realising that you were a proper baby now – and soon you'd be a little girl. It all happened so quickly, without any kind of alarm bell or warning going off. There was no going back.

So, I made a vow that day to slow down and soak it all in.

And do you know what, Bella?

That's exactly what we did.

Love from Mummy x

It was 9.27 a.m. on Friday 20th July – and Jessica and Bella were whizzing towards London at 117 miles per hour. The train carriage was busy and several people had rolled their eyes and tutted as the doors opened at Westcombe Park and she'd attempted to squeeze inside with Bella in her buggy. 'Sorry,' she'd called into the carriage as she pushed Bella onto the train, 'Any chance you could move down just a little? Sorry about this! A bit more? Sorry! Please?'

Eventually they managed to squeeze inside, and as Jessica stood with her back uncomfortably tight against the doors and someone's backpack swinging close to her face, she wondered why she'd ever thought it was a good idea.

It didn't help that she was feeling apprehensive about going to this baby food launch in the first place. But when she'd aired her hesitations with the girls in the park the day before, she'd been met with unanimous encouragement to go.

'Well, it's my idea of hell,' Mel had said, as she took a sip of her takeaway cup of coffee. 'But I think you should go.'

'Me too,' Deena added, with Henny nodding along in agreement.

'Do you? But why?' Jessica asked, surprised at their encouragement.

'Well look,' said Mel. 'You know that none of us knows a great deal about mummy blogging...'

'Me included!' interrupted Jessica, with the girls all laughing in reply.

'But it turns out that you're bloody good at it! And even though you started this blog as a bit of a hobby, you've already got your first paid job and been nominated for one of the biggest awards out there. And if you want to be taken seriously, you're going to have to do the things that bloggers do. So why not just go? Show your face. Put something on your social media bragging about being there. Meet a few of the other big bloggers and tag them. Do all the things that other bloggers do,' Mel said.

'So basically, just pretend I know what I'm doing?' Jessica said, raising her eyebrows at her friend.

'Exactly!' replied Mel. 'You didn't expect to see yourself on that shortlist, but you deserve it. So, go out there and show people that you are the real deal – even if it involves going to events that you'd rather not go to.'

'You're right' Jessica said, realising she needed to accept her fate. 'I'll just suck it up and go. It's only one day in the whole grand scheme of things. It'll be fine.'

The girls nodded along enthusiastically, before Deena added: 'And now the important question. What the hell are you going to wear?'

And with the conversation turning to a debate on whether she should wear heels or flats, the fact that Jessica and Bella would be getting on that train in the morning and making their way to Borough Market seemed decided.

And just twenty-two hours later, she was wedged on the 9.24 a.m. to London Cannon Street, wishing she'd ignored their advice entirely.

The journey into London took twenty minutes. In fear of Bella trying to eject herself from her buggy and escape (and she wouldn't blame her), Jessica relied purely on bribery to get them through it. And whilst leaning into her bag to gather snacks put her dangerously close to head-butting a stranger's crotch, it was well worth the risk to prevent the inevitable meltdown.

When they finally ground to a halt in the station and she could feel fresh air on the back of her neck as the doors opened, the relief in that carriage was so palpable that she could almost hear a collective sigh. She reversed the buggy off the carriage and through the ticket gates, heading towards the station exit. Commuting into London in the morning rush hour was never fun but with a toddler on a warm day, it was pretty much torture.

The journey had been a distraction but now that the two of them were standing on the pavement of Cannon Street, with commuters in sharp suits rushing past, the traffic back-to-back on the road in front of them, and the sound of honks, beeps, and revs filling the air, her mind was firmly back on the objective of their visit. Thinking about where they were heading made her stomach plunge, but her next job was to get there.

The pavement was thick with people and pushing the buggy wasn't easy. 'Sorry!', 'Excuse me!', 'Oops, sorry!', 'Sorry would you mind?', 'Ah thank you!' she said every few seconds, as she found a route through the crowds. Reaching the end of Cannon Street a few minutes later, she crossed the road and swung right towards London Bridge, where the pavement widened and she finally had space to stroll and enjoy the scenery.

It was a mild day; not stiflingly hot thankfully, but warm enough to get away with a dress, cardigan, and sandals. She'd have been a lot more comfortable in her standard uniform of skinny jeans and a striped T-shirt to skim her mum-tum, but the girls had convinced her to dress up a little. 'There might be photographers there!' Henny had suggested, sealing the decision to make a bit more of an effort. So, she'd gone for a summer favourite in her wardrobe; a black cotton dress with delicate neon embroidery. It reached just past her knees and had quite a stylish bohemian look (and most importantly, didn't need ironing), along with metallic gold strappy sandals (flat, because heels would've taken it way too far), and a pale grey cardigan. It was an outfit that still fitted from her pre-Bella days and she felt quite confident in it, which gave her one less thing to worry about as she strolled across London Bridge that morning.

Glancing to her left, she stopped for a moment and paused to admire the view. There was Tower Bridge, with HMS Belfast sat to its right. Beyond it, she could see Shad Thames, City Hall, and the peaks of Canary Wharf in the distance. She had always loved this part of London and missed being able to jump on a train and meet Chris for post-work drinks whenever it took her fancy.

'Look, Bella Boo, there's Tower Bridge', she said, pointing. Bella writhed and moaned in her buggy, eager to keep moving. 'You'll appreciate it one day,' she said, as she peeled her eyes away and began pushing again.

It wasn't long before they reached the end of the bridge and the traffic lights, waiting for them to change so they could cross the road. Borough Market was right in front of her and she knew she was minutes away from reaching the launch. Her stomach flipped as she imagined arriving at the event, before a voice inside her head gave herself a strict pep talk. 'Oh, come on! You're a grown woman! You can handle this! Stop getting so worked up about it!'

As the traffic lights changed, she sighed and crossed the road. And minutes later, she was standing underneath a large red brick building, with a neon-pink sign that read MUNCH! above her head.

'Come on, Bella Boo,' she said, taking a deep breath. 'Let's head inside.'

It was dark in the hallway, which was disorientating having been in the bright sunshine moments before. Jessica pushed the buggy as best she could in the darkness, following a stream of light coming from the main room. As she approached it, her eyes adjusted to see a girl sat behind a reception desk with a list of names to tick off. She must've been seventeen or eighteen at most. Jessica wondered for a second whether she'd come to the right place.

'Oh hi, I'm here for the Squeeze & Gurgle launch?' she said, as she pushed the buggy up to the desk.

'What's your name?' the girl replied, without moving her eyes from the list in her hand, which had been printed on a couple of sheets of A4 paper.

'Oh right, it's Jessica Holmes. Hopefully you'll find me!' she said, with a nervous laugh. But the teenager didn't laugh with her. Instead, she sighed and began reading. Not finding it on the first page, she sighed again and flicked it over, her eyes once again moving down the list. As she searched, Bella let out a screech and made an escape attempt, becoming quickly enraged with the straps of her buggy.

'Shh, it's OK. We'll be inside soon. Shh. Hang on a minute, it won't be long,' Jessica urged, as she rocked the buggy.

'Your name isn't here,' the girl said, finally. 'I'll get my manager.'

'Oh right, I sent my RSVP, I'm not sure why…' she said, as the girl disappeared into the room behind her.

Bella wasn't impressed and was now objecting loudly, so Jessica undid her straps and picked her up. She kissed her on the head in an attempt to ease her own nerves and embarrassment, just as another guest arrived and stood in a queue behind her. Jessica turned to smile, but the lady was busy looking down at her phone.

'Well, this is just bloody awful,' the voice in her head said. 'I'll give it a few minutes and then we're leaving.' And just as her arms were starting to ache from holding Bella, who was putting up a good attempt to ditch to the floor, the teenager reappeared with a blonde lady behind her.

'Hello!' the lady said, with a smile on her face. 'Can I just take your name?'

'It's Jessica Holmes,' she replied. She could feel the eyes of the lady behind glaring into the back of her head and shifted uncomfortably in her sandals at the humiliation. As Bella squawked, she added: 'Sorry, she really wants to get down...'

But the smiling lady was too busy reading through the list to acknowledge her. 'What publication do you work for?' she asked.

'Publication? What do you mean? Oh, no, it's a blog,' Jessica replied. 'Letters to My Daughter?'

'Oh, that explains it,' the lady replied. 'It was probably Victoria who invited you and she left last week, so likely didn't add you to the list in time. No worries! You aren't down here, but why don't you both come inside? We'd love to have you anyway!'

She couldn't have been more embarrassed, but smiled awkwardly and followed the lady inside the room, struggling with Bella in her arms and the buggy to push, while re-adjusting her eyes to the brightness.

Jessica had eaten at MUNCH! in the past and imagined they'd be inside the main restaurant, but she found herself standing in a function room instead. It was quite a small room, with a large stand on the far side displaying the different flavours of Squeeze & Gurgle baby food pouches. A big advertising board was propped behind the table with their logo and a picture of a baby sucking from a pouch. To the right of that, there was a small table set out for manicures or face painting, with one little girl (probably about three years old) sitting quietly while her face was painted and her mother chatted behind her.

Jessica realised pretty quickly that there wasn't much for Bella to do and inwardly sighed at the thought of her running around the room and knocking over the displays. But with her arms now aching from her weight, she had no choice but to put her down and then find a space to park the buggy under a window.

'Shall I show you the new pouches?' the blonde lady said, with the smile still fixed on her face. 'Don't worry about the little one! Let her run around!'

'Yes, sure,' Jessica said hesitantly, watching Bella toddle straight towards the little girl having her face painted.

'So here we go,' the lady said. 'There are ten flavours in total and they are all totally organic! I've been trying them out with my own daughter and she *loves* them! You'll be getting each of these flavours in your bag as you leave, so your little one can have a try! Shall I leave you to have a little look?'

'Thanks, that's great,' Jessica said, picking up a pouch

to look closer, while simultaneously watching Bella, who was still fascinated by the little girl being transformed into a tiger.

'Take your time!' the lady said. 'I'll be right back!' She waved at a few ladies that had just walked into the room and strolled away, leaving Jess studying the pouches.

With Bella still glued to the spot, Jessica picked up each of the ten pouches in turn, feeling it was her duty given she'd come all this way to see them. As she focused on perfecting her 'I'm interested in the ingredients list' face, the tiger's mother approached her.

'Sorry to ask, but are you Jessica from "Letters to My Daughter?"' the lady asked, smiling warmly at her.

'Yes!' Jessica replied, her eyes opening with the shock of realising she was face-to-face with a blogger she'd been following since she first found out she was pregnant. It was Wendy from the blog 'Hiding in the Bathroom!' – and somehow she knew Jessica's name.

'I thought it was you! I'm Wendy – I think we're nominated for the same award? Congratulations! I've been reading your blog since I saw the list and it's really, really good!'

Jessica realised her face was frozen into a shocked smile. 'Oh hi, Wendy! It's lovely to meet you…' she stuttered. 'I have to admit I've been reading your blog for quite a while. It's really nice to meet you!'

'Ah really? Well you'll already know that's my little girl Adeline being turned into a tiger then,' Wendy said, glancing over her shoulder at the two girls. 'And your little one is….?'

'Bella,' Jessica replied. 'And she wants to have her face painted next, by the looks of it!'

'Of course,' Wendy said, as she smiled at the girls, before turning back to Jessica and adding with raised eyebrows: 'It doesn't seem like anybody else brought their kids!'

Jessica laughed and looked around the room. It was getting busy now, with other guests standing in groups chatting or studying the pouches on the table. But Wendy was right; Adeline and Bella were the only children.

'This always happens at launches,' Wendy said, raising her hand and talking behind it in a loud whisper. 'Nobody ever brings their kids and I am left wondering where the hell they all are!'

'I guess they're all at school and nursery?' Jessica asked, genuinely surprised.

'Or at home with the nanny while their mother blogs about being their mother,' Wendy added behind her hand, before howling loudly with laughter. A few of the ladies at the table next to them turned to stare, prompting Wendy to raise her eyebrows at Jessica and smile.

Jessica warmed to Wendy instantly and was relieved that the first real life blogger she'd met hadn't disappointed. She was warm, bubbly, and friendly – exactly how she came across in her blog.

Adeline's tiger face was now finished and she jumped down and ran to her mother. Wendy crouched down and caught her. 'You're terrifying!' she said, as the little girl held up her hands and growled. Out the corner of her eye, Jessica spotted Bella trying to climb up into the chair.

She made her way there quickly. 'Does she want a

turn?' the face painter asked, poised with a brush and palette. Turning to Bella, she continued: 'What do you want to be?'

'I think she's probably too young to sit still!' Jessica said, laughing. 'But try if you like? I think she wants to be a tiger like her new friend.'

She crouched behind Bella to stop her falling off the chair, as the face painter got to work. Remarkably, Bella sat still and let her start painting. As she daubed tiger stripes, Jessica took the time to glance around the room at the other guests. Most were chatting to members of staff, while others were studying or sniffing pouches. It was getting quite noisy as the room filled up, with the sound of chatter, laughter and footsteps on the wooden floor.

She quickly recognised a few more of the bloggers in the room, feeling like a starstruck teenager as she watched them move around. There was 'Mother to Twin Terrors' chatting to 'Coffee Survivor' by the pouches like two long-lost friends – and over by the door, Anwen from 'This Is Where The Wild Things Are' had just arrived and was being ushered over to the display table by the blonde lady, who was chatting away enthusiastically, while Anwen stared down at her phone.

It was fascinating to study a room of other bloggers and journalists for the first time. She'd always thought that they'd be far more glamorous, with perfect figures, expensive wardrobes, and gaggles of beautifully behaved children at their feet. But they all looked quite normal. She guessed the average age of the guests was around thirty-five and most were wearing skinny jeans and T-shirts.

Glancing down at her outfit, she felt quite overdressed, and she was thankful she hadn't opted for the high heels she'd been considering.

Wendy was now studying a pouch of baby food, as Adeline hugged her legs and tried to steer her away. Giving into her attempts, she made her way back towards the face painting. 'She wants me to get my face painted too,' she laughed, as she approached them. 'Addie, Mummy isn't quite ready for that level of humiliation today, I'm afraid!'

'Although it would make a great photo for the blog?' Jessica laughed.

'You are right! But still not worth the pain of walking through Borough Market afterwards... At least I don't think it is... Maybe I should reconsider...' Wendy replied.

As predicted, Bella started to squirm in an attempt to escape from the chair. With only one side of her face completed, she was a very lopsided tiger, but her patience had been exhausted. 'I think we'll have to leave it there,' Jessica said to the face painter, picking Bella up. 'And this definitely isn't a look I will be sharing on my social media!'

Wendy laughed. 'Well actually, I think it might go down well. She looks like a very cute tiger-baby hybrid!'

'See, this is why you're a better blogger than me!' Jessica replied.

'Actually, shall we try and get a picture of the two of them together?' Wendy asked.

Jessica nodded and placed Bella on the floor. 'Hold her hand, Addie,' Wendy said, as she snapped away with her phone. Confident she'd got the shot, she turned to Jessica and said: 'I'll send this to you. We can both share it later and tag the brand.' And then behind her hand, she added: 'Let's be honest, it's a lot more interesting than a photo of a baby food pouch – and we're less likely to get hate about posting adverts!'

'You get hate?' Jessica retorted, surprised that somebody as lovely as Wendy would attract it. 'Like, negative comments?'

'Of course!' Wendy replied. 'Don't we all? I think it's just part of being a blogger these days – and the benefits definitely outweigh the negatives!'

'Oh OK, I thought it was just me...' Jessica added, feeling relieved.

'No girl!' Wendy replied. 'It's all of us! And the bigger your following gets, the thicker your skin needs to grow with it. Believe me... But don't let it put you off. You just learn to roll your eyes and ignore it!'

Jessica raised her eyebrows. 'Wow, I didn't realise...' she said, scooping Bella into her arms. 'I'll have to learn how to shrug it off like a pro. Are you sticking around much longer? I think we'll probably head home...'

But Wendy was distracted by somebody walking through the door. 'Oh, it's Tiggy! Better go and say hello, I guess. Have you met? Come with me, I'll introduce you!'

Jessica's stomach fell so quickly to the floor that she thought she was going to throw up.

Wendy was already striding over to the door, but Jessica's feet were planted to the spot. She couldn't talk to Tiggy Blenheim! What would she say? Would she acknowledge the message she'd sent? Should she be friendly or aloof? Should she stroll over and greet her like an old friend? Or pretend she'd never sent the message and hope she didn't work out who she was? She wished she could consult the girls.

But there was no time. Wendy seemed to be deep in conversation, but turned suddenly and gestured to Jessica to join her. And just like that, she found her legs working on autopilot as she walked across the room with Bella in her arms.

She smiled as she reached them but didn't interrupt.

'Oh yes, William was like that for a while,' Tiggy continued 'but I was consistent and he never asked for it again. You have to be consistent! You just can't give them a dummy because they cry for it!'

'You're right. But it's just so bloody hard, isn't it? All they want is their dummy and you know you'll get some peace if you give in.' Wendy said laughing. She turned to Jessica and said: 'Oh sorry, this is Jessica from "Letters to My Daughter". Have you met?'

Tiggy glanced at Jessica, taking time to look her up and down.

Jessica felt her toes curl.

'No, I don't think we have,' Tiggy said finally, without a hint of a smile. 'Nice to meet you.'

But before Jessica could reply, she turned back to Wendy and continued the conversation: 'Honestly, Wendy, you have got to be a little tougher. Stick to your guns. I was like you with Amelia and she had the thing until she was five!'

The conversation continued, while Jessica stood alongside them feeling like a spare part. Surely Tiggy would stop talking about dummies soon and have the decency to make some kind of polite conversation with her. Surely, she'd remember that Jessica lived on the same road as her when she was growing up, and that she'd babysat her as a child. Surely, she'd acknowledge the cuteness of the half-painted tiger in her arms. The rudeness was so staggering and awkward that it hung heavily in the air – and while Wendy had seemed shocked when Tiggy first turned away from Jessica and continued talking, she was now so deep in the conversation that she appeared to have forgotten Jessica was there too.

But as she was forced to stand there silently as they chatted, something was stirring in Jessica.

She was angry now. Angry about the snub at the door. Angry that she'd come all this way to look at baby food pouches that were really no different to the baby food pouches that were already on the shelves of Tesco. Angry that none of the team members in the room deemed her important enough to talk to for more than two minutes. Angry that she'd dragged Bella all the way across London to an event that nobody else had bothered taking their kids to. And angry that a childhood acquaintance was snubbing her so publicly. And as that anger continued to bubble and boil, it was threatening to spill over at any moment – that was the moment she decided to speak up. She wasn't a nobody and she deserved politeness at the very least.

As a sentence came to an end, Jessica pitched in. 'We grew up on the same road, actually Wendy. Tiggy and I! Isn't that funny?'

'What?!' Wendy roared with a big smile on her face. 'No way! What are the chances!'

Tiggy pursed her lips and smiled awkwardly, but said nothing.

'Yes, it was in Mottingham in South East London. Funnily enough, my parents still live in the same house. My sister Fran lives there too now, with her little boy. Do you ever pop back, Tiggy?' Jessica asked, her confident tone propelled entirely by adrenaline.

Wendy turned to Tiggy smiling widely. 'I can't believe this! How small is this world?!'

Tiggy was looking at Jessica now, which was an improvement to a few minutes before, but still, she stayed quiet. Wendy was finally starting to pick up on the tension. Her smile faltered, as she glanced between the two of them and laughed nervously.

And finally, Tiggy spoke up.

'Sorry,' she said, without a hint of emotion in her voice. 'I don't remember you.'

And at that very moment, just as Jessica's mouth dropped open in shock, the blonde lady grabbed Tiggy by the arm. 'Tiggy, darling! So lovely to see you,' she said, kissing her on both cheeks. 'Thank you so much for coming! We really, really appreciate it! Come with me and I'll show you the range?'

As they strode away together, Jessica noticed a photographer for the first time. He was following close behind and snapping Tiggy from every angle, while she did a flawless job of pretending she hadn't noticed.

Adeline ran after them, attempting to grab a lead hanging from the camera, with Wendy in hot pursuit, which left Jessica standing on her own with Bella in her arms, so humiliated and so shocked that the room was practically spinning.

And when tears started to prick and well in her eyes, she knew she had to leave. Spotting her buggy under the window, she dashed to it, strapped Bella in as quickly as she could, and ran out of the room.

As she strode out onto the streets of London, not a single person in that room even noticed that she had gone.

Followers – 9,190
Emails in inbox – 84
Event invitations – 21
Paid collaborations – 1
Award nominations – 1
Blogger friends – 1
Blogger enemies – 1

Dear Bella,

I'd never experienced real loneliness until I was a mother, which sounds silly, doesn't it? Because let's be honest; I was never really alone.

But once we'd got through the whirlwind first few weeks, when we had visitors arriving on our doorstep on a seemingly hourly basis clutching home-cooked casseroles, gifts wrapped in powder pink wrapping paper, and armfuls of pre-loved baby clothes that they'd raided from storage, things slowed down.

And then we had those horrible, dark months after Michael died, when we spent most of our time crying, hugging, or picking flowers to go in funeral displays. We clung together so tightly during those weeks that we were rarely ever alone. So, when Auntie Fran decided that she wanted to be left alone and your grandparents needed to be there for Freddie, I found myself back in the silence of home.

And I struggled, Bella. I really struggled.

You were always with me – on my boob, in your buggy, or lying right next to me in bed. But you couldn't chat to me about the plot in my favourite soap opera. You couldn't discuss the highlights of the weekend over a cup of coffee. You couldn't reassure me when I was worried about snipping your fingers off in the pursuit of trimming tiny fingernails. So instead, I usually picked up the phone and called Daddy. And sometimes I ranted; sometimes I cried; and sometimes I howled with laughter. But mainly, I just talked and talked and talked, while he stood outside his office, staring out at the rooftops of London, listening to every single word and no doubt worrying that his wife had gone mad.

My pre-baby friends were rarely there for me either. I don't think that they meant to abandon me; I just think their lives were in a very different place. They didn't realise that a quick visit to coo over a newborn baby, hand over a gift, and fill me in on the complexities of their love lives wasn't enough. They thought they'd done their bit – and then they left again, with me ticked off their list for another few months. I tried so hard not to blame them for my loneliness, but it was hard. I missed them being in my life. And I missed them wanting me to be in theirs.

When I look back now Bella, the loneliness is probably the thing that surprised me most about motherhood. The long days with just a baby for company. And I know that sounds silly, because it wasn't as if I hadn't been expecting you. My bump had grown as quickly as the stash of tiny pink clothes in your wardrobe, and I was fully aware that a human baby would be arriving at the end of it. I was looking forward to my maternity leave. I spent a long time imagining those lazy days together on the sofa and believed wholeheartedly that it would be bliss. Nowhere that I needed to go and nowhere that I needed to be. I mean it sounds like bliss, doesn't it?

But then you arrived and I dressed you in those powder pink outfits, and we retreated to that sofa for what felt like months on end. And it was bliss in one sense, because I had you in my arms and I felt so lucky to have you. I had never been less alone in my life. I had a shadow; a sidekick; an extension of myself. But it became clearer every single day that being alone and being lonely are two different things entirely.

And I realised that I really needed to make some new friends.

We needed to make some new friends.

For both of us.

Love from Mummy x

Jessica was walking back over the river before she let the tears fall. She was half-expecting somebody to chase after her, but it hadn't happened – and while that would have gone some way towards soothing her bruised ego, she was thankful that she was alone. She had never felt more humiliated and as she pushed the buggy as fast as she could down the pavement, on a mission to get as far away from Borough Market as possible, she didn't even try and hide the heavy, angry tears rolling down her cheeks.

Pausing to cross the road at the end of London Bridge, she reached into her bag to check her phone. A message was staring back at her.

Chris: How did launch go? Got meeting close to Cannon Street at 1 p.m. Want to meet for an early lunch in area? Let me know when done.

Jessica clicked on his name in seconds and two rings later, he was on the other end of the phone.

'Hi honey. All OK?' he said as he picked up.

'Where are you?' she asked, her voice breaking.

'You OK?' he asked. 'What's up?'

'Yep. Well no. It was awful,' she said. 'Where are you?'

'The launch was awful?' he asked.

'Yes. Well, no. Well, yes,' she said, before adding: 'Sorry, I'm a mess. Just tell me where and when to meet you.'

'I'm at work, honey. I'll leave now and be there in ten minutes. Meet you at Xanthe's on Cannon Street? It'll be good for Bella.'

'Fine,' she replied. 'See you then.'

Just five minutes later, she was inside the café. They had beaten the lunchtime rush and she quickly found a table, parking the buggy in a space alongside and nodding when a waitress asked if she'd like a high chair.

Around her, two men in suits were sat chatting at a table, while a lady sat alone typing on a laptop on another. She'd usually worry about heading into a café with a child in this part of town in fear of disturbing business meetings, but today was different. Today, Bella could dance on the table, throw a plate of pasta across the room, and scream so loudly the wine glasses lined up on a shelf cracked one by one and Jessica still wouldn't care. Today, if anyone even dared to tut or raise an eyebrow, she'd happily challenge them to a duel on the pavement outside.

As she gritted her teeth and tried to calm her breathing, she went through the motions of motherhood. She lifted Bella into the high chair, strapped her up, and delved into her bag for snacks that hadn't yet been eaten. Her hand came out covered in something ominously sticky – usually she'd be revolted by that. But today, she couldn't care less and simply pulled a wipe from the packet, cleaned off the goo, and ripped open the pack of rice cakes she'd discovered to keep Bella happy.

Once she'd handed them over, she sat at the table deep in thought, hearing Tiggy's voice over and over again in her head.

'Sorry. I don't remember you.'

'Sorry. I don't remember you.'

'Sorry. I don't remember you.'

Now that she was sitting at that café table, different responses were playing on a loop in her mind.

'Well, that's strange Tiggy, because you sent me a message last weekend! Would you like me to show you on my phone to remind you?'

'Oh, don't be silly Tiggy, of course you remember me! I was the little sister of one of your best friends! You remember Fran, don't you? Of course you do!'

'Remember babysitting me when I was a child? Remember that, Tiggy? Surely you do? I only reminded you a few weeks ago!'

How she wished she'd had the presence of mind to challenge her! To remind her about the years they'd spent as next-door neighbours. To ask her if she'd had a chance to look at her blog, after the message she'd sent a few weeks beforehand. To introduce her to Bella, despite her clear disinterest.

Before long, Chris strode into the café. On a normal day, Jessica would've felt flutters of pride. Dressed in a perfectly cut, dark grey suit, clutching the tan leather laptop case she'd bought him for Christmas, he cut a very stylish figure.

In fact, Jessica would usually be the first person to turn when he walked into a room, especially when he was suited and booted. But as she sat biting her fingernails at the table, distracted by her own thoughts, it was Bella who spotted him first.

'DADADADADA!' she said, as she threw her rice cake across the café in excitement.

His lips curled into a smile as he spotted them, and reaching the table, he kissed Jessica on the back of the head.

'My girls in the big city!' he said, as she turned to him. And that's when he spotted the tears.

'Shit, honey, why are you crying? What happened?' He was searching her face for clues, while Bella banged the tray of her high chair in excitement. Walking to her, he stroked her head and kissed her on the forehead. 'Hello baby girl, what's happened? Talk to me, Jess!'

'I've just been through the most humiliating experience of my life,' she said, as tears welled in her eyes again. She blinked quickly to clear them, determined not to dissolve into sobs in public.

'What the hell happened?' he asked, sitting down at the table. 'Do you want a coffee? I'm going to get a coffee,' he said, turning to the waitress stood behind him by the counter and signalling. After ordering two black coffees, he turned back to his wife. 'So, talk me through it. What happened just now?'

Jessica ripped the top off two sachets of sugar and carefully stirred them into her mug with a teaspoon, inhaling the scent of the coffee as she took a deep breath. She slowly exhaled and began her story.

'And she just looked at me, with no emotion whatsoever, and said "Sorry. I don't remember you."'

Jessica picked up her mug and drank, surprised by the heat of the coffee as it scalded her lips.

Chris pursed his lips and sighed. 'Well, that's pretty nasty.'

'Nasty?' Jessica quipped back, looking up at him.

'Yes. Don't you think so?' Chris looked puzzled.

'Well it's a bit more than "nasty", isn't it, Chris? I mean, it's humiliating, it's rude, it's actually pretty soul destroying when you've dragged your toddler to London on a packed train with everyone shoved in like bloody sardines, walked across the city, stood around looking at some shitty baby food pouches, and met another blogger that you actually really liked. And then this top blogger, who everyone respects – and who you happen to know from childhood – walks in and the whole room turns in her direction. And when you have the audacity to join her and, God forbid, even speak to her, she dismisses you like that. And why? Clearly for no other reason than to make me feel like shit. Maybe it's because she wants me to stop blogging and back out of the awards. Maybe it's because she's scared I'll reveal her humble roots to the world. Or maybe she just thinks I'm so unimportant and so insignificant that I needed to be brought down a peg or two. I don't know Chris, but seriously, it's a bit more than "nasty" isn't it?' she said, struggling to control the volume of her voice as it cracked with emotion.

'Calm down, Jess,' he said, 'I didn't mean…'

'Calm down?' she cut in.

'Yes, Jess, it's not my fault. I'm not Tiggy! Don't take it out on me!' Bella started to shriek, so Chris quickly reached for the packet of rice cakes and gave her another one. 'Do you want to eat? We should order something for Bella.'

'I'm not hungry,' she said, turning her face away.

'Oh, come on, Jess. Yes, I agree. She was a bitch. She embarrassed you. But this isn't you!' he said, picking up the menu from the middle of the table and scanning down as he spoke.

'This isn't me?' she repeated slowly, spitting her words.

'No! You've never cared what people like Tiggy think about you! You're confident! You've got sass! You aren't the girl that cries in a café over something a complete stranger has said to you!'

'I can't believe I'm hearing this! I thought you'd be the first one to stick up for me!' she replied, her words broken with tears. 'And she's not a stranger! I knew her as a child!'

'Jess, don't cry!' he said, cupping her head in his hands and trying to kiss her forehead.

'Get the fuck off! Seriously! I've had enough. I've had the shittiest day...' she said, trying her hardest to hide her tears, aware that the girl typing on her laptop was now staring in their direction.

'Jessica, please! I love you! I have your back! I support you! But I'm worried that the blogging has made your confidence hit rock bottom, when really it should be doing the opposite! This isn't like you!' he said, as he signalled to the waitress again and quickly ordered Bella a plate of kids' macaroni cheese and himself a chicken panini.

'You encouraged me to start this blog, Chris! And I have done nothing wrong! I've tried my best. I've written blog posts that have done really well. I've been nominated for an award that I didn't ask to be nominated for, and now I seem to be on the receiving end of a witch-hunt!' she replied angrily.

'Well, it's not a witch-hunt, is it! She clearly needs work on her manners, but she's hardly started a witch-hunt!' Chris was smiling, which Jessica found infuriating.

'Oh, so you're on Team Tiggy now? Well why don't you just run off into the sunset with her and her seventeen children? You'd look great together,' she spat back. She knew she was being ridiculous now, but she couldn't stop the words tumbling out of her mouth. Chris was the one person she expected to be on her side, always, and hearing him defend Tiggy was too much.

Chris smirked. 'Let's forget it. Can we forget it? I'm not on Team Tiggy. I'm obviously on Team Jessica. And if I ever come face to face with her, I will tell her what I think. But in the meantime, can we not let her ruin our day?'

Jessica sighed and sipped her coffee. 'Fuck. Why is this coffee so hot? I'm going to need a skin graft on my lips at the end of this.'

Chris laughed and passed her a napkin to wipe her tears. 'Honestly honey, I'm sorry about what happened this morning. I'm sorry it was such a waste of time and she embarrassed you like that, but don't let her words upset you like this. She obviously just feels threatened – and that has to be a good thing. I bet you beat her to that award.'

'Well, that's doubtful,' Jessica said, blowing her nose. 'But I would enjoy every second if I did.'

'Will you have half of my panini?' he asked, spotting

the waitress carrying over their two plates. 'Come on, eat something.'

Jessica watched as Chris cut the sandwich in half and passed half to her on a napkin. She ate it slowly, pushing the food around in her mouth for a while before swallowing. She knew she needed to eat, because she felt weak and shaky, but she'd left her appetite in Borough Market, somewhere near to her dignity.

After Bella had eaten some of her lunch and smeared the other half over her high chair and the floor, Chris looked at his watch and announced it was time to get off to his meeting. Jessica kissed him, still not having totally forgiven him, and asked for the bill. And within a few minutes, they were back on the platform at Cannon Street waiting for their train.

Thankfully, they had a whole carriage to themselves on the return leg and that was lucky, as the risk of head-butting a stranger's crotch would have definitely thrown Jessica over the edge that lunchtime.

She had made no plans for the afternoon, but Bella was happy toddling around at home, delighted to be released from the clutches of her buggy. Jessica, on the other hand, spent most of her afternoon tapping away on her phone, filling in the girls and her sister on the events of the morning. She didn't have the energy or emotional stability to talk to anyone, but she must have broken the one-hundred-message mark by the end of the day (most of them filled with expletives), as her friends and sister surrounded her in the hug (albeit virtual) that she'd been hoping for when she met her husband just hours earlier.

Henny: There's more to this. Something is going on here. Why would she say that? Something must've happened in the past. It doesn't make any sense!

Mel: I don't think so, I just think she hates the fact Jessica started a blog and was nominated for the same award as her within months! She's threatened by you. You should be flattered.

Jessica: Flattered? I'm struggling with that one…

Deena: What can we do? I vote we track her down and make her apologise?

Jess: That's the very last thing I want to do. I want to run in the opposite direction, if I'm honest.

And then there was Fran.

Fran: She was always pretty confident and ballsy, but she wasn't rude.

Jessica: Well, she was today.

Fran: Do you want me to message or call her? We haven't spoken for years, but I'd like to think she'd answer the phone.

Jessica: No. Fran, please. Let's just leave it.

Throwing her phone onto the sofa, she made her way into the kitchen to switch the oven on and start Bella's dinner.

So, when her phone beeped with a message, she didn't see it. She was too busy throwing fish fingers and smiley-faced potatoes on a tray (freezer tapas was all she was capable of today). If she had seen that message as it pinged through, however, she'd have seen that it was from her fellow blogger Wendy and that it read:

Hi Jessica, I wanted to send you this picture of Addie and Bella from earlier. How cute do they look as tigers! Sorry I didn't get a chance to say goodbye. Tell me it's none of my business if you like, but I have a feeling I know why Tiggy was so rude to you. Do you fancy meeting soon for a chat so I can share my thoughts? And good luck with the shortlist next week. I reckon you've got it! Wendy x (PS - I grabbed your goody bag when I left, so you can thank me for the 10 pouches of baby food when we meet. There's a shopping voucher in there too, so I'll try my best not to spend it!)

And when she finally saw it at 7.30 p.m. that evening, she didn't hesitate to bash back a reply:

Thank you so much for your message Wendy. It was very strange with Tiggy and I'd love to chat. Yes to wine. You can keep the baby food (you're welcome) but I'll reserve judgement on the shopping voucher until I see it. When are we meeting? Jessica x

And as she sent it, she felt her spirits lift. Maybe she did have a friend in blogging, after all. And on that note, she grabbed her laptop and notebook from the dining room table and settled down on the sofa. She had a letter to type up and publish, and not even a disastrous first foray into the world of blogging events was going to put her off.

12

Followers – 15,794
Emails in inbox – 21
Event invitations – 33
Paid collaborations – 1
Award nominations – 1
Blogger enemies – 1
Blogger friends – 1

Dear Bella,

I knew that I needed to find a new group of friends.

I knew that it would make my days easier and more enjoyable.

I knew that I needed to find a better support network, so that I didn't keep pulling Daddy away from his desk whenever I was worried about the strange colour of your poo.

I knew that you needed friends your own age.

I knew all of this – but the thought of getting out there and making it happen was so much harder than I expected.

It felt like dating all over again, and as the weeks and months ticked on, it played on my mind more than ever.

But one Wednesday morning in July, with the sun shining and a decent night's sleep spurring me on, I finally plucked up the courage to try, and by 9.30 a.m., I was on my way to a coffee morning arranged by the local baby clinic. It was the same place I went to strip you off and listen to you scream as you were plonked on a scale to be weighed (not the highlight of my fortnight, it has to be said). The coffee morning was in a different room from the torture room, I was assured, and there would be soft mats to lie you on and sensory lights, bubbles, and music to keep you entertained. And given that you were still only four months old and unable to escape my clutches, you'd hopefully allow me to get to the bottom of my cup of coffee, so I could make some small talk with the other mothers and possibly, if I was lucky, bag myself a friend.

But as I strolled into the room – late, which was true to form, but admittedly pretty unhelpful in scenarios like this – I immediately wished I could turn and run back out of it again. There were about six or seven other mothers there that day, with children of varying ages. Most were very little babies, curled in arms as they fed from a boob or bottle, with a few older children toddling around the room. Every single one of them was already involved in a conversation, and while a few turned and smiled kindly as I walked in the room ('good start,' I thought), nobody invited me to join them ('what the hell do I do now?').

With you in my arms, I stood, for a moment, like a lemon by the door, frozen to the spot. Glancing around in desperation, I noticed a lady pouring mugs of coffee on the other side of the room. Coffee had been my saviour for a while, so I trotted over to her smiling. 'Ah, can I take one of those?' I said, as I smiled at her (my lip twitching with the nerves). 'Of course you can! Is it your first time here?' she asked. 'Yes!' I said, giving her a grimace-smile. 'Do you work here?' 'Yes', she said 'I'm one of the health visitors.' So, for the next 45 minutes, I threw question after question her way to avoid the awkwardness of trying to butt into a conversation with the other mothers. We started with a discussion about breastfeeding (I knew that would keep her talking for a while), before moving onto a very thorough discussion about weaning (which she was extremely passionate about, giving me the chance to sit back and swig my coffee for a bit).

Time ticked on, and the other mothers in the room stood up one by one, strapping babies into carriers on their front and wandering over to say goodbye to my new buddy. And as each of them walked out of the room, I watched my chances to find a friend disappear with them. 'I'd better go too, I guess,' I said, as I knocked back the now-cold dregs of my mug and scooped you into my arms from your spot on the floor where you were happily studying your toes.

And do you know what I felt as I walked out of the room, Bella? I felt relief. Relief that I hadn't had to introduce myself, relief that I hadn't been forced to make small talk in the manner of speed dating, and relief that I hadn't had to face the awkwardness of asking for a virtual stranger's phone number before I said goodbye. I knew that making friends that day would've been a forward step in our lives, but I just couldn't do it.

I just wasn't ready.

Love from Mummy x

'Can't you reschedule it?' Deena's message read as it pinged through to Jessica's phone as she was applying her lipstick in the mirror. She was meeting Wendy for drinks in Blackheath in twenty minutes and her cab was on its way. After pursing her lips and admiring her handiwork (terrible, but it would be dark in the wine bar so perhaps Wendy wouldn't notice), she picked up her phone, read the message, and sighed before she texted back:

I really can't. Wendy lives in Crystal Palace and will already be on her way.

Deena's message pinged back instantly.

Wendy?

Jessica paused before replying. Admitting to Deena that she was prioritising a blogger she barely knew was awkward, especially given how worried they'd all been about Mel recently, but she couldn't let Wendy down at the last minute. She was her first friend in blogging. And while Mel had messaged them all to say she needed to chat that evening, she knew the other girls would be there for her. If it was anything important, they would pick up their phones and let her know – and in return, Jessica could make her excuses and run.

She's a blogger friend. I'm really sorry Deena, I just can't cancel tonight. But can you call and let me know that she's OK?

Jessica stared at her phone and waited for her reply, but nothing came. Distracted by the sound of a horn outside on the road, she threw the phone into her bag, ran to the sofa to kiss Chris on the lips (already glued to the television, with a bottle of beer in his hands), and ran outside to climb into the cab.

It was Saturday evening and the roads were busy as they wound their way towards Blackheath. With the sun still shining brightly, the heath was busy. Dogs bounded after balls, groups of friends sat around swigging beer from plastic pint glasses, and children chased each other across the lawns. Jessica watched as the summery scene flashed past her window.

She had tried her best to shut the incident with Tiggy out of her mind since the launch a few weeks ago, finding it easier than replaying the conversation over and over again in her mind. After cooling off, she knew there was some truth in what Chris had said to her that lunchtime in the cafe. She had let things get to her. Blogging had seeped into her mind and made her feel far more vulnerable, so she'd tried her best to slow down. She'd only published one letter, tried to check her social media feed less frequently, and spent more time with Bella, with Chris, and with her friends. She felt better, but with the announcement of the awards shortlist looming in the coming days, she could feel the nerves starting to build again.

'That'll be twelve quid, love,' the driver said, turning to Jessica from the front of the cab.

She jumped, suddenly aware that they had pulled up next to Little Sorrento – one of her favourite wine bars in the village and where she'd suggested meeting Wendy. Pulling her wallet from her bag, she grabbed a note and a few coins and paid him, climbing out of the cab as an impatient driver behind beeped to move past.

'Oh, fuck off,' she muttered under her breath, as she shot a glare at the driver and strolled through the doors of the wine bar.

As the door swung closed behind her, the sound of a small bell rang out, and Wendy, who was standing at the bar, turned towards her.

'Hello, hello!' she said, rushing towards her and planting a kiss on each of her cheeks. 'Lovely to see you again! Especially without the small people in tow!'

The wine bar was small and quite dark, with lanterns lined up on the bar housing flickering candles. It was quiet for this time on a Saturday, as most people were still in pub gardens or enjoying the heath, but there was something about this place that Jessica loved.

'Wow, you look amazing!' Jessica said smiling, admiring the glossy black curls bouncing on her shoulders, expertly drawn eyeliner flicks, pillar box red lipstick, and a white flared jumpsuit that looked fantastic against her dark skin.

'We scrub up alright when the kids are in bed!' Wendy replied, accompanied by a laugh. 'Come on, do you want some wine?'

They turned towards the bar, where Wendy had secured two stools and had a glass of red already on the go. 'A glass of Pinot Grigio for me, please?' she said to the barman as she tried her best to gracefully wiggle her bum onto the stool.

'And here is your goody bag!' Wendy said, pointing to a bag at her feet.

'Oh Jesus, it's massive. Did you just carry that on the train?' Jessica asked, feeling guilty.

'No girl, Jason dropped me. Adeline and Dylan are on a sleepover with Granny tonight and he practically had to drive past to drop them. I'm already on my second glass, chin chin,' she said, raising the wine glass. 'And don't forget that bag at the end of the night as there's a shopping voucher in there too – and they were quite generous...'

Jessica raised her eyebrows in surprise, just as her glass of wine was placed in front of her by the barman.

'Thanks Wendy, that's really kind,' she said, as she took her first sip.

'So now we're on the subject,' Wendy started, 'you haven't been letting the attitude of "Queen Bee" Tiggy put you off blogging, have you? I know what it's like to be the newbie...'

'Ah no,' Jessica said, looking down at her nails. 'I mean, well, not really.'

'Well, that's good,' Wendy replied. 'And if it helps at all, I think I know why she was so off with you the other day...'

'Really?' Jessica asked, looking up to meet Wendy's eyes. 'I assume it's because I'm too lowly a blogger to converse with?'

'Well no, probably the opposite actually,' Wendy said, raising her eyebrows.

Jessica frowned. 'How exactly?'

'You're on the new Mama & Me campaign, right?' Wendy asked.

'Yes,' Jessica replied, blushing.

'It's a great campaign, girl! Congrats!' Wendy said, clinking her glass against Jessica's.

'Thank you,' Jessica replied. 'Bella and I have got the shoot for it next week and I'm really nervous, to be honest. But what's it got to do with Tiggy?'

'Well, that was her gig,' Wendy said, pausing to let it sink in. 'She's been on that campaign since the beginning, every year without fail. But this year, she was ditched.'

'Oh.' Jessica said, exhaling loudly and shaking her head in realisation. 'And I replaced her?'

'Yes. They said they were going to change it all up, bring in several new faces, and let a few of the original team go. But when it came down to it, they only got rid of one,' Wendy explained.

'Tiggy,' Jessica said.

'Exactly. And you replaced her,' Wendy replied. 'The only new face on the team.'

Jessica shook her head, letting it all sink in. She didn't know what to say.

'I heard on the grapevine that she didn't even find out until they announced the new team on their social feed,' Wendy continued. 'Which must have been a pretty big kick in the teeth.'

'Oh God,' Jessica said, swallowing. 'I feel terrible.'

'No, stop! Don't feel terrible! This is how blogging works! You win campaigns and you lose campaigns. Running a blog is like running a business – and there are as many rejections as invitations along the way, believe me,' Wendy said, smiling at her.

'It makes sense now. The announcement of the Mama & Me team came a few days before that launch, so she would've seen it just before we met...' Jess said, thinking out loud.

'But it doesn't excuse the way she spoke to you,' Wendy added, shaking her head. 'And between you and me, she's got form...'

'How do you mean?' Jessica snapped back.

'The first year that Tiggy was nominated at the Blog Network Awards was 2015. There weren't so many of us blogging back then and she had been doing really well, so nobody was surprised to see her name make the list. Her social media numbers and subscribers had suddenly gone batshit mental.'

Jessica nodded, swirling her wine in its glass as she listened.

'But a young mummy blogger had appeared on the scene a few months beforehand, after a few posts went viral on social media,' Wendy continued. 'She blogged in a different way to everybody else on that list, telling her readers about motherhood in a really honest way. She blogged about baby poo, about finding it all pretty tough, and about enjoying a glass of wine in the evening when she finally got her baby to bed.'

'And she was nominated too?' Jessica asked.

Wendy nodded. 'Yep. That was the same year that the team at the Blog Network Awards decided to add a new, up-and-coming blogger to every category.'

Jessica nodded, feeling like everything was finally making sense. 'And how did the other bloggers take it?' she asked. 'Her name being on the list?'

'Well, not brilliantly,' Wendy said, catching the barman's eye and smiling. 'One more of these please? It's the Shiraz.' They both watched as the barman poured the wine in silence and after she'd taken the glass, Wendy continued. 'I guess a lot of the most popular bloggers at the time felt a bit threatened by this new style of blogging and the fact it was getting so much attention. But still, this young blogger, who only had one baby at the time and wasn't exactly confident about either blogging or motherhood, tried her best to integrate herself. Most people were a bit indifferent to her and left her to it. But there was one that was especially unfriendly.'

'Tiggy?' asked Jessica.

'Exactly,' Wendy replied. 'She wrote a blog post about the award nomination, with lots of smiley pictures of her and the kids. At the end, she recapped the list of other nominated bloggers and gave a line about why they were brilliant too. On the surface, it looked like the loveliest, most supportive post. But the truth was that she'd left one out.'

'The new blogger?' said Jessica. 'Wow.'

'Exactly... She thought it must be a mistake at first and approached her at a pre-awards event, hoping to share a drink and have a laugh about it. But as she walked up to her, Tiggy turned away and walked off. Again, she assumed it was just a misunderstanding and tried to break the ice later on. But as she approached the second time, Tiggy turned to her and said very quietly: "I'm sorry, I really don't know who you are, but I am busy and would prefer to chat to my friends." And that was that!'

Jessica shook her head and raised her eyebrows. 'And did she win?'

'The new blogger?' replied Wendy. 'No. It went to a Daddy blogger that year. I'm not sure Tiggy was ever expecting to win it, as it was the first year she was nominated too, but she certainly didn't want that young blogger to get it either.'

'I don't know if all this information makes me feel better or worse,' Jessica said, staring into her wine glass. 'But how do you know about it all?'

'Well,' said Wendy, taking a large gulp of wine. 'That new blogger was me.'

Jessica's eyes snapped up. 'What? But how? You and Tiggy are friends, aren't you?'

'Well no, not really. But she respects me,' Wendy replied.

'So, what changed?' she asked. 'How did you get to the point of chatting like buddies at a press launch?'

'I stood up to her,' Wendy said, smiling. 'I was invited to a dinner shortly after that awards ceremony and they put me next to her. That was torture for Tiggy because she couldn't escape or make a scene at the table without everybody hearing. So, I forced her to have a conversation with me and when she tried to turn away, I told her that I wasn't going anywhere, I deserved my spot on that nomination list, and she might as well start accepting it.'

'That was brave,' Jessica said.

'No, that was four vodka sodas before we sat down for dinner!' Wendy replied, raising her eyebrows.

Jessica laughed loudly.

'But honestly, I think this is part of the problem with blogging. And you'll have to excuse me for getting all deep, because I've probably already had too much Shiraz – but the problem is that we think the person in the photos and behind the blog posts is as confident as their smile or their words communicate. But actually, we all suffer from the same shitty moments when we feel like death, the baby hasn't slept properly, and we compare ourselves to everyone else.'

'So, what are you saying?' Jessica asked. 'That Tiggy is human, after all?'

'Yes,' Wendy replied. 'She is – not that she'd want you to know it. Maybe she found out that she'd been ditched from that campaign when she was having a really shit day with the kids and feeling massively low in confidence for some reason. And maybe she's worried you'll go on to win that award, which would totally validate the brand's decision to bring you in and replace her.'

Jessica smiled uncomfortably and sipped her wine.

'Look girl, I'm not telling you that she's a wonderful human. She probably isn't! Definitely isn't! None of us are! I'm just saying that she clearly feels threatened by you and doesn't know how to deal with it. And do you want to know how I'd personally feel about that, knowing what I do now?' Wendy asked.

'Go on.'

'I'd be flattered,' Wendy said with a smile.

Jessica frowned.

'I know it sounds nuts, but if she thought you were a nobody, she wouldn't bother. I think you've got a really good chance of winning that award – and to treat you like that, Tiggy must do too.'

Knots twisted in Jessica's stomach as she allowed herself to imagine her name would be on the award shortlist for a moment, but no sooner had she let the thought creep into her mind, then she shut it out again. She didn't want to set herself up for a fall, especially since realising how vulnerable blogging had made her feel. So instead, she steered the conversation to Wendy, asking more about how she got into blogging and what she'd seen change over the years. And for the next hour, they chatted happily as they sipped their wine and tucked into bowls of dry roasted peanuts and stuffed olives.

'I'm just popping to the bathroom,' Wendy said. 'Shall we have one more for the road when I get back?'

'Excellent idea,' Jessica replied, reaching into her bag to check the time on her phone.

And that was the moment that she remembered that Deena and Henny were heading over to spend the evening with Mel at her house.

And the moment she remembered that Mel had something important that she needed to discuss.

And the moment that she noticed there were two messages from Deena and two from Henny, plus a couple of missed calls from both of them staring back at her from the locked screen.

'Oh shit!' she said out loud, quickly unlocking the phone with her thumbprint and scrolling down to read the messages.

19:45 – Henny: You not coming tonight babe?

20:05 – Henny: You coming later?

20:15 – Deena: It's not good news. Can you join?

21:30 – Henny: Could you call when you get a moment babe?

It was now 9.53 p.m. and she was sat in a wine bar with somebody she had only met once before, when there was clearly a crisis situation developing with her nearest and dearest. The realisation hit her hard. Trying to work out what to do, she took a deep breath and glanced around the room, just as Wendy was bounding towards her with a smile on her face.

'Same again?' she asked, as she got to the bar.

'God, I'm sorry Wendy. I'd love to, but I think I'd better go,' she replied.

'Oh, is everything OK? Is Bella playing up?' Wendy asked.

'Exactly,' she said, realising it sounded far less offensive than the truth.

Wendy was characteristically lovely and five minutes later, they were outside the bar hailing cabs. Wendy insisted that Jessica jumped in the first one, and as she climbed inside, they shared words of encouragement about the awards shortlist announcement a few days later. 'Good luck to you!' Wendy called, before slamming the door shut from the pavement.

'And same to you!' Jessica called back as she waved.

'Right, where we going?' the driver asked her, leaving Jessica stumped.

'I'm not sure,' she replied, 'But head towards Westcombe Park for now.'

Did she want to head home? Or join the girls? She was feeling quite irritated that they all needed her desperately. Wasn't she allowed to have a drink with a friend without being interrupted? But on the flip side, what if something had happened? She pulled out her phone to call Henny, who answered on the second ring.

'Hi babe, you OK?' she asked.

'I'm on my way,' Jessica replied, making a split decision to join them. 'What's going on?'

'Hang on,' Henny said, getting up to leave the room. Reaching the kitchen, she spoke in a whisper. 'It's Steven, babe.'

'What? What happened? Is Steven OK?' Jessica asked, suddenly feeling sick with worry.

'He's fine, babe. He's a dickhead, but he's fine,' Henny whispered.

'Oh God. Can you just tell me what's going on before I walk through the door?'

'He's having an affair,' Henny said, hearing Jessica exhale loudly on the other end of the line.

'What?' she managed to say, suddenly lost for words.

'And he's having that affair with his ex-wife,' Henny continued.

Jessica gasped. 'The one in Sweden?'

'That's right, babe. And that's not all,' Henny continued in her loud whisper.

'How can it possibly be worse than that?' Jessica asked, wishing she'd drunk less over the past few hours and had a clearer head.

Henny paused and sighed.

'Mel is pregnant.'

13

Followers – 14,294
Emails in inbox – 78
Event invitations – 40
Paid collaborations – 1
Award nominations – 1
Blogger enemies – 1
Blogger friends – 1

Dear Bella,

Suddenly we had friends.

Friends that made time tick a hundred times faster.

Friends that replied instantly, when I felt like I was failing at motherhood and needed a few words of reassurance.

Friends that laughed hysterically as we took turns sniffing baby bums as they crawled round the room.

Friends that offered each other coffee by day – and wine by night.

Real friends.

It all started one Tuesday morning in September, when I plucked up the courage to go to a music class with you. But while it was my feet that did the walking, it was Daddy that was pushing us out of the door. 'You have to go, Jess,' he said that morning as we lay in bed. 'Bella needs a few friends as she's growing up – and more importantly, you're bored. Fran doesn't come any more and your parents are rarely here either. You need something to get you through the day and make it all a bit easier. And look, it doesn't matter if you don't meet them today, but it'll get you out the house for a few hours. It has to be worth it for that alone.'

I had immediately rolled my eyes and turned over. 'Don't turn away,' he said. 'You know it makes sense.'

'It's easy for you to say, isn't it?' I said to the wall. 'You'll be on a train to London in half an hour, then happily working away at your desk. It isn't you that has to walk into a room full of strangers!' Even the thought made me feel sick with nerves. It had been a few months since I'd last tried – and this time, I wouldn't be able to hide in the shadows with a hapless health visitor.

'I know, Jess!' he replied. 'And if I could do it for you, I would! But I can't, so just go! You may not hate it as much as you expect. Wait and see.'

Despite wanting to punch him on the nose, I knew he was right. You were six months old now and needed more than the stuffed woodland creatures on your baby gym swinging in your face to fill the day. One class every week wouldn't be too bad. And maybe the fact it was a structured class would make it easier to integrate myself. Or maybe not. But whatever was in store, I knew I needed to walk out our front door that morning. So I did, despite wishing I could run back inside and cuddle up with you on the sofa.

That was the day we met our gang, Bella. And it was hard walking into that church hall on that first morning – but it's amazing how talk of baby poo, sleepless nights, and the absolute love/hate relationship we all had with breastfeeding bonded us tighter than super glue within a matter of weeks. Within hours, I was telling those ladies things that I would never dream of muttering to near-strangers, and at times, I even shocked myself with my openness. But there was something about mutual motherhood that made it all seem totally acceptable. No subject was off limits for conversation. And when one of us needed help – either physically, in the form of childcare for a few hours, or mentally, on the days when we wished we were tapping away at a computer in an office full of other adults, rather than changing our third nappy of the day at 9 a.m. – we were there in a second. It was wonderfully, exhaustingly, amazingly brilliant.

You were still so little, Bella but I didn't doubt for a second that you'd grow up with those little friends. You saw those little faces more often than you saw your own grandparents and they quickly became surrogate cousins. You may have only laid next to them at first, studying your toes, but that changed as time ticked on. They became your playmates, your sparring partners, and your partners in crime. I watched those little people grow up nearly as closely as I watched you.

It's like a family.

Just like a family.

And I have thanked my lucky stars that we walked into that church hall every day since September.

It was the best decision I ever made.

Love from Mummy x

As the taxi approached Mel's road, Jessica's mind was whirring.

Mel was pregnant.

And her husband was having an affair.

With his ex-wife.

Who had married someone else and was living in Stockholm with him and the children.

How was all this even possible? How had he managed it? And how long had it all been going on?

Mel had always been vocal about only wanting one child. She had met Steven at work, when she was in her late thirties, and they had a whirlwind engagement and marriage, eloping to New York without telling friends and family. Their wedding photos were posed in Times Square and Central Park on a cold December day, with Mel wearing a gold lace dress under thick, white fur. And then came Lara, and despite not being part of the plan, she had been very welcome. But Mel knew from the very moment that she saw the word 'PREGNANT' on the test that she only wanted to do it once.

Mel had had a successful career as a legal counsel before her maternity leave and it had always been the plan for her to go back to work. So when Jessica had heard that Mel wanted to chat that evening, she had assumed that would be the news. She imagined Mel would sit them down and break it to them that their Tuesday morning coffees were coming to an end. She had assumed it wasn't urgent. She had assumed she could wait and hear it all tomorrow.

But it *had* been urgent, and as her taxi wound down dark streets towards the house with the climbing roses, Jessica wished she'd sent an apology to Wendy and rushed off to be with the girls instead. But you couldn't deal backwards and she was here now, handing over a note to the driver and climbing out of the cab. She held her breath as she knocked on the door, biting her lip with nerves as she heard footsteps rushing towards it.

'Hi, babe,' Henny said, allowing just the corner of her mouth to curl into a smile. 'Come in, we're in the lounge.'

'How is she?' Jessica asked in a loud whisper. 'I'm really sorry for not being here!'

Henny stopped and turned, smiling the same smile she always smiled. 'Don't worry! You didn't know!'

Jessica exhaled deeply and smiled back.

Mel's house was never usually quiet. It was filled with the sound of toddler babble, the whistle of a kettle, and the radio playing softly in the background. It felt strange to step into the silence, as Jessica followed Henny through the hallway. It suddenly occurred to her that it was very similar to the sound of her parents' house after Michael died.

Yes, it was just like someone had died – and she guessed for Mel, it felt like they had.

As they walked into the lounge, Mel and Deena turned towards them.

'I'm so sorry, Mel,' Jessica said, fighting to compose herself but she couldn't stop a single tear rolling down her cheek, trying to wipe it away with her hand before it was noticed.

'Hey, what are you crying for?' Mel said, followed by her characteristic laugh. But her eyes weren't laughing. As Jessica hugged her and looked into them, she could see they were puffy and red. 'Tell me what happened.'

Mel took a deep breath. 'I feel like a broken record, but I'll tell you the story again. I guess I'm going to have to at some point.' She cleared her throat and took a sip from a glass. Jessica watched as she did it, wondering what was inside as the ice clinked against the side.

'It's tonic water, in case you were wondering,' she snapped, reading her mind.

'Oh no, I wasn't…' Jessica said, swallowing. 'Sorry Mel.'

Mel laughed quietly, then cleared her throat with two small coughs. 'I've had my suspicions something has been going on for a while. Steven has been in Sweden a lot and I get it, because his kids are there. But when Lara and I are alone a lot of the time and he refuses to employ a sodding nanny to help me get back to work, that's pretty hard to swallow. But anyway, the constant trips to Sweden have been worrying me for a while, but I guess I put it to the back of my mind. I just treated it like another business trip.'

'I knew he was away a lot,' Jessica said. 'I just didn't realise quite how often.'

'Jess, he's barely here! What with the monthly trips out to the Middle East for work and the fortnightly trips to his ex and the kids in Sweden…'

'Fortnightly?' Jessica cut in. 'Jesus.'

'Well, exactly – and it all makes sense now. It was obviously a problem for us and we were arguing a lot. I wanted to go back to work, but the logistics of being a working mum just wouldn't work if he couldn't commit to being here more often. He was either at his desk in London, out of the country on business, or arguing with me at home. I spent the days entertaining Lara and the evenings worrying about where my husband was and what exactly he was doing. It's been pretty miserable, to be honest.'

'So, you suspected something was going on?' Jessica asked.

'Well, I did after I got a message from Jenny,' Mel explained.

'Jenny?' Jessica asked, trying to place the name.

'Oh, I don't think you know her. Steven and his ex-wife Emily met at university, and Jenny was on their course too. They all hung out together, but Jenny was always better friends with Steven and I don't think she's seen Emily since the divorce. They stayed connected on social media though and a few months ago, a message arrived in my inbox from her asking whether I knew Steven was hanging out with Emily that weekend. Of course I did, as he was in Sweden seeing the kids. I was actually quite irritated by Jenny's message as she'd caught me at a bad moment with Lara and I was probably a bit short in my reply so she backed off and I forgot about it. But then she messaged me again a fortnight later.'

'What did it say?' Henny asked,

'She asked if I knew he was staying in the house with Emily and the kids. We have an apartment over there, which I was obviously under the impression he was sleeping in – so I typed back saying I didn't think that was the case. I added that I thought Emily's husband may find it all a bit strange if her ex was sleeping under the same roof and did one of those laughing face emojis. I was pissed off with her to be honest. I felt like she was trying to stir things up for no reason. So I rolled my eyes and closed the message, carrying on with running Lara's bath. But then a reply instantly popped up on my phone from Jenny saying that she was pretty sure Emily had recently separated from her new husband (something Steven hadn't obviously told me) and I started to shake. She went on to send me screenshots of the photos Emily had shared online; Steven eating breakfast with the kids in his pyjamas in their kitchen, the whole lot of them playing happy families at the zoo, and smiley family selfies on the beach. Lara was happily splashing in the bath at this point and I felt like I'd been punched in the stomach.'

'I still can't believe it,' Deena said. 'Fuck. I never saw it coming.'

'Tell me about it,' Mel said, shaking her head. 'Do you want to see the photos she sent?' The girls nodded and she passed over her phone.

And she was right; they were incriminating. The two children were the perfect blend of Steven and Emily. Her eyes, his blond hair, her freckles, his chin dent, her golden tan, his chiselled cheekbones. And there they were; the four of them beaming with happiness, as if a divorce and two remarriages had never happened.

'I can't believe he thought he'd get away with it...' Jessica said, as she passed back the phone. 'So, did you call him? What happened?'

'He'd flown out to Stockholm the day after the barbecue we hosted last month, and the next day, you invited us all for drinks at your house Henny. That was the day she messaged me.'

'I wish you'd told us babe. I *really* wish you'd told us,' Henny said, her eyes filling with tears.

'I know Hen, but I couldn't even think straight. I didn't want to believe it. He wasn't due home for another couple of days, but I couldn't just sit and wait for him. I knew he was in her house, pretending life was like the old days. And meanwhile, Lara and I were home alone in London. I went through so many emotions trying to decide what to do, but I was mainly angry. So, the next morning, after a totally sleepless night, I decided to call him. Now you know me girls – I'm not a shrinking violet and I've dealt with some tough shit in my career, but this was something else. I literally saw my life flash before my eyes as the phone rang and until he answered, I didn't know whether I was going to shout, cry, or completely lose the ability to talk. I was a mess.'

'I don't know if I could've made that phone call,' Henny said, shaking her head. 'I'd have bottled out.'

'He answered after about five rings and told me he'd have to call back as he was with the kids. So, without thinking, I shot back, "And Emily, I assume?" That stopped him in his tracks and he told the kids to sit tight for a moment and left the room. Then he was all like "What's wrong, darling? Everything is fine darling! No, those pictures are just misleading, because the truth is that Emily would love everything to be back like it used to be." He said of course, he hadn't been staying the night. He was wearing his pyjama bottoms because the kids wanted to have a pyjama party and watch a movie as a family and he didn't want to say no, because they already missed out on so much since the divorce. And the family photos were taken for the benefit of the children. And "honestly darling, everything is fine". And he missed Lara and he couldn't wait to get home.'

'And you believed him?' Jessica asked.

'I let myself fall for it. I didn't want this world of ours to fall apart. I loved him and I wanted to make it work, for Lara if nobody else. I put down the phone and I tried my best to put it out of my mind and trust him over the next few days. He sent me lots more messages than usual and picked up the phone to call so he could say goodnight to Lara for the first time in forever. I mean, looking back now it's ridiculous – of course he was trying to cover something up. But I wanted to believe him so I let myself fall for his lies.'

'Shit,' Jessica said. 'He's good.'

'Yep,' Mel replied. 'But just before he got home, the unthinkable happened.'

'You found out about the baby?' Jessica asked.

Mel nodded, her eyes filling with tears for the first time. To her side, Deena squeezed her arm and Mel turned to smile at her.

'God, I wish I could have a stiff drink. This is torture!' Mel said, with the girls smiling sympathetically. She cleared her throat and carried on. 'Yes, I mean it had crossed my mind for a few weeks. I had moments where nausea suddenly swept over me, but as soon as I acknowledged it, it disappeared again. I'd been sick from the beginning with Lara and it was pretty relentless, so I convinced myself I was just getting poorly. But then I started getting a horrible metallic taste in my mouth, and that was it. I knew I had to get a test.'

'Shit, I got that too,' Deena replied. 'First thing I noticed.'

'Me too,' said Henny, on the sofa next to her. 'Not so much with Thomas, but definitely with Tallulah.'

'So, I got one of those digital tests and managed to put it out of my mind until Lara was in bed that evening,' Mel continued. 'I kept busy that afternoon doing crafty stuff and going for a walk and once she was in bed, I ran a bath. While it was running, I did the test. I thought I was going to get five minutes or so to pluck up the courage to look at it but nearly as soon as my wee hit the end of the stick, the result flashed up that I was bloody pregnant. I was so horrified that I threw the test on the floor and it landed face up, taunting me with the word. PREGNANT, PREGNANT, PREGNANT. It seemed like a really cruel joke.'

'How did you tell him?' Jessica asked.

'He got back the next day, clutching a gigantic bunch of flowers. I mean, seriously... He played along with the cliché of a cheating husband so perfectly. It should've been such a red flag, but knowing that I now had the cells of Lara's sibling multiplying inside me, I wanted to believe him more than ever. He grovelled a lot at the beginning and I let him convince me. I really wanted everything to be OK. I kept wondering when I should tell him about the pregnancy, but it was getting late and he wanted to go to bed. I tried to convince him to stay up a bit, but he was falling asleep so I left it. I figured I'd tell him the next day,' Mel explained.

'But he was back to work the next morning. He left early and had clients to entertain in the evening, so came home after I was already in bed,' she continued. 'And the same happened the next day. And the next. And then he was off to Abu Dhabi on a business trip. Life just carried on, with him pretty absent in our life and although I wanted him to be at home, it gave me the chance to carry on ignoring the fact I was pregnant. I didn't want anybody to know about it – not him, not any of you, nobody. Because if I told everybody, it suddenly became real.'

'I get it,' Deena said. 'I was the same with Finley. I totally, totally get it,' Deena said, squeezing her arm again.

'But I was starting to feel really sick with this pregnancy and it was getting harder and harder to ignore,' Mel said. 'Plus, I was starting to get a bump. I think I'm double the size I was with Lara at this stage and I knew it wouldn't be long before Steven noticed. And more importantly, his next trip to Sweden was coming up and I couldn't let him go back there without telling him.'

'So, you told him?' Jessica asked.

Mel nodded in reply.

'When?' she asked. 'Today?'

Mel nodded again and continued. 'His flight to Stockholm wasn't until this afternoon, so we had a few hours together this morning. I decided it would be best to go to the park, because we could stroll as we talked. I didn't think being at home would work so well, because he'd probably be distracted tapping away messages on his phone – as he always bloody does. So off we went to the park, with Lara in the buggy. I felt sick with something – I'm not sure if it was pregnancy or nerves, but it was bloody awful – and about five minutes in, I had to turn and puke into a bush. Steven was staggered, muttering about how he didn't know I was ill and that we should go back towards home. I realised it was my chance. It was now or never.

'So, I told him. "Actually no, the thing is, I'm pregnant…" He replied: "Pardon?" So I repeated: "I'm pregnant." And then there was silence. Total silence. No hugs, or tears, or even screams. We kept walking and I could feel my heart pounding with every step. And after what felt like a lifetime, he calmly turned to me and said, "Well, that isn't going to work."'

Jessica gasped. 'You're kidding?'

'No, sadly not. I kind of laughed and said, "What do you mean? I know it's not ideal, but it's going to have to work, isn't it?" But he didn't even look at me. He just stared ahead as he walked with a cold, glazed over expression, and then he took a deep breath and said: "Mel, I didn't want it to come out like this, but I'm in love with Emily and I want to be a family again. I love Lara too and I'll always be there for her, but this new baby can't happen. It isn't in the plan."'

Jessica knew she should say something, but she was lost for words.

Mel paused for a moment and shook her head. 'I didn't say a word. I stopped walking, composed myself for a second, then turned around with the buggy and walked as fast as I could back home. I knew I had to get back through the door before I broke down. I didn't want him to see me lose it. I didn't want to have to dodge people's eyes as I sobbed big, angry tears in public. I knew that once I started, I probably wasn't going to be able to stop. He didn't chase after me. I wasn't sure if I wanted him to, but he didn't bother. And then when I got home, I bolted the doors so he couldn't use his key. I assume he's in Stockholm now, but his passport could still be here. I haven't even bothered to check.'

Jessica stood up and strode over to her friend, sitting next to her on the sofa and pulling her into a hug. She didn't know what to say. There was nothing she could say.

'This would all be a lot easier if we could share a few bottles together, wouldn't it?' Mel said, laughing through her tears.

'Too right, babe,' Henny said, joining the three of them on the sofa. 'But do you know what? We're going to get you through this, with or without alcohol.'

'We bloody are,' Deena added. 'In fact, I'm going to message Ian now and tell him I'm staying here tonight.'

'Me, too,' added Jessica.

'Me three,' replied Henny.

'Now lead us to your pyjama drawer my dear, as we've got the whole night ahead,' Deena said, beckoning to the door.

'Thank fuck for you girls,' Mel replied, standing up and leading the three of them out of the room. 'What would I do without you?'

And with that, they were heading up the stairs.

14

Followers – 19,794
Emails in inbox – 149
Event invitations – 39
Paid collaborations – 1
Award nominations – 1
Blogger enemies – 1
Blogger friends – 1

Dear Bella,

In the movies, having a baby is the end part. The bit after
you fall in love, have a beautiful white wedding, and grow
a baby bump, glamorously. The movie usually ends with a
shot of a hospital bed, babe in arms, and two parents gazing
adoringly into each other's eyes. That was pretty much how
all my favourite movies came to an end in the 1990s and so
I grew up believing that it would happen to me, too. I'd fall
in love (check), get married (check), get pregnant (check),
and pop that baby out without even smudging my mascara

(first half checked, second half definitely not checked). And after that? I didn't know, but I fully expected to be gazing into Daddy's eyes adoringly while doing it.

But the truth is Bella that there's no idyllic rosy glow cast over your life when you have a baby. There weren't petals strewn across our king-size bed when we got you home from hospital. In fact, if Daddy had even attempted to touch me for the first few months postpartum, I would probably have clobbered him. We spoke mainly to debate whose turn it was to change your nappy or for me to demand he scurried off to hunt for another pack of giant maternity pads. My body was bloated and bleeding, my hair went days between washes, and I hadn't seen my make-up bag since the day I'd gone into labour. I have vague memories of trying to make eye contact one evening on the sofa but it was less about 'gazing adoringly' and more about 'needing a bar of chocolate from the fridge'.

It wasn't romantic, Bella. It was far from it. And in the weeks that followed your birth, it often crossed my mind that Hollywood had done mothers a disservice by allowing us to believe it would be. As time went on, we argued a lot too – because essentially, I wanted and needed him home with us, but work, life, commitments didn't always allow it. I've never been so angry with someone I love so much, and at times, that floored me.

But on the good days – the days I could string a sentence

together and see clearly through the fog of tiredness – it occurred to me that the way that our relationship had changed made it so much stronger, so much closer, and I guess so much better.

I didn't wear lace underwear any more (even the thought made me shudder) and we hadn't been on a date since I was thirty-three weeks' pregnant and nearly fell asleep in my bowl of spaghetti – but we had you now. We were a family. We were together.

It was about having a newfound respect for each other. It was about seeing Daddy's protectiveness as I grew you, his calmness as labour swept over me, and the love wash over his face as he cradled you in his arms for the first time. Suddenly everything felt different. Suddenly it made sense. And while we may have argued more frequently and had more than our fair share of moments when we seriously wondered if the other was living on the same planet (mainly me, admittedly), our relationship had still never felt closer.

So no Bella, he hasn't always been the perfect husband – as I haven't always been the perfect wife.

But he has, without fail, always been the perfect daddy to you.

And watching that happen has made me fall in love with him all over again.

Even on the days he's late home from work.

I promise.

Love from Mummy x

*

'Here you go ladies,' Henny said, as she placed three mugs on the breakfast bar.

It was the morning after, and while Mel slept upstairs, after finally drifting off when daylight peeked through the curtains, the girls were gathered in the kitchen wearing pairs of her pyjamas and looking after her baffled, but rather excited toddler.

After much persuasion, Mel had called her mother late the night before. She was convinced that she'd laugh and say 'I told you so!' having never been a fan of Steven, but the reality had been very different. In fact, she'd immediately cleared her diary and booked a flight to London the next morning. Within hours, she would be sweeping through the door to look after her daughter and granddaughter.

'Do you think she'll be OK?' Jessica asked, as Henny pulled a stool up to join them.

Deena shrugged her shoulders. 'She puts on a brave face, but she's broken. I think the thought of heading back to work was keeping her going to be honest. I don't know what she'll do now.'

'Will she keep the baby, do you think?' Henny asked.

The question made Jessica flinch, the alternative having never crossed her mind.

Deena blew on her coffee and took a sip, as the question hung heavily between them. 'I think she'll have the baby, but let's see. She probably needs some time to think.'

'I still can't believe it,' Henny said, staring into her mug. 'I mean, if I'm totally honest with you girls, I never really warmed to him and hearing him speak to Mel like that at the barbecue just confirmed it. But I just don't know how she's going to move on. She really loved him.'

'I feel bad, because I knew she was on her own a lot of the time and I feel like I should've done more now. Like be here more? Do you know what I mean?' Jessica asked, swirling the coffee in her mug as she spoke.

'Nah, don't feel bad,' Deena said. 'Mel has always been brilliant at putting on a brave face – and if she'd wanted more support, she would've asked. She knew we'd all be here in a flash if she needed us.'

Jessica swallowed. 'I wish I'd been here earlier,' she replied awkwardly.

'Oh, stop it! How were any of us supposed to know? You had plans, don't beat yourself up, babe,' Henny said, as Lara toddled up to the table and handed her a piece of a puzzle. 'Do you want to do the puzzle, Lara Lou? OK, Auntie Henny will do it with you.' Deena and Jessica smiled as they walked off hand-in-hand towards the lounge.

'So how did it go with your blogger friend last night?' Deena asked, as the two of them were left on their own in the kitchen.

'Oh, it doesn't seem to matter now,' Jess said, sipping

her mug of coffee. 'Blogging felt so important last night but this has put it all in perspective.'

'Don't say that. We do care about your blogging, girl! We all want you to get through to that awards ceremony. In fact, we're considering gatecrashing and cheerleading in the corner!'

Jessica shook her head and laughed. 'Well, that's something I'd like to witness... Thank you... You are all lovely friends, but I think we all know the chances of me making it through to that ceremony are pretty slim!'

'Well, we all reckon you're going to win it,' Deena replied, raising her eyebrows.

'You would say that! You're my mates,' Jess said, rolling her eyes and laughing. 'But seriously, half the people aren't even going to make it to the awards ceremony. The shortlist comes out on Tuesday.'

'Oh wow, it's all happening soon. What time?' Deena asked.

'I don't know actually. I've tried not to think about it too much,' Jessica replied.

'But generally, how is the blogging going? Are you enjoying it?' Deena asked.

Jessica paused to think. Nobody had asked her that question before and she wasn't sure how to reply. She knew it was going well – the rising follower numbers, paid collaboration, and award nomination spoke for themselves, after all. She hadn't been prepared for the speed of how quickly her blog would take off and she had to pinch herself on a daily basis. Having an audience listening to her words was a dream come true. It was what she'd always wanted.

But was she enjoying it? Really enjoying it?

Tiggy's voice played in her mind at the launch: 'Sorry, I don't remember you', quickly followed by a vision of Felicity Macdonald tapping away her comment: 'You should be ashamed of yourself!', and then Chris' voice rang in her ears in the café: 'You aren't the girl that cries in a café over something a complete stranger has said to you! This isn't you! You've got sass!'

She sighed. 'Honestly? I don't know.'

Deena looked surprised. 'You aren't going to stop, are you?'

'I don't think so,' Jessica replied. 'I love writing. I really, really love it. But I always imagined I'd be dashing around London reporting on important events, rather than blogging about how I sent Chris out to get me another pack of maternity pads...'

Deena laughed. 'But that's our life, isn't it? It's not glamorous any more! And so many other mums read your blog posts and understand exactly what you're getting at. It makes them feel better! The one that you wrote about finding your friends made me cry! And I never bloody cry!'

'Really?' Jessica asked, surprised.

'Yes! Honestly. I know I'm your mate, but I enjoy reading it.'

'I knew you all read it, but I wasn't sure if it was just moral support,' said Jessica, laughing.

'Well, it's true. I really enjoy reading it. So don't stop,

OK? Get your next letter up today when you get home. And I'll be keeping my fingers and toes crossed for good news on Tuesday,' Deena said, as they both turned to a knock at the door.

BANG! BANG!

'I didn't think her mum was going to be here for another few hours,' Deena said, strolling towards the front door. But as she strolled down the hallway, Lara had made it to the door first.

BANG! BANG! BANG! BANG!

'Dad-dy! Dad-dy! Dad-dy!' Lara called, looking through the glass panel at the bottom of the door.

Deena stopped in her tracks, her blood suddenly running cold.

'Deena? Let me in please! The door is bolted!' Steven shouted loudly from the other side. He pushed his key into the lock and turned it repeatedly, the sound of metal grinding on metal cutting through the air.

'Dad-dy! Dad-dy! Dad-dy!' Lara repeated, banging her fists on the other side of the door. Henny reached the door, opened her eyes wide in surprise at Deena, and scooped Lara into her arms.

'Come on baby girl, let's go play in the other room!' she said gently, as Jessica strolled over to join them. As she walked away, Lara screeched loudly, flailing in Henny's arms and crying loudly as she was carried into the lounge.

'What the fuck do we do?' Deena whispered to Jessica. 'We can't let him in!'

'Deena? I can see you stood there, for fuck's sake! Let me in my house, please! Unbolt the bloody door!' Steven yelled. He turned the key again, pushing the door with a thud.

BANG! BANG! BANG! BANG!

'Bad idea!' Deena yelled back. 'It won't be helpful! Just go away and give her some time!'

'It's my fucking house, Deena! You can't lock me out of my own fucking house! Where is she? I want to talk to her!'

'She's upstairs! She's finally sleeping! I really think it's better if you leave her alone!' Deena shouted back, looking at Jessica and shrugging. 'We can't let him in, can we?' she mouthed at her.

Jessica shook her head and mouthed back 'No!' thinking for a moment before adding in a whisper: 'Is the back door locked? I'm just going to check.'

BANG! BANG! BANG! BANG! BANG!

'I'm going around the back!' Steven shouted, prompting Jessica to turn her fast walk into a run. Seconds later, she was there and one pull of the handle reassured her that the door was locked fast. As she turned to run back to the front door, she could hear him at the side gate trying to force it open.

'Open this gate! Seriously? This is my own fucking house!' he shouted, using his shoulder to barge against the gate. Unsuccessful, he was back at the front door seconds later. 'I'll call the police, Deena. For fuck's sake! Unbolt the door and let me in!'

BANG! BANG! BANG! BANG! BANG!

'I'll call the police too and tell them you're harassing your wife,' she shouted back, as they all turned to the sound of footsteps coming down the stairs.

'Why don't you just fuck off, Steven?' Mel shouted, as she reached the bottom of the stairs and walked slowly towards the door, her hair messy and eyes streaked with yesterday's mascara.

'Let me in, Melanie. Please? I just want to grab my passport,' Steven yelled, his voice lowered.

'Of course you do!' Mel spat back loudly. 'You didn't want to come and see your daughter or check whether your pregnant wife is doing OK after telling her you've been screwing someone else! No! Of course not! You just want to grab your passport so you can fly back to that whore!'

At that, she turned and stormed down the hallway towards the kitchen, with Jessica close behind her. Deena stood firm by the door, while Henny had switched the television up loudly in the lounge and shut the door.

BANG, BANG, BANG, BANG, BANG!

'Teletubbies! Teletubbies! Say Hello! Eh-Oh!'

BANG, BANG, BANG, BANG, BANG!

'That fucking bastard,' Mel said under her breath, as she reached the kitchen and opened the cupboard above the microwave. Grabbing a black leather wallet from inside, she hastily unzipped it and flicked through the passports. Finding Steven's, she threw the wallet down and turned on her heels back towards the door.

'You're not going to give it to him?' Jessica asked, as she followed behind her.

'Yes, Jess,' Mel replied without even turning. 'I just want him to go!'

BANG! BANG! BANG! BANG!

'Where the fuck are you, Melanie? Last chance or I'll call the fucking police!' Steven yelled, his voice hissing with rage.

Without a word, Mel posted the passport through the letterbox, so that it fell at Steven's feet, and turned back towards the kitchen.

'Come on girls,' she said, as she strolled away. 'I need a bloody coffee.'

And they followed, with their hearts thumping and nerves frayed.

An hour later, Jessica was strolling home. Deena had happily volunteered to stay with Mel until her mother arrived, as her partner Ian had taken Finley to his parents for the day and Henny was already on a train to spend the rest of the day at The Science Museum with Dan and the children. So, Jessica walked home alone, deep in thought.

She often moaned about Chris and the fact he got home late from work. She honestly wished he was around more often. And they had arguments – quite often actually, since Bella had arrived. But seeing Steven that morning and the way he had shouted at Mel, ignored Lara, and pounded on the door so aggressively, she suddenly appreciated how lucky she was. Especially when her phone pinged during the post-Steven-turning-up coffee and she glanced down to see selfies of Chris and Bella in their favourite café next to Greenwich Park, scoffing pancakes and blowing kisses at the camera. He loved his little girl and thinking about their relationship filled her eyes with soppy, thankful, tired tears.

Jessica had only spent one other night away from Bella before last night, when she had stayed with Fran at her parents' house after Michael's funeral, and she was nearly bursting with excitement to see her little girl again as she approached her front door. So when she opened it and wasn't greeted by her daughter running towards her legs at top speed, she felt momentarily deflated. But Chris was there and she was happy to see him.

'Hi honey,' he said with a smile, turning towards the front door from his position on the sofa watching football. 'How is she? What's happening?'

'Hi,' she said, sitting next to him and kissing him on the lips. 'I missed you both. Is she sleeping?'

'Yes, and it only took an hour for her to settle and go to sleep. How do you have the patience for that every day?!' he asked.

'I'm surprised you did, to be honest,' she replied, laughing.

'You underestimate my determination when I've got food to eat and sport to watch,' Chris said. 'So, tell me about Steven. What the hell is going on?'

So, Jessica began the story of what had happened – right from the moment she walked into the wine bar in Blackheath, to saying goodbye to the girls earlier that morning. And when she came to the end, they sat together in silence.

'I'm not surprised,' Chris eventually said. 'I've never liked him.'

'Well, me neither, but today was different,' Jessica replied, as the memory of him banging on the door thumped over and over again in her mind. 'He was so cold and aggressive. It was scary.'

Chris squeezed her hand.

'But it's good about your blogger friend Wendy, isn't it?' Chris asked. 'You had a good time with her? And the shortlist comes out on Tuesday?'

Jessica flinched. 'It's supposed to, yes, but talking to Wendy last night has made me realise how little chance I have to get on it. I'm not expecting to be on that list. I don't really want to think about it.'

'Not expecting to be? Or not wanting to be?' Chris asked.

Jessica sighed loudly. 'Of course, I bloody want to be! It would be amazing! But I don't think I will. I really don't.'

'Surely it's about who's the best, though,' Chris replied. 'Not about who's been doing it for the longest. They wouldn't have added a newcomer to each category if they didn't think they had a chance to win it...'

Jessica shrugged.

'Do you want to do some blogging this afternoon?'

'I'd love to,' Jessica replied. 'But maybe we should get outdoors with Bella?'

'We've been out,' Chris replied. 'I didn't know what time you'd be back, but I planned to stay here this afternoon and let the mesmerising pig entertain her for a while.'

Jessica laughed out loud. 'Good idea,' she said. 'But I'm not moving until she wakes up.'

'Deal,' Chris said, kissing the top of her head as she sank into his arms.

Jessica had been thankful that the shortlist was being published on a Tuesday as that was the busiest day of the week for her and she'd be distracted as the hours ticked away.

But this Tuesday would be different, as they'd be missing a member of their team while they danced around the church hall to dubious pieces of music. Because despite the girls encouraging Mel to come to the class as usual, they knew the chances were slim. So instead, they promised to drop round afterwards for coffee. A little bit of normality in the gloom, and the chance to come together and support her.

That was exactly what happened, the three of them parking their buggies underneath the white climbing roses, knocking on the door, and being invited inside as usual. They drank the same coffee, sat on the same sofas, and watched the same babies potter around and play.

In fact, the only difference to the average Tuesday was that Mel's mother was there too, helping to make coffee and playing with the toddlers as the four of them chatted in the kitchen. That and the fact that Mel hadn't bothered to get dressed and had made her excuses to run to the toilet to vomit at least three times during their conversation.

The time passed quickly and before she knew it, Jessica was strolling home with Henny and the babies as usual.

'You checked whether the shortlist has come out yet, babe?' Henny asked, as they pushed their buggies side by side. The heat of the previous few weeks had finally broken and they were both shivering in thin summer dresses.

'I've checked lots, but there's nothing yet! I guess it'll come out this afternoon.'

But it didn't.

Jessica had to do a supermarket trip, which filled an hour. But the list still hadn't been announced when she got home.

She sat on the floor and built towers with Bella. But when Bella inevitably got bored and knocked them all down in a fit of toddler rage, it still hadn't been announced.

She cooked a shepherd's pie from scratch for dinner but it still hadn't been announced when she came to scrape most of Bella's portion into the bin.

She ran a bath for Bella, put her in it, washed her hair, took her out, dried her, got her dressed for bed, and read a story on the armchair in her nursery. And as she lay alongside the cot waiting for Bella to fall asleep, with her arm poked through the bars so that she knew she was there, she convinced herself that the shortlist would finally be up online when she made it downstairs.

But it wasn't.

Annoyed with herself for letting it dominate her thoughts, she busied herself by typing up the letter from her notebook about her relationship with Chris, finding the perfect picture of their wedding day, and publishing it to the blog and social media.

And when she'd finished all that, Chris had finally made it home, and she'd warmed up dinner and eaten it, she glanced back at her laptop to see if the list was finally up.

She reloaded the page, watching it re-appear on the page agonisingly slowly. And when it was finally back, her eyes darted down the page to check.

But still, nothing.

'Oh, fuck it,' she said, under her breath, slamming the lid of her laptop down.

'Still not been announced?' Chris asked.

She shook her head.

Maybe it was delayed and wouldn't be out until Wednesday. Maybe she'd go to bed and have a good sleep and be better prepared for the disappointment when her name wasn't there in the morning. Maybe it was better that way. Maybe it would be easier to take the disappointment.

That's it, she thought. *I'm not going to look again tonight. I'll just leave it until the morning.* And she kept her promise, sinking into Chris to watch the end of a film.

So, when her phone rang at 11.05 p.m., she jumped with shock.

'Who's that?' Chris asked. 'Bit late to be calling,'

'It's Fran,' Jessica said, staring at her name on the screen. 'I'd better take it. She probably just wants to know if I've heard anything.'

Chris nodded and turned his attention back to the film.

'Hello sister,' Jessica said as she answered. 'And before

you ask, the answer is no. I still haven't heard and I'm trying not to think about it.'

'Well, that isn't what I was going to ask, but…'

'Oh, what were you going to ask then?' Jessica interrupted.

'I just wanted to know what you were planning to wear?' Fran replied.

'What for?' Jessica snapped back.

'The awards ceremony,' Fran replied.

Jessica froze on the spot. 'Pardon?'

'I just wanted to know what you were planning to wear?' Fran repeated slowly.

'What exactly are you saying?' Jessica asked, her words slow and calm.

'I have to spell it out? Seriously Jessy?' Fran replied. 'I just wanted to know what you were going to wear to the awards ceremony, because I've just seen your name on the shortlist!'

Jessica jumped up from the sofa and stood in front of Chris with her eyes wide open in shock.

'No fucking way!' she finally managed to reply.

'Yes way, little sister!' Fran shouted down the phone. 'It's time to shop for a dress, because you've got an awards ceremony to attend.'

15

Followers – 25,701
Emails in inbox – 35
Event invitations – 41
Paid collaborations – 1
Awards nominations – 1
Award shortlists – 1
Blogger enemies – 1
Blogger friends – 1

Dear Bella,

Put it this way, your mother wasn't born to be a supermodel.
I was neither willowy tall, nor effortlessly skinny. My hair
could be described as 'OK' on a good day, but 'losing a
battle with frizz' on the average day. I was still prone to
hormonal zits and I was well past the stage of blaming
teenage hormones. But do you know what, Bella? I
was always pretty confident about the way I looked. I
occasionally donned my trainers to run around the heath to

keep my thighs toned, but I never felt pressure to squeeze into a smaller size of clothing, nor to turn down a slice of chocolate cake. I think my self-image and I always had a pretty good relationship. We were on good terms. We were mates. And I expected it to always be that way.

But from the moment I reached down and felt my empty stomach on that hospital bed, with you lying newly-born and wrinkled on my chest, my relationship with my body changed. My tummy felt and looked like a sack of jelly, jiggling as I poked and prodded it. I wasn't revolted by it – how could I be, when it had housed you moments before? But I just didn't feel like it was mine any more. The body I had got to know over the last three decades vanished the day I became a mother and I knew that accepting the new one was going to take some time.

I watched that tummy deflate slowly over the course of the next few weeks, taking selfies in the mirror to compare against the previous one. 'Oh look, my tummy is going down!' I'd say to Daddy as I stood in front of the mirror side on, to which he looked up every time and without fail replied: 'You look amazing, Jess!' I always appreciated his kindness, but deep down, I didn't believe him. I was at least a couple of sizes bigger than before, still wearing my maternity jeans and pyjamas on the sly, and often caught myself looking down and feeling like I was looking at somebody else's thighs. I didn't go on any crazy diets, Bella, or start pounding the pavements again (I'd need a nanny for that, as Daddy left so early in the morning and got back so late) but I did have 'losing weight' on the to-do list, always somewhere at the back of my mind.

Well Bella, they say 'nine months on, nine months off' – and nearly bang on that milestone, you started to crawl. And suddenly, I was on my feet most of the day. I didn't even know that I was starting to lose the weight, because I was so exhausted by this new stage of motherhood that I rarely had the time to sit and think – but when I found myself pulling up my jeans over and over again over the course of the day, I decided to treat myself to a pair a size smaller. And that's when I knew it was happening, Bella; I was slowly morphing back into the old me.

The baby weight hasn't gone completely, but I'm OK with that – because when I look in the mirror, I finally see some of myself staring back. And maybe one day, I'll pull on those trainers and head out for a run. Or maybe I won't. But either way, I want you to know that I'm cool with it – and you should be too.

Bodies change when you have babies. Some spring back quickly. And others, like mine, come out the other side with a little extra padding.

A few extra pounds. A few extra curves.

But either way, it's all so worth it.

I am still me.

And now I have you.

Love from Mummy x

Jessica had been smiling for so long that her cheeks ached.

'That's great! Can you just move a little to your left? No, not quite like that. Just move your left foot and twist your hips? That's perfect. Yep, perfect. OK, freeze like that! And smile! A bit more! Can you smile too, Bella? Look at the silly teddy bear right above my head and smile! Can you see him? Yeah! Isn't he funny! That's right! Good girl! Perfect! Jessica, look back at the camera quickly! Hold it! Stay still! Perfect! Brilliant! Smile! Stay like that! OK, great! I think we're done! I think we've got it! Stay there for one moment and let me check!'

The photographer put down her camera and turned to the laptop set up on the table next to her, scrolling through the digital shots and chatting quietly with her assistant.

'So we're done?' Jessica asked, taking a step forward. She had been stood against the giant white backdrop for the last twenty minutes, holding Bella's hand in various poses as the photographer snapped away. She was amazed Bella hadn't made a dramatic escape attempt halfway through the shoot or decided it was the perfect time for a tantrum. She held her breath as she waited for the photographer to deliver a verdict, hoping she would be able to quit while ahead.

'Let me just check, but I think we've got it!' the photographer called back, with her eyes fixed on the screen.

Losing patience, Bella sat down and picked at the strips of masking tape that were securing the giant backdrop to the wooden floor. 'No, Bella,' Jessica said, as she swatted her hand away. 'Stop! Don't touch that! Good girl, we're nearly done now!' She had visions of the whole thing peeling away and landing on their heads, and with three other bloggers waiting for their turn in front of the camera, that would be public humiliation at its finest.

Jessica had been nervous about the Mama & Me photoshoot since she'd been told it was happening this week, but finding out she'd made it onto the awards shortlist had given her the confidence she needed to get on the train that morning and make her way to the head office in Islington. She finally felt like she might deserve a spot on the campaign, and in turn, felt a little less guilty about Tiggy's departure from it.

And since she'd got to the swanky offices just after 10 a.m., she'd been treated like a VIP, and that was a welcome relief after her last disastrous foray into London to look at pouches of baby food. After arriving in the big, shiny reception area and giving her name to one of the three sharply-dressed receptionists, she had been greeted warmly by Maria (breathing a sigh of relief that at least they were expecting her this time). She'd then been taken up in the lift to the third floor and through to the big photography studio, invited to sit down in a leather chair and had had her make-up and hair professionally styled (while Bella played in a makeshift toddler corner, filled with plastic toys and board books). She'd helped the stylist to choose outfits for them both to wear, and then she had been made to feel totally at ease in front of the camera by the lovely photographer (when she had fully expected to awkwardly giggle her way through it).

And when the photographer finally looked up and said: 'We've got it! Thank you, Jessica! Can I have my next lady please, Maria?' Jessica exhaled in relief.

'Well done,' Maria called from her left, clapping her hands. 'That was brilliant! You can go and get changed!' In turn, everyone else in the studio stopped what they were doing, looked up, and clapped in unison too. Feeling her cheeks flush red, Jessica picked up Bella and strolled towards the dressing room. Emerging a few minutes later in their original outfits of the day, she went over and joined the other bloggers waiting on sofas at the back of the studio.

'Well done, babe,' Michelle said with a smile, her little girl, Felicia looking adorable in a white linen dress on her lap as they waited for their turn. She wrote the blog 'The Single Mum Diaries', which Jessica had always loved.

'Thank you, it wasn't nearly as bad as I expected!' Jessica replied, letting Bella run off to the toys that had been moved to the corner of the studio to keep the little ones busy.

A blogger called Katherine (aka 'The London Mumbles') was now standing against the backdrop with her little girl, as the photographer snapped away. Every time a shot was taken, there was bright flash from the studio lights, accompanied by a loud pop. The photographer and stylist were giving her a stream of instructions, just as they had with Jessica a few moments before, but Katherine seemed totally comfortable from the moment she stepped into the spotlight, changing poses quickly and smiling down at her daughter.

Jessica could tell she'd done it before.

Pearl and Michelle had been deep in conversation as Jessica strode over, so the fact it was now so quiet made her feel uneasy. Maybe it was her that needed to break the ice.

'So, all three of you were on this campaign last year, too?' Jessica asked, as Michelle and Pearl turned to look at her.

'We've all been on it for a few years now,' Pearl replied, with Michelle nodding alongside her. 'It's been a good gig actually. The girls running it are pretty sound and we've all become quite good friends.'

'There's been a few good nights out!' Michelle added, raising her eyebrows.

'There certainly have!' Pearl replied, laughing.

'Oh wow, so you went out together as a team?' Jessica asked, as Tiggy's face flashed into her mind.

'Yep, lots of times over the years,' Pearl said, glancing into the pram alongside her to check her baby was still sleeping.

Jessica's eyes immediately moved to the sleeping newborn, who was dressed in a striped nautical dress just like her elder sister, who was playing alongside Bella on the floor.

'How old is she?' Jessica asked, smiling. Pearl wrote the blog 'Octavia and Me' and it suddenly struck Jessica that she might have to change the name.

'Only six weeks,' Pearl replied.

'Ah congrats,' Jessica said. 'She's gorgeous!'

'I know I keep saying it, but I think it's bloody amazing you've made it here, babe!' Michelle said. 'I was still in full-on pyjama mode when Felicia was six weeks old!'

'Me too with Bella...' Jessica added, smiling.

'You can't get away with that with a second though,' Pearl replied. 'Octavia would be running up the walls if I stuck to Delilah's schedule!'

'Oh, I love her name! I love both of their names!' Jessica said.

'Thank you', Pearl replied, her eyes moving back to her newborn. For a moment the three ladies sat in silence, with the sound of the light popping loudly over and over again, as Katherine smiled and posed.

'You happy to join the team?' Michelle asked, turning to Jessica.

'Oh, well, yeah,' Jessica replied. 'Surprised really, I guess. I didn't expect to get campaigns, so it was a bit of a shock when I got the call.'

'How long you been blogging then? I mean, I know it hasn't been long, but when exactly did you start?' Pearl asked.

'Oh, not long... About three months ago,' Jessica replied, feeling uncomfortable.

'Wow, you've done well,' Michelle replied flatly. 'And nominated for the Blog Network Award too?'

'Yes,' Jessica replied, wiggling her toes in her sandals. 'In the newcomer spot.'

'Well, that's good going,' Michelle replied, flicking her dark hair over her shoulder as she glanced down at Felicia.

'I haven't seen the list this year,' Pearl said. 'I've been totally out of the loop with Delilah arriving. Who else got on it?'

Jessica wasn't imagining it; there was definitely an atmosphere between the three of them. And how could she be surprised when she'd taken the place of their friend on the team? Meeting Wendy had given her hope that other bloggers would be as friendly and welcoming as she integrated herself but she was starting to realise it was going to be hard work to be accepted into their gang.

'So it's Jessica,' Michelle began, holding out a finger. 'Then obviously Tig, Jackson from "And Then Came The Kids" and Wendy from "Hiding in the Bathroom."' Coming to the end of the shortlist, Michelle had four fingers extended, which they all stared at for a moment, as they visualised each blogger in turn.

'No real surprises Jackson and Wendy are on there. Jackson has been working with some big names recently,' Pearl said, as Michelle dropped her fingers.

Jessica shifted in her seat.

'Congrats, love!' Pearl said, turning to look at her. 'You must be made up to make that list and get this spot in the team too.'

'Thank you,' Jessica replied, trying to keep her voice pretty casual. 'It's just a shame they couldn't expand the team, rather than cut people out.'

'Look, I'll be honest,' Pearl replied, holding both hands in the air. 'Tiggy is a mate, but we know it's not your fault! You didn't make the decision!'

'It wasn't Maria's decision either, by all accounts,' added Michelle, lowering the volume of her voice. 'We heard it came straight from the top, as they wanted to align the brands with younger faces.'

Jessica didn't know what to say. Her mind turned to Mama & Me nights out, imagining Pearl, Michelle, Katherine and Tiggy bonding over drinks at the bar. She thought back to the photoshoot she'd seen of the previous year in this same studio; the four of them laughing together as their children posed at their feet. She imagined them working together as a team, congratulating each other when babies were born, and being invited to each other's houses for coffees.

'I feel bad about it,' Jessica finally said. 'Really bad.'

'Don't feel bad,' Michelle replied. Her eyes darted to Pearl, but they looked away again so quickly that Jessica doubted if she'd seen it. 'I'm sure there'll be another night out soon. Where are you based? In London?'

'Yes,' Jessica replied, welcoming the change of subject. 'Westcombe Park.'

'Great,' Pearl replied. 'I'm in Lewisham.'

'Not far from me then!' Jessica said, taking a deep breath and looking down to watch Bella fitting wooden jigsaw pieces together with Octavia's help. Out of the corner of her eye, she saw Maria making her way over to them from the far side of the studio.

'Hi ladies!' she said breathlessly, clutching her clipboard under her arm. 'How are you all doing?'

'Good babe,' Michelle replied. 'Seems to be going well?'

'Yes, we're bang on schedule, which is just the way I like it! Michelle, you'll be up next. Then Pearl, you'll be last to go, which should give Delilah a chance to sleep before her big moment. Does that work OK with everyone?'

Michelle and Pearl nodded.

'Great! Katherine will be finished soon, then we'll move on,' Maria said, smiling widely. She turned to Jessica and added: 'Jessica and Bella, you both did brilliantly and you are free to go whenever you like. But first, let's have a quick chat about the posts you're going to put up, as it's your first time. Have you got time to stroll to my office quickly? It'll only take a few minutes and I can show you what all the girls shared last year to give you an idea?'

'OK yep, of course. Shall I bring the buggy and my bag?' Jessica asked, reaching down for Bella's hand.

'Oh yes, great idea, bring them both and you can head straight off,' Maria said, pausing as Jessica said goodbye to Pearl and Michelle, and mouthed 'bye!' at Katherine as she paused posing briefly to wave.

The office was just along the corridor from the studio, light and bright, with sunshine streaming through the window and a radio playing on a low volume in the corner. There was a large silver vase on the windowsill, filled with the most beautiful coral-pink peonies. As they walked through the door, Bella rushed towards them and cupped a flower in her hands. 'Bella, baby, no!' Jessica said, picking her up and sitting her on her lap as she sat down on the seat opposite Maria's desk.

'Oh, don't worry about them! My flowers never survive very long. My kids are in here a couple of times a week!'

Jessica smiled, catching sight of a photo frame on her desk with two boys posing in primary school uniforms.

Maria was obviously slightly older than she had assumed. And with this office all to herself, probably more senior than she'd assumed too.

Outside the office, the desks were arranged in a large, open-plan space. It was nearly lunchtime and staff were milling around, carrying sandwiches and coffees back to their desk, and chatting in pairs as they passed.

'OK so...' Maria said, sitting down behind her desk and opening a big black folder in front of her. 'Here are some of last year's posts, which we've compiled for you to have a look at. We'll be sending you across the photos from today's shoot in the next few days and you can just pick your favourite and share it, using the text below here as inspiration. Does that all make sense? I'll send some pointers over on email when I send the shots, so no need to memorise it.'

Jessica nodded as Maria slid the folder across the desk. The folder was open on a page with one of Pearl's posts from last year, just a hint of a bump showing in her maxi dress. Tall and willowy, with shortly cropped blonde hair and dramatic black eye make-up, she was certainly photogenic.

After scanning the page, Jessica flicked over – and there was Tiggy. In that split second, without even being aware she was doing it, she took a sharp intake of breath.

Maria looked up at her. 'You OK?'

'Oh sorry, yes,' Jessica said, embarrassed. But with nothing to lose, she decided to open up. 'I do feel bad that I'm the one who replaced Tiggy, to be honest. I wish we could both be on the team.'

Maria sat back in her seat and smiled. She stood up, walked over to the door of her office and shut it gently. 'We all do, Jessica,' she said, lowering her voice as she walked back to her desk, 'but it's just one of those things that came from the top. Our Managing Director is really passionate about the Mama & Me image being about young, fashionable mummies matching their younger daughters. So naturally, we were going to change the team at some point. He made the decision it would be happening this year – and as Marketing Manager, I have to respect that. It wasn't much fun delivering the news, as we've all bonded as a team over the past few years. But that's business, I'm afraid. That's how it works sometimes. And we are all absolutely delighted that you agreed to come and join us. You – and Bella – fit the brand perfectly and we're excited about seeing the content on your feed in the next few weeks.'

'I understand,' Jessica said, kissing the back of Bella's head as she sat quietly in her lap. 'I just feel terrible for her.'

'Look, Jessica,' Maria replied, shaking her head. 'She hasn't been as gracious about it as I had hoped, and she probably doesn't deserve your sympathy. But maybe it's best if we all just move on now and focus on this year's campaign...'

'How do you mean?' Jessica interrupted.

'Pardon?' Maria asked.

'How do you mean "she hasn't been as gracious as you had hoped"?' Jessica asked, surprised at her own confidence.

'You've read her interview with *The Daily Gossip*, haven't you?' Maria asked, raising her eyebrows.

Jessica swallowed. 'No, what did it say?'

'Oh, I'm sorry, Jessica. I just assumed you'd seen it,' Maria said, averting her eyes down to look at her nails. 'I'll leave it for you to read in a quiet moment. But please don't worry too much when you read it. And believe me, the rest of the team are on board with the new set-up. We've spoken extensively about it and I really do think we're going to have a great year!'

Jessica smiled weakly, looking back down to the folder as Bella tried to yank the printed sheet from inside. Pulling it back, she took a deep breath and tried to read the words to commit them to memory but they were swimming around the page.

'OK, I've got to head back to the studio as Katherine will be finishing up any second. You can stay and look over these a little longer if you like? Just let yourself out when you're ready to go. You just need the floor "P" to get back down to the plaza in the lift and make sure you hand your visitor pass over to our receptionist on your way out!'

'OK,' Jessica replied, struggling for words. 'Thank you.'

'No, thank *you*, Jessica! And Bella! You were both brilliant today! And we can't wait to see your post go up and see what all your followers think! See you soon, OK? You can expect an email from me later in the week and we'll take it from there!' Maria kissed Jessica on both cheeks, leant down to say goodbye to Bella, and left the office with her clipboard under her arm.

And as Maria gave them a final wave from behind the glass of her office window as she strolled back past, Jessica wasn't sure if she wanted to know what was in that interview at all.

16

Followers – 31,031
Emails in inbox – 91
Event invitations – 52
Paid collaborations – 1
Award nominations – 1
Award shortlists – 1
Blogger enemies – 1
Blogger friends – 1

Dear Bella,

When you were nine months old, I took you to the park on a crisp and sunny December day. You were wrapped up like a baby burrito in your snowsuit and blankets and exhausted from your ridiculously early morning (I think it was a 5 a.m.-er that day), you fell fast asleep as I pushed you in your buggy towards the park. I had a thermos of coffee in my bag, so I strode up to the hill to my favourite bench and sat down in the sunshine, admiring the view of

London in front of me. I often sat on that bench in the first year of your life and took in that sight as you slept, constantly reminding myself what a beautiful part of the world I lived in. In the foreground, trees stripped bare by winter, dog walkers strolling across the green lawn in giant coats and bobble hats, and my breath smoking around me in the air. In the background, boats moving slowly and silently down the Thames, the chestnut brown rooftops of apartment blocks lining it, and the peak of Canary Wharf glinting in the sunshine. After a difficult morning with an overtired baby, I sat back and enjoyed the peace for a while, pulling my scarf higher and my coat around me for warmth.

But after twenty minutes or so, you started to stir, and knowing that you would be hungry when you woke, I reached into my bag and started to make a bottle of milk. Tipping the powder into the pre-boiled water, replacing the teat, and shaking it all together so it was ready for you to drink. And with the bottle ready, I looked back at you. Your arms were flinching now and your eyes were starting to open, and at that very moment, two new mothers walked past me. Each was pushing a very tiny newborn baby in a basket, and once a pang of 'oh wow, so tiny' had crossed my mind, I looked up at the mothers to smile. But instead of smiling back at me as I doted on their babies, I noticed they were looking directly at the bottle of milk in my hands with surprised eyes.

They were in the middle of a conversation and didn't break their step, their words inaudible to me as they disappeared off down the path. But suddenly, I felt so aware of that bottle of milk in my hands. 'Were they judging me?' I wondered, as I glanced back at them. 'Did they think you were still a tiny baby and that I should be breastfeeding?' I asked myself, as I looked down at the bottle in my hand. And the pangs of guilt started to stir in my mind.

I had stopped breastfeeding you when you were about six months old, Bella. We had got to grips with it after the difficulties in the early days and found a rhythm together, but the truth is that I never really liked doing it (even typing that makes me feel bad, but I was so proud of myself to get that far). And since I made the decision to move to bottles, we haven't looked back. Life somehow became easier. I felt more like myself again. In fact, I even suggested to Daddy that we burnt my feeding bras on a bonfire in the garden in celebration – and whilst this was disappointingly vetoed, he did agree to join me on a shopping trip to buy some new lingerie. And I enjoyed wearing it, Bella! No clips on my shoulder, no milk stains on the cups, and no lingering aroma whenever I pulled off my bra at the end of the day.

But it was about more than just new bras. It was about getting my body back. It was about being able to plan my day without making pit stops in places I felt confident enough to whip a boob out and feed you. It was about not having to plan my outfits around buttons to unbutton, tops to lift, or zips to unzip. Don't get me wrong, Bella – I know how lucky I was to breastfeed you for so long, but I was ready to stop. Very ready to stop. And since that last feedback in September, when you confirmed everything by grabbing and scratching me in frustration as you fed before bed, I hadn't regretted it for a second.

Until that moment on a park bench, that is. Seeing those new mothers glance down at your ready-made bottle as they strolled along. Of course, I don't know what they were thinking. They were probably deep in conversation and weren't really seeing the bottle at all. But I felt it. I felt judged.

And as I sat there holding the bottle, I suddenly felt the December chill and started to shiver. I pulled you from your buggy and you sat in my lap, barely able to move in your ridiculously bulky snowsuit, feeding hungrily and happily from your bottle.

And as I stared down into your eyes, I told you I was sorry.

Even though I wasn't really sorry at all.

Love from Mummy x

Jessica was still sitting in Maria's office - and her mind was now very firmly on *The Daily Gossip*. She had dipped into that website occasionally in the past when a headline grabbed her attention – and she was aware that they had started to treat bloggers with the same interest as celebrities. She knew they wouldn't be worried about stirring up a bit of drama – and if Tiggy was as offended as Jessica feared she was, she doubted her feelings would have been considered at all.

Finding it impossible to focus on the folder in front of her, Jessica decided it was time to head home. Moments later, Bella was back in her buggy with a box of raisins in her hands and the two of them began their journey back to the station and towards home.

Jessica knew that reading that interview wasn't going to make her feel better, but still, she couldn't stop herself needing to read it. And if Bella fell asleep in her buggy on the journey home, she was planning to pull her phone out of her bag and try and find it.

And that was exactly what happened.

As the train hurtled towards Westcombe Park, with Bella snoring gently in the buggy next to her, Jessica started searching, scrolling, and clicking. Frustratingly, the interview took a few minutes to load as the train weaved its way in and out of mobile coverage. But finally, there it was on the page, the full interview, complete with one of the photos of last year's Mama & Me shoot that Jessica had been staring at in the black folder only an hour before.

TIGGY TALKS MOTHERHOOD!

Tiggy Blenheim is no stranger to blogger highs, blogger spats, and blogger grudges – and she reveals all to *Daily Gossip* in this tell-all interview!

Jessica skim read the beginning of the interview, scanning her eyes down the page quickly to find the part Maria was alluding to.

And it was then that she saw it.

TDG: OK, so we've heard about the highs that come with blogging. But what about the lows?

T: The lows?

TDG: Oh, come on Tiggy, there must be some!

T: Oh, there's plenty. Believe me, there's plenty...

TDG: Now we're talking!

T: (raises eyebrows).

TDG: Come on! Spill! What has bothered you?

T: I'm not sure how much I should say...

TDG: Tell us everything!

T: OK, well there is something.

TDG: We knew it!

T: You know what, I'm only human. And when I lose a campaign I've been part of for years because apparently my face is too old, it stings a little.

TDG: Too old?! But you're a spring chicken!

T: Ha ha, well thanks. But apparently not…

TDG: Well, that's outrageous. So are you going to name and shame the company? We do like a bit of a name and shame here at *The Daily Gossip*!

T: No, because I'm a professional. I enjoyed working with them. It was a long-term thing. But they know who they are. And they know exactly what they've done.

TDG: So did they replace you?

T: (nods)

TDG: Wow, it gets worse. Who with?

T: (shrugging) Oh, I can't remember her name – but she knows who she is. It's clear that she agreed to take my place, knowing why I was being thrown off the campaign. And I don't tend to forget things like that.

TDG: Somehow we aren't surprised that you're holding a grudge on this one Tiggy… So it isn't a blog we'll know about?

T: I very much doubt it.

TDG: (laughing) It's rubbish, isn't it?

T: (stays silent)

TDG: Come on Tiggy! This is *The Daily Gossip*!

T: Let's just say that your time is probably better spent reading something else, yes.

As the train sped towards home, Jessica read it over and over again. And when she didn't think she could read any more, she sat back in the seat and stared out of the window. Bridges daubed in graffiti, skyscrapers reflecting the sun like beacons, station signs passing so quickly the words blurred, and postage-stamp back gardens with children jumping on trampolines. It all flashed past but Jessica didn't see any of it. She was lost in her own world, imagining Tiggy sitting on a sofa chatting to the interviewer. Smirking at the thought of Jessica trying to take her place.

It was clear now; Tiggy thought Jessica shouldn't have accepted her place on the campaign. She thought Jessica knew who she was replacing. She was hurt and embarrassed. Professionally and personally.

She knew she'd been naïve. She should have done some research before she agreed to take the job. She should've been a bit more aware of what was going on in the world of blogging, bloggers, and brands. She shouldn't have stepped into the middle of a storm with a smile on her face.

But despite it all, she hadn't meant to hurt her.

As hard as it was to read that interview, Jessica knew it didn't solve anything to sit there brooding about it. Over the hours that followed, she tried her best to shut it all out and focus on Bella. She distracted herself by putting together a giant jigsaw on the floor, building towers and letting Bella smash them down again, and pretending to feed her doll a bottle as Bella squealed in appreciation. She let her watch television for a while, enjoying the comforting smell of her hair and weight of her cuddle as they both zoned out on the sofa.

She knew she only had to get through the afternoon and she could chat it all through with the girls. Because that evening, they had dinner planned, and she'd never been so desperate to see them.

It was all thanks to an email that had arrived in Jessica's inbox a few weeks ago, offering a complimentary meal for herself and her friends at a local restaurant. In exchange, she just had to do a quick mention on her social media feed. She wasn't sure whether to accept the invitation at first, but the girls were so excited when she mentioned it that they made the decision to book it for that evening, so Jessica could give them a full debrief of the Mama & Me photoshoot. 'I don't know,' Henny had said when the booking confirmation came through. 'Photoshoot in the morning and dinner review in the evening… I think this is called "The Big Time", babe!'

And as soon as she greeted the girls in the small restaurant just a few hours later, she felt like herself again.

'I know it's shit,' Deena said, looking over her menu at Jessica, 'But not many people can say they've been the main talking point of an interview on *The Daily Gossip*…'

'Well, my name wasn't mentioned…' Jessica replied. 'But yes, I guess this is true.'

'Except nineties boy band members,' Mel chipped in.

'And desperate reality TV stars,' Henny continued.

'And anyone who has ever met the Kardashians,' Mel added.

'Or their second cousins, twice removed,' Deena said, with a smile.

'Oi!' Jessica laughed. 'This is not helping!' But as the girls all laughed along with her, she knew it *was* helping. She was feeling better by the second.

'I read it as soon as you sent the link,' Henny said. 'And she clearly thinks you took the job to spite her, doesn't she?'

Jessica sighed. 'I think so. She probably assumes I've done everything in my power to claw my way to the top. But it couldn't be further from the truth. I feel totally unprepared for all this.'

'I think you should be flattered,' Deena said. 'This confirms that she sees you as a massive threat.'

Jessica shrugged. 'That's pretty much what Wendy said about it all.'

'But she's shot herself in the foot,' Mel added. 'Does she seriously think the people in charge of the awards won't be reading this shit?'

'Maybe,' Jessica replied. 'It's made me feel like such a bitch, though.'

'Babe!' Henny shot back. 'Stop it! The fact you're even worrying about it shows that you aren't at all!'

Jessica smiled. 'Thanks Hen. I just can't help feeling a bit sorry for her, though... Despite everything.'

'That's because you've got a heart,' Mel said, as she picked up her glass of soda water. 'Unlike that bitch!'

The girls all laughed in unison, taking sips from their drinks.

'Anyway, let's forget it,' Jessica said, shaking her head. 'It's been a really long day.'

'Tell me about it,' Mel replied. 'Another day goes by and I still haven't heard from my arsehole of a husband.'

'Fucking hell,' Deena said. 'Really? Nothing?'

Mel shook her head.

'So what's it been now? A week?' Henny asked.

'Ten days,' Mel replied quickly, biting her lip.

'And you've got no idea when he's flying back?' Jessica asked.

'Not a clue,' Mel replied. 'But I know it's over. I've changed the locks, so he can't just let himself in. I've messaged to tell him I've already contacted my solicitor and I'll be communicating through her ongoing. I assume he'll want to see Lara at some point, so we need to work that all out. Well, I mean I assume so but to be honest, nothing would surprise me any more.'

'Wow,' Deena said, staring down at her menu. 'It's crazy how quickly this has all happened. It only seems like yesterday that we were all at your house and he was lighting the barbecue.'

'Completely crazy,' Mel replied, shaking her head.

'And what... what about the baby?' Henny asked apprehensively.

'This one?' Mel asked, pointing at her stomach.

Henny nodded.

'I'm still not totally sure but the one thing that keeps going round my head is that this pregnancy might be a setback for me and a major inconvenience for Steven, but it's probably the best thing that could happen for Lara. To grow up with a full brother or sister... Well, this is going to be her only chance now, isn't it?' Mel said, folding and unfolding her napkin as she spoke. 'And maybe she needs a sibling, being shunted around different houses every weekend, every school holiday, and every Christmas. I don't know, maybe she needs a little brother or sister so she doesn't have to do that all alone.'

'So maybe it's a blessing?' Henny asked.

'Maybe.' Mel shrugged her shoulders. 'And at least I can go ahead and get a nanny now he's out of the picture. He won't be able to tell me I'm a shit excuse for a mother any more, just because I want to return to the career ladder I spent years trying to climb...'

'He didn't actually say that, did he?' Jessica asked, holding her knife and fork still. 'That you're a shit mother?'

'Pretty much,' Mel replied, shaking her head.

'Well, you know we are all here for you,' Henny replied.

'I'll drink to that,' Deena said, lifting her wine glass towards her friends.

'Me too.' Jessica raised her glass.

'And me,' Henny joined in.

'Here's to a life without my wanker husband, surrounded by my three best friends,' Mel replied, chinking her glass of tonic water.

'And here's to one of those friends being gossiped about, alongside the boy band members, reality stars, and

Kardashian-meeter-and-greeters!' Deena added, as the four of them chinked their glasses again.

'At least life isn't boring!' Jessica said, laughing.

'And thank fuck for that!' Mel replied, smiling at her friends.

17

Followers – 39,978
Emails in inbox – 199
Event invitations – 61
Award nominations – 1
Award shortlists – 1
Blogger enemies – 1
Blogger friends – 1
Newspaper features – 1
Spotted by followers – 1

Dear Bella,

When you were ten months old, you taught me a valuable
lesson about motherhood. Distracted by the chicken soup
I was making for my lunch, which was bubbling and spilling
out of the saucepan, I forgot about you for a moment. Just
a few moments, when my attention was totally focused on
saving that soup. I lifted the pan, turned down the heat,
and tested a little bit to see whether it needed seasoning.

And when I was happy with the flavour and had left it to simmer gently on the hob, I was distracted by a dirty dish on the side that I'd been soaking all morning, so I washed it up. And then a recipe book caught my eye, propped between the microwave and the wall, and I flicked through for a few minutes, suddenly feeling inspired to cook something warming for Daddy and me for dinner. I was humming something to myself, probably something I'd been listening to on the radio moments before, when I suddenly realised I'd forgotten about you.

Sheer panic coursed through my body as I darted out the kitchen to find you. And there you were, sat at the very top of the stairs, so proud and triumphant that you'd managed it. And there was me at the bottom, frozen to the spot for a split second in panic, before calling your name and screaming. 'DON'T MOVE! BELLA! STAY THERE!' as I ran up three steps at a time, nearly tripping myself up in the process, and carried you down to safety with my heart pounding and my legs shaking with nerves.

I was lucky that day. Very lucky. I knew that. It was the first time you'd ever discovered the stairs and if you'd decided to reverse, or turn, or come back down, you would have fallen – and I would have heard the thuds as I was reading through a list of ingredients for a beef stroganoff in the kitchen. Until then, I'd been adamant we didn't need to get a safety gate, because I was always with you. You were never on your own. But that evening, before he'd even had a chance to eat his dinner, Daddy grabbed the car keys and drove to a DIY superstore to buy a stair gate – and I stayed at home on the sofa, filled with guilt, and worry, and a horrible sense of failure.

But that day I learnt something, Bella. I learnt that despite someone's determination to be the very best mother in the world, everybody makes mistakes. I learnt that I may be a mother now, but I am still Jessica and I don't come equipped with a superhero cape. And as the months have ticked on and you have got braver and more inquisitive, similar things have happened. A fall off the sofa onto your head; a split second in the supermarket when you ran from my sight; a pebble grabbed hastily from your mouth. Lapses of concentration. Chinks in my armour. And ultimately reminders that the goalposts will keep changing and that I am bound to make mistakes.

As the years tick on, I will make more of them.

And while that fills me with dread, I know it's all part of being a mother and that you will continue teaching me lessons, day after day, month after month, year after year.

But know this; I will always try my best, Bella.

To keep you safe.

To keep you from harm.

I will do my best, every single day.

I promise.

Love from Mummy x

*

It was Thursday 31st August and the awards ceremony was just two days away.

Jessica was strolling alongside the grass in Blackheath, with the sun shining warmly on her shoulders and a cool breeze in her hair. She had the whole day reserved to spend with Fran; shopping for a dress to wear together and then heading out for drinks to properly catch up. And Jessica couldn't wait. She couldn't wait for the freedom to be childfree again for the day. For the opportunity to chat. For the chance to buy an item of clothing that was actually for her and not for her daughter. It was going to be a good day. She just had a feeling about it.

The sisters had arranged to head for coffee first and Jessica had suggested meeting in Spill the Bean. She missed stepping through those familiar wooden doors every day and smiling at the baristas behind the counter, while ordering her usual coffee to take back to her desk. Return visits to the village weren't complete without a pit stop, and she was just a few steps away when she felt a hand on her shoulder.

'Hi!' she said happily, turning towards the person she assumed was Fran. 'Oh sorry, I thought you were my sister...'

'I'm so sorry,' the blonde lady said, blushing a little as she spoke. 'But do you mind me asking if you write the blog "Letters to My Daughter"?'

'Uh, yes…' Jessica stuttered.

'God, I'm so embarrassed,' the lady said, nervously fiddling with her hair. 'I never do things like this, but I just had to ask! I feel like I know you! I've been reading your blog since the beginning and I love it! I really, really love it!'

'Oh wow, this is the first time this has happened,' Jessica replied, feeling her own cheeks start to turn red. 'Well hello, it's lovely to meet you!'

'I'm so sorry, I feel like an absolute tit now. But I couldn't just let you walk past without telling you! I was just reading about you in the paper this morning, so it's really strange that I've bumped into you! I'm a big fan!'

'The paper?' Jessica asked.

'Yes, you know, the feature in *The Scoop* this morning,' the lady replied.

'No. What? Sorry, No, I didn't know. What was it about?' Jessica asked, stuttering her words.

'You haven't seen it?' the lady asked. 'It's about the awards you've been shortlisted for. Anyway, I'm late to collect my little boy so I'd better go but I'm so happy to meet you! Good luck at the awards! You deserve to win it!'

'Lovely to meet you,' Jessica replied, watching the lady stroll away with her mouth open in shock.

She walked through the doors of the café on autopilot. She was a few minutes late, but true to form, Fran was nowhere to be seen, so Jessica chose a table and sat down.

Pulling her phone from her bag, she typed a message to Fran as quickly as she could.

Hi, I'm here. Can you grab a copy of *The Scoop* when you walk past the newsagent? It's important. Thanks.

'Hey!' a voice suddenly said, strolling towards her table.

Jessica looked up. 'Meryl! Hi! How are you?' She stood up and kissed her on the cheek, smiling widely.

'How are you, darling?!' Meryl asked, drying her hands on her apron as she spoke. 'And where's the baby?'

'Oh, I left her with her granny today! It's mummy-only time!' Jessica replied with a smile.

Meryl smiled. 'What do you want, darling? Black coffee, two sugars?'

'Exactly,' Jessica said, feeling very at home. 'You haven't lost your touch!'

'How could I forget?' Meryl called to her, as she walked back to the counter. 'It'll be with you in a few moments, darling!'

Left on her own, Jessica glanced down at her phone – and suddenly a newspaper was slammed down on the table next to it. It was *The Scoop*.

'Hey, Jessy,' Fran said, as her sister stood up to hug her. 'What did you want this rag for?'

'Well,' Jessica replied. 'Apparently I'm in it!'

'What the fuck? Why?' Fran replied quickly, grabbing the paper off the table.

Jessica grabbed it back. 'No way! I'm looking first!'

Sitting down, Jessica spread out the paper on the table and began flicking through the pages. As each page opened, the two of them studied every inch of text, unsure whether it would be a small column or a larger piece. And just before they reached the middle of the paper, there it was. In full colour. Two whole pages. A spread.

TOP PARENTING BLOGGERS FIGHT IT OUT

The headline read, with colour images of the four bloggers in the shortlist underneath.

'Fucking hell!' Jessica blurted out, as her eyes scanned over the page.

Jessica was pictured second from left, standing in Henny's lounge on that alcohol-fuelled night, raising her champagne glass to the camera. Flushed cheeks, a couple of blemishes visible on her chin, hair that probably needed a brush, and a slightly blurred finish to the photo, thanks to it being taken on a phone camera that should probably have been upgraded a few years ago.

Next to her, Tiggy was pictured on the far left of the page, her blonde hair styled perfectly as she smiled with her bright, white teeth. She was standing in her kitchen, with mint green kitchen appliances surrounding her. Her hands were covered in flour as she kneaded dough, with a child in an apron smiling next to her. Jessica inwardly groaned at the perfection of the photo. She just looked so happy and wholesome. Her kitchen so perfect and bright. Her activities so fun and educational. Pretty much the opposite of Jessica's photo.

On the right-hand page of the spread, Jackson was pictured first. Sitting in the driving seat of a car, with the photo taken through the open driver door. It looked like a promotional photo for a family car, with his wife slightly blurred in the passenger seat, and their children visible in the back. He looked cool in skinny jeans and a leather jacket, a pair of aviator sunglasses attached to his top.

And finally, Wendy was pictured on the far right of the page. Her photo was taken in the park, and Jessica remembered seeing it in a recent blog post. It didn't look professionally lit or composed, but it was certainly better than Jessica's effort. Dressed in a nautical striped jumper, skinny jeans and black ballet pumps, her black curls tumbling free and her bright white smile wide, she was looking proudly at Adeline as she held her hand.

Underneath each photo, the journalist had summarised their blogs...

Much-loved blogger, Tiggy Blenheim, documents her life in the countryside in Tiggy Does Motherhood! Head over to her blog to read about child-friendly adventures, fun activities, Mama-and-me style, and chic interiors – be prepared to fall in love with everything in Tiggy's world.

A new addition to the blogging scene, Jessica Holmes writes through the medium of letters to her young daughter. These insights are brutally honest, about the highs and lows of motherhood: pregnancy haemorrhoids, expanding thighs, or sending her husband out to buy more maternity pads!

Jackson Freeman is the dad that all fathers wish they could be! His blog drips with cool, from the most stylish cars to drive the brood around in, to the most fashionable togs for heading outdoors to entertain them, and the most delicious restaurants in Yorkshire to feed them!

Wendy Felicia Cooper writes the laugh-out-loud parenting blog Hiding in the Bathroom, where she documents the life of a stay-at-home mother of two in South East London. But despite being a great comic, you'll read along with Wendy and think 'ME TOO!' – and we think that's the measure of a fantastic blog!

'Wow,' Jessica said, as they came to the end of the text. 'They hate me!'

'Come on, Jess! It's pretty cool to have your picture and name splashed in a national paper!' Fran said.

Jessica looked up at her sister and raised her eyebrows. 'Seriously, Fran? Every other photo has a child in the shot – and I look like a total pisshead. And the words? Everyone else gets words like "fun", "chic", "laugh-out-loud'", and "drips with cool'",' she said, trailing her finger under the words as she read. 'And what do I get?'

Fran shrugged.

'Haemorrhoids, fat thighs, and maternity pads...'

'Well, they say you're brutally honest, which is true! Surely that's a good thing?' Fran said, struggling not to laugh. 'Look, I don't think it's too bad, Jess! They obviously like your honesty'.

Distracted by Jessica's coffee arriving and Fran giving

her order, they sat in silence for a few minutes staring at the paper lying open on the table.

'How are you feeling about seeing Tiggy on Saturday?' Fran asked, as they both turned their eyes to her picture on the left. 'Honestly?'

Jessica sighed and looked up at her sister. 'I'll give myself a pep talk on the night to get through it... It took me a good few days to calm down about that stupid interview, but honestly, everything that is happening with Mel has given me a huge wake-up call and it seems petty to be stressing over something another blogger said to a gossip website. She didn't reveal my name, so it could've been a lot worse...'

Fran didn't take her eyes off her little sister, searching her face for clues. 'Well if you're sure,' she said finally, 'but I'm here if you want to sound things out.'

'I know,' Jessica replied. 'But you've got enough to worry about, Franny! You don't need to hear about blogger dramas!'

'Don't be silly. You were there whenever I bloody needed you over the last year!'

'It's hardly the same!' Jessica said, shaking her head.

Fran smiled at her sister. 'All I'm going to say is that this blogging thing is going really well for you and nobody should be allowed to piss on your bonfire!'

Jessica laughed. 'I'll make sure of it. To be honest, the blogging thing all feels a bit surreal now. A lady just recognised me on the street.'

'What? You're kidding?' Fran shot back. 'She reads your blog? And she stopped you?'

'Yes, and she reads *The Scoop* too, so I have her to thank for informing me of this disaster...' Jessica said, glancing down again at the paper.

'Get you, Jessy!' Fran said, raising her eyebrows. 'My little sister is getting famous! Is it the first time you've been recognised?'

'Well yes, but... well...' Jessica paused and picked up her coffee. 'No, it's silly.'

'But what?' Fran asked.

'I've noticed a few people do a double-take when I'm in the park with Bella and whisper to their friends. I thought I was just being paranoid, but meeting that lady outside today... I mean, maybe I wasn't imagining it?'

'You probably weren't, to be honest. Bloggers are like celebrities these days. I mean, think about the ones you follow – you'd recognise them if you walked past them on the street, wouldn't you?'

'Well yes, of course, but... I guess you're right. It just seems hard to believe when we're talking about me,' Jessica replied.

'It's not *just you* though, is it Jessy. You're the writer behind "Letters to My Daughter"! I mean, how many followers do you have now?'

'Nearly 40,000,' Jessica said. 'Last time I checked...'

'OK so, I happen to know this, as the mother of a Chelsea FC fan. Do you know how many people fit inside Stamford Bridge Stadium?'

'Oh God, I don't know... I wouldn't have any idea,' Jessica replied.

'It's 41,000 people, Jess. Now imagine a football

stadium in your mind, and imagine you are stood in the middle of the pitch. Everyone's eyes in that stadium would be on you – and that's what it's like every time you write a blog post and every time you post a picture,' Fran said, with wide eyes.

'That's insane…' Jessica said, shaking her head.

'And that's also why we have to find the perfect dress,' Fran added. 'There's going to be a lot of eyes on you when you accept the award on Saturday!'

'That. Is. Not. Going. To. Happen,' Jess said, tutting and laughing. 'But I get your point. And I haven't shopped for myself for a long time, so I'm looking forward to it.'

'Too right,' Fran replied. 'And once we've found *the dress*, we'll head to a pub garden to celebrate. That's still the plan, right?'

'I can't wait,' Jessica said, nodding in agreement. 'Mum said she might pop in to say hello quickly. They're planning on heading to the village to have a wander this afternoon and let Bella play on the heath.'

'Ah, I'd love to see her,' Fran replied, smiling. 'But you haven't forgotten that this is supposed to be your day off? You'll let Mum and Dad take her home again afterwards?'

'Hell yeah,' Jessica said. 'I've been looking forward to it for weeks!'

'Me, too. So let's finish these coffees and find that dress, little sister!' Fran replied.

And that was exactly what they did. Once they'd drained their mugs, stashed the newspaper in Jessica's bag, and made their way back out onto the street, they started hunting for the dress she would wear to the awards ceremony.

Jessica already had a vision in her mind for the kind of thing that she wanted to wear. The thought of anything too short or too clingy gave her shivers of horror. It had to be knee-length, it couldn't cling to her curves, and ideally it would cover at least the top of her arms. She didn't really want to wear black, but she definitely didn't want anything too bright either. She didn't think it was going to be easy to find, which was why she'd asked Fran to help her. Naturally more confident, fashionable, and daring about what she wore, Fran would lend Jessica a shot of confidence.

But when Fran pulled a dress entirely covered in silver sequins from the rail and held it up to Jessica, she laughed and shook her head. 'No way!' Jessica said. 'I'd turn every head in the room and that is the opposite of what I want to happen!'

'Fuck that! You're the star of the show,' Fran replied, forcing the hanger into her hand. 'Just try it on. Just for fun. Go on, Jessy, you'll look amazing in it.'

'OK,' Jessica said, taking the hanger. 'But it's just for fun! There is no way I am wearing this dress to the ball!'

And she meant it too. She wasn't going to wear it.

But just seconds later, standing in front of the changing room mirror, she realised she quite liked it.

Possibly even loved it.

Heavy enough for the fabric to fall beautifully and flatter her figure, long enough to cover her knees, and with slightly fluted sleeves to her wrists to cover the bits of her arms she didn't feel confident to show off, the shape was perfect. And even though the sequins naturally caught the light, the effect was far more muted than she imagined. If she paired it with black heels and a clutch bag, she'd still be in her comfort zone.

Suddenly the changing room curtain was pulled open, and from behind it, Fran gasped.

'Jesus! You look bloody amazing!' she said, looking her sister up and down. 'It's *the one!*'

'I like it,' Jess said quietly.

'You what?' Fran replied.

'I like it' Jess repeated.

'Oh my God!' Fran shouted. 'She bloody likes it!'

'Shut up!' Jess said, embarrassed by the commotion. 'I'll get it, OK? Just keep your voice down and clear a route to the till.'

Just five minutes later, they were strolling in the sunshine, with Jessica clutching a paper bag containing a dress that shimmered and shined in the sunlight.

And just forty-eight hours later, it would be her turn.

18

Blog subscribers – 44,031
Emails in inbox – 146
Event invitations – 53
Award nominations – 1
Award shortlists – 1
Blogger enemies – 1
Blogger friends – 1
Newspaper features – 1
Spotted by followers – 1

Dear Bella,

We weren't planning on having a party at first but as
the weeks ticked closer to your first birthday, I started to
realise how important it was that we marked it in some
way. I wanted your friends and family to make a fuss of
you, to sing 'happy birthday' as I carried a home-made
birthday cake to the table, and to see your shy smile when
you realised the whole day was about you. So a decision

was made to organise a small gathering at home with our closest friends and family – and it would all happen on the Saturday that fell just after your birthday. I chose a theme of rainbows, designed colourful invitations on my phone, and researched cakes and decoration ideas endlessly in the weeks beforehand. I was so excited, Bella – for you and for me.

Because here is the thing. Before you arrived, I thought mothers made an effort for birthdays just for their child. To spoil them, I guess. To show them how much they loved them. But as we started nearing the end of your first year, I suddenly realised that it was a celebration for me too. I knew I couldn't let that day pass without marking it in some way, even if you were too young to commit those rainbows, or that cake, or the sound of those voices singing 'happy birthday' to your memory forever. I realised it didn't matter. We still had to celebrate, because it was too special. It was too big. Your birthday, yes. But my birth day too. It was the day that we met. The day that life changed forever. The day the world stopped spinning as you were placed on my chest.

So you had a party – and despite the weather being overcast and a bit chilly (which I fear will always probably be the way with a birthday in March), it was a beautiful day. Daddy popped open bottles of prosecco, I displayed a cake that hadn't gone remotely to plan but was still enthusiastically admired, and you were showered with kisses and love by your family and all of your friends.

And at the end of the day, as you slept peacefully in my arms with the remnants of rainbow crumbs around your mouth, Daddy leaned towards me, kissed my forehead, and whispered 'bloody hell, we made it!' And as I turned towards him and smiled, not entirely sure whether he meant the day or the year, I realised that I've never felt more thankful that we did.

We made it.

And it was amazing.

Love from Mummy x

'I assume we're heading to the Princess?' Fran asked, as the two sisters strolled together in the sunshine. It was mid-afternoon now, but the sun still felt warm on their skin.

'I think it's a good idea, don't you?' replied Jess. 'It feels like the perfect afternoon for a pub garden.'

A few minutes later, they arrived at the Princess of Wales and walked through the side gate to the garden. It was the most popular pub in Blackheath and, unsurprisingly on such a beautiful afternoon, every table was already filled. And it wasn't just the tables, with crowds of people standing on the patio and chatting noisily, pouring glasses from large jugs, and tucking into sausages in buns from the barbecue, with sweet-smelling onions and dollops of tomato sauce.

'Oh crap. Do we have a Plan B?' Fran asked, as Jessica stood on her tiptoes and craned her neck to see whether there was anything free at the back.

'We're just leaving if you want to take our table?' a smartly-dressed young man said, pointing to a picnic bench in the far corner.

'Ah, thank you!' Fran replied, not quite believing their luck. 'That's perfect!'

'No problem,' he said. 'Follow me!'

'We really appreciate it,' Jessica said loudly, over the noise of the crowd as they wound their way through.

His friends were already standing up and getting ready to leave, their table filled with four empty jugs of Pimms and glasses of discarded apple chunks and cucumber slices. 'Wow, you've been busy!' Fran said, as she glanced down at her watch and saw that it was just past 4 p.m.

'We graduated this morning,' their new friend replied, to which both the girls cheered and congratulated them. And with a couple of dramatic bows and dons of imaginary hats, they had vacated the table and were heading out of the garden, leaving the two sisters with one of the best tables in the house.

'So, what do you fancy?' Fran asked, as they sat down.

'Shall we share a jug of Pimms?' Jessica asked. 'It seems appropriate when the sun is shining!'

'Great idea. And it's my shout, as a celebration of finding the perfect dress! Hopefully the bar won't be too busy,' Fran said, as she stood up and made her way inside.

Watching her sister make her way across the garden, Jessica's thoughts turned to Bella. It wasn't often that she got to spend time on her own and she had to admit it felt amazing to only have to think about herself for an afternoon. She didn't need to worry about pushing the buggy through crowds on the pavement, through narrow gaps between the rails in shops, or finding child-friendly places to eat with enough highchairs and spaces to park the buggy. She didn't need to stash snacks in her bag, or bottles of water that were likely to leak – and there was no looming deadline of cooking Bella her dinner, running her bath, or contorting herself through the bars of the cot at bedtime. Part of her missed her daughter, of course, but most of her was enjoying every second.

She was so deep in thought at the table that when her phone buzzed in her bag, it made her jump. She pulled it out and found a message from her mum flashing on the home screen:

IN BLACKHEATH. LOVELY TIME ON GRASS. BELLA IN FINE SPIRITS. ANY LUCK WITH THE DRESS. WHERE R U. WE WILL SAY HELLO.

She typed back quickly:

We're in the Princess. It's quite busy, so probably not ideal for Bella but you could pop in quickly to say hello?

She threw her phone back in her bag – and with no sign of Fran emerging from inside the pub, she found herself with more time to think and her mind wandered back to being recognised on the street earlier in the day. She was still stunned that somebody had recognised her, and whilst it was flattering, it was unnerving too. She'd never considered that people might connect her and her blog in public before. She could be Jessica and Bella's mummy when they were out of the house, and a blogger when she was at home, with her laptop on her knee and the front door shutting the rest of the world out. *But with the lines blurred, did she need to be wary about who was watching?*

Was someone watching her now? Were they wondering who was looking after her daughter? Were they disappointed that she wasn't taller, skinnier, or more stylish? Should she ask a member of staff to clear up the empty glasses on the table in case somebody thought she had drunk them all?

She suddenly felt very self-conscious and as a waitress walked past with an empty tray in her hand, she caught her eye and smiled.

'Would you mind clearing a few of the empties away?' Jessica asked. 'It wasn't us, I promise! We just sat down.'

'No worries at all,' she replied laughing, piling the empty glasses onto her tray. 'I'd be impressed if it was you! I'll be back for the jugs in a moment!'

'Thank you!' Jessica replied laughing, glancing around the garden and realising that nearly everybody else was student age. None of these people had babies! None of them would be interested in her blog! She relaxed and turned her face to the sunshine, enjoying the feeling on her skin. Moments later, Fran arrived back at the table with the jug and two glasses.

'You took a while,' Jessica said, as she picked up the jug to pour.

'Yes, I got chatting to an old friend at the bar. Do you remember Kerry Matthews? You were probably too young actually, but I used to play netball with her and have bumped into her every now and again through the years. She's lovely, you should meet her! We were chatting about your blog. It turns out she's a reader!'

Jessica swallowed and blushed. 'OK, that's enough publicity for one day,' she said, raising her hands in the air. 'It's all too weird! Let's drink while we can. I've already had word that the parents may be in the area!'

Fran laughed and picked up her glass. 'To the dress!' she said, clinking her glass against Jessica's.

'To the dress!' Jessica replied smiling.

But they'd barely got to the bottom of that first glass before her parents appeared at the entrance to the garden with Bella strapped into her buggy.

'COOOOO-EEEEE,' her mother called over, waving wildly to get their attention.

'Oh God, here we go,' Fran said, laughing. 'How the hell is she going to push that buggy through those people!'

'I don't think I can even watch,' Jessica replied, putting her head in her hands.

'COOOOOO-EEEEEEE,' her mum called again, starting her mission to head over. 'Excuse me! Sorry! Excuse me? So sorry! So sorry, could you move slightly? Oh, terribly sorry! I'm trying to get through to my daughters in the corner! Sorry! Oops sorry! Terribly sorry! Could you move to the right slightly? So sorry!

You'll have to move your chair for me to get through! So sorry! My fault! Very sorry!'

As Fran and Jessica watched with horror, their dad trailed behind looking embarrassed and apologising profusely to everyone that moved out of the way – and thanks to her mother's effective technique of steaming ahead regardless, they arrived at the table within about a minute.

'MA-MA-MA-MA!' Bella called, as they approached.

'Oh, hi baby girl! Have you been good?' Jessica said, unclipping her straps and scooping her out of the buggy.

'Hello, hello!' her mother said, loudly enough to turn heads at the tables surrounding them. 'And how are you both? Any luck with the dress?'

'Yes actually,' Fran replied, reaching under the table for the paper bag. As she unfolded the dress and held it out, their mother gasped dramatically and clasped her hands to her chest.

'It's perfect!' she said, 'Exactly how I imagine they dress in Hollywood at these big award shows! And perfect for accepting an award in, too.' At that, she winked dramatically at Jessica.

'Mum! Stop it!' Jessica said, shaking her head. She took the dress out of Fran's hands and folded it carefully, placing it back in the bag. 'Actually, could you stash this under the buggy and take it home? It's probably less likely to end up covered in Pimms!'

'I'll take it, dear,' her dad said, reaching for the bag. 'It's very nice, Jessica. Very nice indeed! You will look lovely in that!'

'Thank you, Dad,' she said, handing it over and smiling fondly at him. She knew it would be safe in his hands.

The conversation continued, but it didn't take long for Bella to lose patience, making grabs for Pimms-infused strawberries in Jessica's glass, so the decision was made to take her home for her tea. Chris had promised to be back by her bedtime, saving her parents from a battle to get her to sleep (they had that job to look forward to on Saturday night, of course). So off they went, retracing their steps through the crowds in the pub garden, making Jessica and Fran grimace and cringe as innocent bystanders were forced to jump out of the way of the buggy.

And once again, they were alone at the table, pouring a second glass of Pimms.

'So, how's Mel?' Fran asked.

Jessica sighed and looked down at her glass. 'Honestly, I don't know. She always puts a brave face on things, but I don't know how this can ever resolve itself. She's a single mum, with another baby on the way and no chance of heading back to her career any time soon.'

'She'll manage,' Fran said. 'She has no choice but to manage.'

Jessica looked up at her sister. She'd felt the similarities on the night she'd walked into Mel's house – the kind of devastation that she'd witnessed when Michael died – but since then, it hadn't occurred to her that Mel had been thrust into single motherhood in much the same way. She'd had a warning, but she'd chosen not to believe it and suddenly there she was, alone with her child, wondering how life was ever going to be the same again.

'When does it start feeling normal again?' Jessica asked.

'I've no idea,' Fran replied. 'It still doesn't for me. I wake up every morning and for a split second, I think I'm in our bed in Dulwich and expect him to be sleeping next to me. And then I open my eyes and realise I'm in my teenage bedroom at Mum and Dad's and he isn't here. It's like I've been kicked hard in the stomach, every single day.'

'I know I've said this hundreds of times before,' Jessica said, 'but it's just really sad. Like really, really sad. Michael was such a good man and you had such a perfect life together. It could've happened to a bad person... I mean, it shouldn't happen to anyone, but if it's going to happen, why does it happen to the good people? People who have families? And children? And only ever do kind things? We never know when life is going to change in a split second and it just isn't fair.'

'No,' Fran said, before looking up and smiling at her sister. 'But that's the difference, isn't it? Michael was such a bloody good man. He loved me and he loved Freddie. And he would've done anything to stay here with us. But Mel's husband? He had no idea how lucky he was! I only met him a few times but from what you've told me, he's treated her like shit.'

Jessica nodded. 'He really has,' she said, as she picked a piece of cucumber from her glass and popped it into her mouth. 'So, it'll be easier? She might feel like herself again, a bit sooner?'

'Well listen, I've been through heartbreak before. I thought Gary was the bloody bee's knees! I thought he was the man! Meanwhile, he was too busy racing around on motorbikes to even notice me most days. And then I had a baby with him, thinking it was the perfect way to tame him, and off he went, into the sunset on his prize motorbike, without so much as fucking goodbye.'

'His loss,' Jessica quipped back.

'Too bloody right,' Fran replied, taking a sip.

'I mean, seriously! What a twat!' Jessica continued loudly, prompting Fran to laugh so hard that she nearly sprayed Pimms across the table.

When they'd both composed themselves, Jessica sighed and said: 'So you think she'll be OK?'

'God yeah,' Fran replied. 'She'll get there.'

'And you?' Jessica asked.

'I guess I will, too. I've got a little boy who needs me.'

Jessica smiled at the mention of her nephew. 'When does he get back from his football tour?' she asked. 'Is he having fun?'

Fran laughed. 'I think so. I gave him a retro Nokia mobile phone of mine before he left and he's so chuffed with himself! I keep getting text messages that must take him at least half an hour to write!'

Jessica howled with laughter. 'Do you remember how you had to push the button four times to get the right letter?'

'Exactly that!' Fran said. 'That's the exact phone! I think it's twenty years old! I was surprised when it charged up to be honest, but I think the old ones are quite robust! Anyway, he's back on Sunday and I can't wait to see him. I miss him far more than I expected to!'

The conversation continued until they'd got to the end of the jug of Pimms, laughing and chatting as the sun lowered and softened. The garden was still busy, but the clientele had changed in the past hour. The students had gradually drifted away and there were now tables of office workers in suits surrounding them, all sipping glasses of wine and pints of beer and tucking into plates of bar snacks.

'Fancy another jug of Pimms?' Fran asked, pointing to the entrance to the pub.

'Better not,' Jessica replied, looking at her watch. 'Shall we have something soft instead? I think I'm going to need quite a lot of alcohol to survive the night on Saturday, so I'd rather save myself for then.'

'No worries, lightweight! What do you fancy? I think I'll move onto spritzer.' Fran stood up and grabbed her bag.

'No, this one is on me,' Jessica said, standing up and pointing at the bench for her sister to sit back down. 'I'll get you a spritzer and I'll grab something to eat, too. You stay here and save base...'

But just as she was approaching the bar, she felt a hand on her shoulder.

'My wife tells me that you're a famous blogger,' a man said to her, his work shirt stretched over a beer belly, face ruddy, and hand clutching a half-drunk pint of ale.

Jessica laughed nervously, already looking around for a space at the bar to escape. 'Oh, I wouldn't say that...'

'That's what she says...' he continued, his speech slurred. 'She says that she reads your blog and you have millions of followers!'

'Oh, that's not true!' Jessica said, hoping nobody was listening in.

'She says that you've been in the pub all afternoon and that you've been through several jugs of Pimms. And that your baby daughter was here for most of it! You naughty girl! Naughty, naughty girl!' Her new friend hiccupped and swayed into her.

Jessica turned to him. 'Well, that's not true. My daughter was here for ten minutes. And I've had a couple of glasses of Pimms. That's all! I'm already on the soft drinks!'

'Oh, so she *was* here!' he replied, hiccupping again. 'I bet that wouldn't go down well with your mummy readers!'

'Oh fuck off,' Jessica said, suddenly filled with rage.

'Pardon?' her friend said, his eyes wide and bloodshot.

'Seriously! Fuck off! I am allowed to go to the pub with my sister! I am allowed to say hello to my daughter quickly if she's passing the pub garden with her grandparents! I am allowed to go out for the day without my child in tow! Just fuck off! I don't have to answer to you!'

She managed to negotiate her way into a spot at the bar, leaving the man swaying behind her.

'God, I didn't realise these blogger types were so touchy! I'm going to do my wife a favour and tell her not to bother reading it any more if you don't want to take a bit of honest feedback!'

'You do that,' Jessica quipped back, refusing to turn around.

Ordering a white wine spritzer and an elderflower soda, she watched as they were made by the barmaid. She was hoping that by the time she had paid and had to turn around again, he might have got bored and disappeared – but she could still hear him hiccupping as he stood behind her.

'You'll have to get used to the criticism though, won't you darling?' he piped up again. 'If you want to be a big blogger, you've got to grow some thicker skin.'

Jessica snapped round. 'Why's that?'

The man looked pleased with himself. 'Oh, I knew you wanted to chat to me! Maybe that thick skin is growing already!' He steadied himself on the back of the stall in front of him as he stumbled to the left.

'Why do I need to get used to criticism?' Jessica shot back.

'You choose to put yourself out there and you have to accept what people think,' he slurred in reply.

'You're a jerk. A total jerk. And for your information, if I choose to put myself out there, you still have to show a modicum of decency and respect. I don't have to accept anything. And it doesn't give you permission to accost a stranger in a bar and try to knock them out with the alcohol units of your breath.'

Hearing the drinks clink on the bar in front of her, she paid with a note, picked up the glasses, and pushed past her sweating friend.

'Oh, and by the way?'

'Yes darling?' he slurred.

'If you really want to do your wife a favour, make that your last pint and fuck off home. You can't even stand up straight, seriously. You're an embarrassment.'

But as she stormed out of the pub and back towards

Fran, she already knew he was right about one thing. She needed to grow thicker skin fast. She needed to be better prepared, because she had a feeling it wouldn't be the last time somebody forced their opinions on her.

She didn't get home that evening until past 10 p.m.

'Hi stranger,' Chris said, as she walked through the door. 'How was your day? Your parents dropped off your dress earlier and it is now hanging up in our room. It is quite frankly exquisite'.

'Do you think so?' she asked, as she kicked off her flip-flops in the hallway.

'Yes, honey! Honestly! You are going to look so good in it. In fact, I will be mainly looking forward to removing it later that evening,' he replied, with a wink.

'Oi!' she laughed.

'But seriously, I can't wait to see you wearing it on that stage!'

'I wish everyone would stop saying that I'm going to win this thing!' Jessica said, starting to feel quite irritated. 'The more you say it, the more I worry that I'll be disappointed when my name isn't the one called out! Because it won't be! I haven't been blogging long enough! It's lovely to make it to this stage – but *I am not going to win.*'

'And if it isn't your name,' he continued, standing up to kiss her on the lips, 'that is absolutely fine. Because you have still done amazingly well. You have still got to the final four parenting bloggers to win the biggest award in the whole year!'

'Yes, exactly!' Jessica said, nodding.

'But if it is your name,' he added quickly, 'you are going

to look a million dollars collecting your award…'

Jessica scowled and playfully kicked him on the shin. 'Enough! But thank you. I'm glad you like it!'

She was. She really was.

And in just a couple of days, she would be stepping into it and heading to one of the biggest nights of her life.

19

Followers – 47,878
Emails in inbox – 228
Event invitations – 61
Paid collaborations – 1
Award nominations – 1
Award shortlists – 1
Blogger enemies – 1
Blogger friends – 1
Newspaper features – 1
Spotted by followers – 2

Dear Bella,

I'm writing this letter to you on the train. I can't breathe, because I'm wearing giant pants to suck in my tummy and they seem to be restricting blood flow to my entire upper torso, but it's worth the discomfort, because I'm feeling more confident in this dress than I've felt for a long time.

And as I sit here and watch the outskirts of London flash past the train window, I am filled with such a mixture of emotions. I'm excited, because it's not every day you are invited to attend a glittering awards ceremony. I'm tired, because you've managed to pick up a snotty cold and I'm not sure how much I've actually slept in the last few days. But most of all, I'm feeling sick with nerves. Like properly sick. Butterflies are fluttering angrily in my stomach, my legs feel like jelly, and my whole body shivers when I remember where we are going tonight.

Life has changed so much, Bella. Six months ago, the only date in our diary all week was a music class every Tuesday morning where we danced around with your little friends – but suddenly, it's not unusual to be getting phone calls from marketing managers inviting us to model in fashion campaigns, emails from restaurants inviting me for dinner, and invites to swanky product launches (even if they don't turn out very swanky, after all). And tonight, here I am travelling to an awards ceremony in a dress covered in silver sequins. It's all got a bit nuts, hasn't it? And if I'm honest, there have been moments when I have wondered if it's all for the best. Moments where I've wondered: 'Why am I doing this? Is it really worth it? Do I really want to be a blogger? Do I really want to reveal so much online?' Moments when I've considered stopping altogether. So many moments of doubt.

I worry that I'm not doing the right thing.

So tonight, as I sit on this train, I want to remind myself about why I started these letters. About why I first sat down, opened this yellow notebook, and starting writing to you.

I've always wanted to write, but I didn't know where to start.

But then I met you, and suddenly I found the words.

I was always waiting for you.

You are my inspiration. My motivation. My muse.

And as I walk into this awards ceremony this evening, shaking like a leaf with nerves, I promise to keep you in my mind every single second.

It's all been for you.

All of it, Bella...

Every single word.

Love from Mummy x

'You ready?' Chris asked, as the train came to a stop at London Cannon Street.

Jessica looked up and sighed loudly. 'I guess so,' she said, steadying herself for a moment on her high heels as she stood up. It had been a long time since she'd last worn them and it took her a while to find her centre of gravity. When she found it, she followed Chris slowly off the train.

'Are we walking?' she asked, linking arms with him as they strolled through the busy station concourse.

'To Old Billingsgate? No, too far in those heels! We'll jump in a cab,' he said, dodging the crowd of people stood looking up at the departure boards. Seconds later, they were out on the street, walking against a flow of people rushing towards the station.

'We stick out like sore thumbs,' Jessica said, laughing.

And it was true. Everybody else was dressed in summer dresses, shorts, and flip-flops, carrying bags of shopping after spending a day of their weekend in the capital. And there they were, quite literally shimmering and shining in the early evening sunshine.

It didn't take long for a black cab to pull up alongside them and they were soon on their way to the awards ceremony, winding their way along Cannon Street.

'You OK, honey?' Chris asked, putting his hand on her knee. Jessica looked down at it, noticing his wedding ring catch the light, before placing her own hand on top and squeezing it.

'I think so,' she said. 'I'm nervous, but I'll be OK.'

'Not worried about seeing Tiggy?' he asked, searching her face.

Jessica turned to the window and sighed. 'Well, yes, obviously. A little bit. I'll chat to her if I get the opportunity. I'd quite like to tell her that I didn't know anything about her being ditched from the campaign. But if I don't get the chance, I'm not going to stamp my feet like a toddler! I hereby promise to stay dignified at all times!'

Chris squeezed Jessica's knee and turned to kiss her on the lips. 'I think that's the perfect plan – and you make me very proud Mrs Holmes!'

Jessica smiled. 'Just don't let me drink too much or we'll risk the plan imploding!'

Jessica knew they would be arriving in a matter of minutes, so reached into her bag for her phone to check there hadn't been any panicked messages from her parents at Bella's bedtime. To her surprise, there were five messages flashing up on the screen.

Mum: ALL OK HERE. SHE IS SLEEPING. GOOD LUCK. WE ARE VERY PROUD.

Fran: GO JESSY! I will be thinking about you all night! Let me know how it goes – and if Tiggy isn't friendly, give her a bitch slap from me!

Mel: The girls are coming round so we can wait for news together! Good luck! Send us a message every few minutes, OK?

Deena: Good Luck, Girl! We can't wait to hear!

Henny: We are so proud of you babe! You are going to smash it tonight! We have a bottle of Pinot chilling in your honour (Mel is on the fizzy apple juice, but we're going to pretend by putting it in a wine glass!) Let us know as soon as you hear! So excited for you! Yay!

'Bella OK?' Chris asked.

'Mum messaged and she's fine. She's sleeping already. I had a message from Fran too, and one from each of the girls. They're all gathering at Mel's tonight to wait for news,' Jessica smiled, zipping the phone back in her bag as the cab pulled up alongside Old Billingsgate Market.

'They really are the best group of girls, aren't they?' Chris said, pulling his wallet from his back pocket.

'The best,' Jessica replied. 'The absolute best.'

They had arrived. As Chris paid for the journey, Jessica took a deep breath and tried to climb out of the cab as gracefully as possible. There were people in dresses and tuxedos all around them, chatting in groups on the pavement, and gathering in the entrance to Old Billingsgate. Jessica clung to Chris' arm tightly as he slammed the cab door and they turned to walk inside. Her legs wobbled with a sudden attack of nerves and she leaned into him to steady herself as they strolled.

Reaching the entrance, a lady in a long, green cocktail dress and a clipboard under her arm greeted them. 'Welcome to the Blog Network Awards!' she said with a big smile. 'Can I take your names, please?'

'Oh, it's Jessica Holmes from "Letters to My Daughter."' Jessica swallowed her nerves. 'And my husband, Christopher Holmes.' *What if they didn't have them on the list, just like the baby food launch? What if she had to endure the humiliation of standing at the door as they called someone more senior to come and check the list again? What if Tiggy started queuing behind her, sniggering at the fact Jessica was stood like a nobody at the door, begging to be let in?*

'Ah yes, of course! Welcome Jessica! It's nice to meet you! You're one of our VIPs tonight, so I've got six tokens here for drinks at the bar,' she said, handing them over. 'You'll be on Table 17, so make your way straight there when it's time for dinner at exactly 8 p.m. Congratulations on making the shortlist and very best of luck!'

Jessica thanked her and walked ahead, the grandeur of the place taking her breath away. Old Billingsgate was quite simply gigantic. Once a large fish market, it had a sky-high vaulted ceiling and pillars running down each side of the hall. It was still light outside at 7.30 p.m., but there was no natural light inside at all. Instead, the place was lit by a striking rose-pink light, with four giant crystal chandeliers hanging from the ceiling and bouncing the light. There were tables as far as Jessica could see, closely packed together, with the large vases in the centre of each table, filled with arrangements of exotic lilies. And to their left was a stage, with a screen behind it reading 'BLOG NETWORK AWARDS' in giant letters and a microphone rigged up.

All the arriving guests seemed to be walking through the giant pillars on the right-hand side of the hall and towards the bar for a pre-ceremony drink, so after one last quick gaze around with open-mouthed amazement, Chris and Jessica followed them. As they got closer, the echoey sound of people chatting, laughing, and clinking glasses got louder and louder.

'You OK, honey?' Chris asked, squeezing her hand. 'This place is amazing, isn't it? I've been here for a few events with clients.'

'It's amazing,' Jessica said. 'But also pretty overwhelming. There are just so many tables and that means this giant place is going to be totally filled with people...'

Chris laughed and turned to kiss her quickly. 'You'll be fine. Honestly, you'll be fine. Just try and enjoy it. It's going to be a good night.'

Jessica smiled, wishing she could believe him.

The bar area was small in comparison to the main hall and people were packed in, standing around in groups or sat at low tables on sofas chatting. After queuing at the bar for a while to be served, they wound their way back through the crowds and found a tall table to stand by near the back of the bar. Jessica was holding a large fish-bowl style glass of gin and tonic, complete with a slice of red grapefruit. As she sipped, she took the opportunity to people watch for a while.

The thing that really struck her was that most of the crowd seemed to know each other, enthusiastically greeting each other and standing around in groups. In fact, so many people were kissing, hugging and calling names across the room that Jessica realised they stood out as a couple on their own.

'I feel like a bit of a loner!' she shouted across to Chris, but he couldn't hear her above the noise.

Jessica was sipping her drink slowly, but it wasn't going down well. And as she looked down and stirred it with the straw, a voice rang out on overhead speakers: 'Good evening everyone! There are just five minutes until dinner will be served, so please drink up and make your way through to the main hall! The show is about to start!'

'Shall we take our drinks to the table?' Chris shouted above the din.

Jessica sighed and shouted back: 'I guess so... Let's do

that'. She took his hand as they strolled out of the bar, looking down at her feet.

The main hall was getting busy now, with people trying to find their seats and milling about the tables. Table 17 was positioned right in the centre, nearly the closest they could be to the stage. As they approached, Jessica was relieved to see Wendy already sitting at the table with her husband.

'Jessica!' she called out as they arrived at their seats, standing up to reveal a floor-length red jumpsuit, white heels, and matching red lipstick. 'Babe! It's so nice to see you! Swit-Swoo! Look at you! You are looking seriously amazing!'

'Ah, hi Wendy, I am so pleased to see you,' she said, hugging her warmly. 'And check you out! Your jumpsuit is incredible! You look gorgeous!'

'Nah, thank you! Nothing like an excuse to get dressed up! And sorry, I'm being really rude. Is this your husband?' she asked, holding out her hand.

'Yes hi, Wendy, I'm Chris,' he said, shaking it and following with a quick kiss on the cheek. 'Lovely to meet you, I've heard lots about you! And this must be…?'

'Jason!' Wendy's husband replied, shaking his hand. 'Great to meet you! Is your wife as nervous about tonight as mine is?'

'Ha ha, you could say that!' Chris replied, stroking his eyebrow and looking down at the floor. Jessica shot him a look and then followed with a laugh.

As the men chatted, Wendy turned to Jessica. 'How are you doing? Honestly?'

'Bricking it!' Jessica laughed. 'You?'

'I'm OK,' Wendy replied. 'I know I'm not going to win it, so I'm just here for the drinks!'

'Ah, don't say that. Your blog is amazing! I bet you win it, Wendy! Honestly!'

'Thanks babe,' Wendy replied. 'I just have a feeling it's not my year. But I'm totally game for a big night, anyway! Shall we sit down? Your place name was over there on the other side of the table, so I moved it. Couldn't have you sat next to Tiggy, could we?' She laughed and winked.

'Oh, thank fuck! Seriously! I was literally dreading...' But she stopped mid-sentence as she saw Jackson from 'And Then Came The Kids' arriving at the table and experienced a fresh wave of nerves.

'Jackson!' Wendy said, jumping up again. Saying hello, Jackson hugged and kissed her, before Wendy turned to Jessica and said: 'Come, meet Jessica from "Letters to My Daughter"!'

Jessica had been reading Jackson's blog and watching his video diaries since the first awards list was published, so she felt starstruck to see him in the flesh. He was shorter than she imagined, probably around 5 ft 8, with tattoos just visible on his wrists and above the collar of his shirt. She knew from posts online that he loved heading to the gym – and he had the bulk to prove it. He was quite a striking man; definitely good-looking, and despite a tuxedo not being his usual attire, it suited him.

Feeling like she already knew his family, she felt a pang of disappointment that his wife wasn't with him (she'd become mildly obsessed with her wardrobe over the past few weeks). Instead, Jackson had an equally dashing suited-and-booted friend alongside him.

'Jessica, it's great to meet you. Good luck tonight!' Jackson said in a thick Yorkshire accent, as he shook her hand.

'Thank you,' Jessica replied. 'And the same to you!'

As Jackson and his friend introduced themselves to Chris and Jason, Wendy and Jessica sat back down at the table. Filled with adrenaline, she sighed loudly and glanced over to Tiggy's empty place. She knew it was only a matter of time before she arrived.

With the men chatting away behind them, Jessica wondered if she should take the opportunity to chat to Wendy about the interview in *The Daily Gossip*. She wondered if she'd already seen it, keeping it from Jessica to save her embarrassment. She closed her eyes for a second and rubbed her forehead in thought. Her own voice in the cab played in her head. *I'm not going to make a scene tonight.* And she knew that she should take her own advice. So instead of bringing it up, she asked Wendy about Adeline and Dylan, and she concentrated on calming her breathing as she listened to stories about cuddly toys diving into (unflushed) toilets and a trip to A & E when a marble needed to be extracted from a nostril.

At exactly 8 p.m., the lights dimmed, music started playing, and those standing around tables started to take their seats. 'Here we go, babe!' Wendy shouted above the music, before gritting her teeth and laughing. 'They usually do the parenting award close to the end, so let's get stuck into the wine! White or red for you?'

'I don't think I'm going to drink much,' Jessica shouted back. 'It's making me feel a bit sick with nerves!'

'Sorry babe?' Wendy shouted back, trying to be heard. 'Did you say white or red?'

'I guess, well, maybe, OK, pour me a white,' Jessica said, pointing at the bottle of white in her left hand. Wendy sloshed it into her glass, and behind the bottle, Jessica noticed that Tiggy's seat was still empty.

As Chris sat down, Jessica turned to him and smiled but she was so nervous, the edge of her mouth twitched.

'You OK, honey?' he asked, and Jessica nodded.

Suddenly a voice rang out loudly across the hall. 'Ladies and Gentlemen! Bloggers and Guests! Agencies and Brand Partners! We are delighted to welcome you to the Blog Network Awards 2018! Please do take your seats if you haven't already! Our host Ricardo Mendez is about to take to the stage!'

'Shit! Ricardo Mendez?' she said out loud.

Wendy laughed. 'Yeah, they always find a Z-Lister! Are you a fan?'

'Ha ha, well no I wouldn't say that...' she said, blushing. Glancing to her left, Chris took the opportunity to wink at her, fully aware of her crush on the *Late Night Natter* presenter.

And as she looked back to the stage, there he was strutting across it with a microphone. Dressed in a slim-fit grey metallic suit, which shone shades of purple under the light, he was everything Jessica had imagined and more. 'Good evening, ladies and gentlemen!' he said loudly. 'It is my pleasure to be joining you this evening to present these awards! And let me just take the opportunity to congratu-late each and every one of the shortlisted bloggers tonight for making it this far! You are all winners! All of you! But I am told we have so many awards tonight that we need to push on quickly before I get a slap on the wrist! So, without further ado, here are the shortlisted bloggers in the "Best Technology Blog" category for 2018!'

Jessica watched as the faces of each of the four bloggers in the category were flashed up on the giant screen, and Ricardo read a brief introduction to each of their blogs. A drumroll then filled the hall, before the winner was announced to rapturous cheering and clapping from a table behind them. The sound system burst into music as a man, probably still in his early twenties, made his way to the stage. After much congratulating and shaking of hands, Ricardo handed over a gold trophy to the winner, who smiled and posed for photos, before being chaperoned off the stage and out of the hall by a glamorous lady in a purple dress.

Jessica stared at her wine glass in front of her, wondering if she should down it quickly for a little Dutch courage. As she stared through that wine glass, she suddenly saw a flash of white. She looked up, and there she was. Dressed in a body-hugging, floor-length, jaw-droppingly beautiful white dress, with perfectly blow-dried hair, and an equally head-turning husband on her arm.

Tiggy.

Ricardo was already announcing the next award for 'Best Travel Blogger', so Tiggy and her husband rushed to sit down in their seats. Jessica didn't know where to look when Wendy mouthed 'Hi! How are you?' across the table, while Jackson turned to kiss her on the cheek from his seat next to her. Tiggy smiled and mouthed 'Hi!' at everyone around the table, stopping at Jessica and giving her the smallest nod of recognition. Jessica allowed her lips to curl slightly, just for a second, in acknowledgement.

Under the table, Chris squeezed Jessica's knee in support. There was no doubt that Tiggy was prepared to win that night. Jessica wouldn't have been surprised if she'd spent the whole day in a salon chair being beautified, with perfect hair, flawless make-up, and a dress that looked like it had been made for her. She would fit in perfectly on a Hollywood red carpet and Jessica suddenly felt embarrassingly frumpy, glancing down at her mid-calf length dress and black velvet heels.

Reading her mind, Chris put his mouth to her ear and said: 'You look amazing! Keep smiling!' Jessica turned and smiled back at him.

It was far too loud for the table to have a conversation, which made things easier for Jessica as the awards continued. She could happily watch the stage and avoid making eye contact across the table. Before long, a line of waiters appeared carrying plates and they were each handed a starter of tomato soup and fresh bread rolls, but Jessica felt far too nervous to eat it. A main course of salmon, new potatoes, and fancy vegetables followed, but she could hardly touch that either, picking at it occasionally with her fork. The awards carried on, through travel bloggers, and fashion bloggers, beauty bloggers, and political bloggers – she knew that their turn was edging ever closer.

And she was right. Just as a line of plated chocolate soufflés arrived at their table, Ricardo Mendez announced the next award was the Parenting Blogger category. 'Sorry, ladies and gents on that table! You've probably got the earliest wake-up call tomorrow morning and for some reason, the organisers of these awards thought it would be a brilliant idea to leave you until nearly the end! How inspired! Good luck with the headaches tomorrow morning, guys!' to which laughter rippled around the hall.

Jessica's nerves were out of control now and she was pretty sure she was going to be sick. 'Oh God,' she muttered under her breath, trying to swallow the nausea down.

'You OK?' Chris asked, but she could only nod in reply.

Ricardo's voice rang out loudly. 'So, the four nominees in the "Best Parenting Blog of 2018" category are as follows... TIGGY BLENHEIM, who writes the brilliant blog TIGGY DOES MOTHERHOOD!' As applause rippled through the hall, pictures of Tiggy flashed on the screen. Jessica snatched a glimpse at her across the table. She was watching the screen with a small smile on her face, while her husband alongside her gazed at her adoringly.

She doesn't feel any nerves, Jessica thought to herself. *It's like she already knows she's won it!*

Ricardo continued. 'JESSICA HOLMES, who writes the popular blog LETTERS TO MY DAUGHTER!' Jessica blushed and smiled shyly at Chris, as pictures of her and Bella were projected on the big screen.

As Ricardo continued onto Jackson and then Wendy's blog, it occurred to Jessica that Tiggy had to acknowledge her now. Even if Tiggy won this award, as everyone expected, she had seen Jessica sitting at that table. She had seen her picture flash up on the screen. She couldn't pretend she was a nobody any more. She couldn't pretend she had no idea who she was.

Ricardo's voice rang out. 'And now to announce the winner!'

Jessica could hear the drumroll thumping around the hall, but her mind was focused on breathing through the nausea. *Don't be sick*, she thought to herself. *Don't be sick! Just smile when the winner is announced and be gracious! You can say congratulations, then make your excuses and go home! Then you get to hug Bella! You just have to get through the next few minutes! Breathe! Breathe!*

The drumroll stopped and silence fell amongst the tables.

And after clearing his throat with a quick cough, Ricardo continued: 'I'm delighted to announce that the winner is…'

Jessica held her breath, Tiggy smiled at the stage, Wendy pursed her lips, and Jackson's friend slapped him across the back for support.

And that was the moment that everything changed.

'JESSICA HOLMES OF LETTERS TO MY DAUGHTER!'

20

Blog Subscribers – 61,888
Emails in inbox – 299
Event invitations – 65
Award nominations – 1
Award shortlists – 1
Blogger enemies – 1
Blogger friends – 1
Newspaper features – 1
Spotted by followers – 2
Award wins – 1

Dear Bella,

I heard my name called out on the stage – but I couldn't move. I was frozen to the spot. 'Oh my God,' I finally said, as applause rippled through the hall and Wendy leant in to kiss me. 'Congratulations, babe!' she said warmly. 'Get up! Go! Go get your award!' I turned to Daddy, who was beaming warmly at me. 'I knew you'd do it! I am so proud of you!' he said, kissing me on the lips.

I scraped my chair back and walked to the steps up to the stage in a daze. 'This is nuts,' I muttered to myself under my breath. 'This is totally nuts.'

I walked towards Ricardo Mendez on the stage, and I had a moment where I felt like I'd stepped outside my own body. I kept thinking: 'How can this be happening?' and 'How could I have won?' I reached him and he took both of my hands and smiled at me, before dropping one and kissing me on the cheek. 'Well done Jessica Holmes of Letters to My Daughter! Well done to you!'

Here was a man that I'd watched so many times on television saying my name. MY name, Bella! And then he passed me a gold award, which was far heavier than I had imagined, and there I was, standing on a stage, with hundreds of eyes on me and cameras flashing in my face. And no sooner had I got up there, than I was being led off the stage again by a lady in a purple dress, following her through the hall and out towards the bar.

'Where are we going?' I asked, as I heard Ricardo's voice on the stage introducing the next award. She looked back at me and smiled. 'We'll take a few publicity shots and then you can head back to your table!'

'Publicity shots?' I asked, but she didn't turn back to explain.

It soon became apparent that I was being led into an area for winners – and as I approached, a man in a suit walked over to me. 'Jessica! Congratulations!' he said, shaking my hand with one hand and stroking his moustache with the other. 'My name is Bob Thomas and I'm the Chief Executive of the Blog Network Awards.' I was in such a daze, Bella, but I managed to thank him for the award, to which he replied: 'Our pleasure. Your blog really stood out for its honesty. It's really quite...' He paused and continued stroking his moustache '... It's really quite exceptional. So, congratulations! Now would you mind standing against this backdrop for a photo for our website and social media channels? We will tag you of course!'

Of course, I didn't mind. I was in such a daze that he could've asked me to go on a murderous rampage with him and I probably would've agreed. I walked to the spot marked 'X' on the floor, as instructed, and smiled as the camera flashed. 'Thank you!' a voice called out from behind the camera. 'Can I go now?' I replied, to which Bob Thomas replied: 'Of course!'

But just when I didn't think the night could get any more surreal, a lady in a red suit tapped me on the shoulder. 'Hi Jessica – and congratulations! Would you mind if I gave you my card?' 'Umm, no of course not!' I replied. 'Oh wonderful! Because my name is Dalia Simpson-Wright and I am the Marketing Executive for Beachy Waves Family Holidays. I'm looking for a blogger to review a holiday to Dubai and I wondered if you'd like to discuss it? I'll give you time to think it over, but my details are right here at the bottom of the card!' I must've been staring at her with an open mouth, because she thrust the card into my hand, smiled, and walked away. I glanced down at that card, without even seeing the words, and put one foot in front of the other to find my way back to the table.

When I wrote to you earlier that night, I told you that you'd never be far from my mind, and I meant it, Bella. As I strolled back to the table, I felt so baffled and so shocked that I deliberately turned my thoughts to you. I imagined you sleeping at home in your cot, with Granny and Grandad downstairs on the sofa. I imagined your snuffly breathing, the way your lips part into a bow when you sleep, the smell of lavender bubble bath on your skin, your cuddly bunny rabbit gripped tightly in your fist. And, as I walked back through the hall, with heads turning as my dress flashed under the bright lights, you were the very reason I managed to keep going.

I owe this award to you.

All of it.

Every word that I've written.

Every picture that I've posted.

Every time I've sat down at my laptop to write.

And I promise to give you the biggest hug to thank you when I wake up in the morning.

It's all been for you, Bella.

Remember that? OK?

It's all been for you.

Love from Mummy x

As Jessica walked back through the hall towards their table, her grip around the award grew tighter and tighter.

She could see Chris chatting to Wendy, his hand on the back of Jessica's empty chair as he leant across to talk to her. To their right, Jason was chatting to Jackson and his friend Clive. Across the table, Tiggy was tapping away on her phone, while her husband was nowhere to be seen.

As Jessica approached, Chris rushed over and kissed her on the lips. 'You bloody superstar!' he said, picking her up off her feet and swinging her.

'Chris!' she said, embarrassed that he was making a scene.

'What?' he replied, 'I'm allowed to be proud of my wife!'

As Jessica blushed and strolled back towards her seat, Wendy stood up to meet her. 'Well done! Seriously, babe! Well done! Amazing! I'm so, so happy for you!' As Jessica hugged her, Wendy whispered in her ear. 'Your husband is as proud as punch! It's really sweet. He absolutely adores you. And Bella!'

Jessica smiled at her, unsure how to reply. Just as she was about to sit down, there was a tap on her shoulder.

She swung round to see Jackson stood behind her. 'Well done, Jessica! Very well deserved! Can I see that award?' Jessica passed it over and he stood it up in the palm of his hand to admire it. 'Jeez, that's a lot heavier than it looks! Wow. What a beauty!'

After he handed it back and Jessica sat down at the table, both his friend Clive and Jason congratulated her and she could feel her complexion turning a shade of crimson.

But across the table, Tiggy didn't even look up from her phone.

'I've ordered a bottle of champagne for the table!' Chris announced loudly and Jessica smiled.

'I don't know much about blogging,' Jackson's friend Clive suddenly piped up loudly, 'but I've heard about your blog, Jessica! And I was told by several different friends of mine that they love it, so you must be doing something right!'

'Oh thank y—' Jessica began, but she was interrupted by Tiggy standing up, scraping her chair back, and muttering, 'What a crock of shit...' under her breath as she stormed away.

Silence fell across the table as every head turned to watch her strutting across the room.

Jessica felt like she'd been punched in the stomach. Humiliating her at the baby food launch was one thing. Alluding to her in a gossipy interview was another. But embarrassing her moments after she won her award? Jessica felt the blood roar in her ears, willing herself to follow her. Willing herself to try and clear the air, once and for all.

'Was it something I said?' Clive laughed, picking up the pint of beer in front of him and sipping.

Jessica shot him a glare, snatched her clutch bag from the table in one hand and her gold award in the other, and stood up.

'You OK, honey?' Chris said, placing his hand on her back.

'I'm fine,' she said. 'I'll see you in a minute.'

'Jess…' Chris said, reaching out for her – but she was already making her way back across the hall.

Seconds later, she arrived in the bar, which was empty now, apart from two men stood over pints of beer at one of the high tables. Jessica paused for a moment to think and out of the corner of her eye, she caught a flash of white as Tiggy's dress swept behind her as she turned towards the toilets.

She took a deep breath and carried on behind her.

As she walked through the doors to the ladies' toilets, Jessica was met with a large powder room lined with mirrors, each framed in a row of single, bright lights – and beyond it, the toilet cubicles. One was now engaged and Jessica felt nerves flutter in her stomach as she realised it was only a matter of time before her nemesis walked out of it.

With a moment to stand still, she unzipped her clutch bag and pulled out her phone. 'Jesus,' she said under her breath, as she saw she had ten new messages.

Henny: ARRGGHHHHHHHHH! Chris just texted Dan who texted me! YOU ONLY BLOODY WON IT! WELL DONE

BABE!!!!!!!! We have popped the champagne here! Call as soon as you can!

Deena: You bloody superstar! Well done! What time does it all finish? Fancy coming here for a glass to celebrate?

Mel: Never doubted you for a second! If you have time to pop over at the end of the night, let me know. We will wait up!

Mum: CHRIS SENT NEWS AND HEAR YOU WON! WE ARE SO HAPPY FOR YOU!

Fran: So bloody proud! Have a glass of something strong and sparkling for me please! I'll call first thing tomorrow!

Henny: God I am a bit pissed now probably, but I wanted to say how happy I am! Can you come here? Sorry bit pissed now probably. Sorry.

Mel: Conversation has now turned to Tiggy Does Motherhood. We are all waiting for the humble congratulations post on her page. It hasn't come yet…

Deena: Is she there? How did she react? We are dying to know!!

Mum: STAY OUT LATE IF YOU WANT TO CELEBRATE. WE ARE OK HERE. DAD NOW OPENING BOTTLE OF SOMETHING IN FRIDGE. HOPE THAT IS OK.

Mum: WE THINK WE JUST OPENED YOR BEST CHAMPERS SORRY.

Jessica smiled, but her attention was suddenly snapped back with the sound of the toilet flushing. Seconds later, the door opened and there she was, flicking her hair off her shoulder as she left the cubicle, already fixed on her own reflection in the mirror above the sinks as she walked towards them.

The conversation Jessica had had with Wendy on their night out was playing on a loop in her mind: 'So what changed?' she had asked. 'I stood up to her,' Wendy had replied.

And now it was her turn.

Jessica moved her arm slightly and silver sequins flashed brightly in the mirror. Tiggy's eyes shot up to meet her, before snapping straight back down to the running water.

'Hi, Tiggy,' Jessica said calmly.

Tiggy turned off the tap and shook her hands, walking towards the paper towel dispenser. She pulled out three towels without looking up and didn't utter a word.

Silence hung between them.

'I'm sorry about the Mama & Me thing,' Jessica said finally. 'I genuinely had no idea I was replacing you. This was not some kind of campaign to usurp you.'

Tiggy moved her eyes up but stayed silent.

'I never meant to do anything to hurt you! I just started typing up a notebook of letters I wrote to my daughter in my pyjamas one evening from my sofa, while my little girl slept upstairs. Because I loved writing. That's all. I loved

316

writing! I didn't mean to step on any toes! I didn't mean to upset anyone! I just wanted to write.'

Tiggy shook her head and laughed quietly under her breath.

'Look, if you are not going to be adult about this and talk to me, I don't even know why I'm bothering,' Jessica continued. 'I mean, I could be out there celebrating with my husband but instead I'm in here, arguing in the toilet!'

'You call this an argument?' Tiggy snapped back.

'No!' Jessica replied quickly. 'You're right! It isn't! Because it takes two people to have an argument, and right now I am talking to myself!'

'Please stand out of my way,' Tiggy replied, rolling her eyes. 'I'd like to go home to my children.'

'No,' Jessica said, surprising even herself.

'Excuse me?' Tiggy replied, moving towards her.

'No.' Jessica repeated.

'You're going to hold me hostage in the ladies' toilets?' Tiggy asked, with a laugh.

'If I have to,' Jessica said. She needed to clear the air tonight. She needed things to be OK between them. And if she let Tiggy push past and storm out of the toilets, that would be it. The moment would be gone. And every time Jessica attended an event or was invited to an awards ceremony in the future, she'd feel the same sense of dread at the thought of Tiggy arriving. She didn't want that to happen. It was silly. It had to stop now. She had to clear everything up, right here in the toilets, with this award in her hand.

Jessica softened her tone. 'I just want to sort things out. I need you to understand that I never did anything to hurt you!'

'Please stand out of my way,' Tiggy repeated, definitely not softening hers. 'This is pathetic!'

'Pathetic?' Jessica exploded. 'Pathetic? No, this isn't pathetic! Pathetic is publicly humiliating me at a launch, pretending you don't know me when you used to bloody babysit me as a child! Come on, Tiggy! You know exactly who I am! Pathetic is telling a trashy gossip website that I had an agenda to steal your place on a campaign – when the truth is that I got an email to invite me one day, accepted the next, and it was as simple as that! It's refusing to congratulate me and then storming away from the table like a child! It's refusing to accept my apology and then laughing at me like a bloody playground bully! I'm sorry that my success has upset you, but it was never a deliberate thing. I've been really lucky, I know that, but I still think I deserve this award, Tiggy. And maybe you'll realise one day that I'm not the person you think I am!'

'Do you want to know how I really feel, Jessica?' Tiggy said, moving to within an inch from her face. 'I am sick of this! I am sick of this industry. I'm sick of sharing my life, my children, my every move! I will never win! It doesn't matter how long I do it! I will never, ever win! My face isn't young enough! My words aren't hard-hitting enough! My pictures aren't unique enough! And it doesn't matter how many years I do it, how many expensive dresses I buy hoping my name might finally be read out on that stage, or how many times I post to my followers and ask for votes! I will never win, because people like you come along and the whole world falls at their feet!'

Jessica didn't know what to say. She looked down at the award in her hand and suddenly felt like she didn't deserve any of it.

'Move out of my way!' Tiggy suddenly shouted loudly, and Jessica was so shocked that she stepped aside and let her push past her and straight out of the bathroom. As the white skirt of her dress flew behind her and the door slammed shut, Jessica stumbled backwards until she met the wall and allowed herself to sink down to the floor. And that was where she stayed, staring down at the award in her hand and replaying the conversation in her mind.

Tiggy wasn't warm, or understanding, or kind. She had probably never read Jessica's blog and clearly didn't think she had a scrap of talent or deserved any of it. But maybe she was right. Maybe Jessica didn't deserve the recognition. The Mama & Me campaign. The growing tribe of readers and followers, or the offer of a holiday in Dubai. As she sat there on the floor drowning in feelings of self-doubt, the door swung open. Jessica was relieved to look up and see Wendy standing above her.

'What the fuck?' she said, looking down at Jessica. 'Are you OK? What happened? Did you talk to her?'

Jessica looked up at Wendy, who was stood with a look of horror on her face. She sighed loudly. 'I don't think it was ever about me,' she said finally, tracing the engraving of her name on the award with her thumb. 'It was always about her. I'm just a convenient person to blame it all on.'

'Well, I know that already, Jessica,' Wendy replied. 'I've been in your shoes before, you know that! And do you know what else I know?'

'No?' Jessica replied, looking up at her.

'That you should be out there celebrating, rather than sitting on the floor of the toilet! This is your night! And there is no place for bad losers! So forget her – honestly, just forget her! And let's head back to that table and drink that expensive bottle of champagne your husband is passing round!'

'You're right,' Jessica replied, taking Wendy's hand and pulling herself up to her feet. 'I shouldn't even let her get to me. It's stupid. Is Chris worried?'

'Fuck yeah. I am the designated search party, and I was told to take my role extremely seriously and not to return empty handed!'

'Oh shit,' Jessica replied, just as she was hit by another wave of nausea. Forced to make a split-second decision, she ran to a cubicle, barged the door open, and promptly threw up in the toilet.

'What's that all about babe?' Wendy said, as she emerged a few minutes later. 'You hit the drink a bit too hard?'

'I haven't been drinking,' Jessica replied. 'I've only had a few sips! I'm not used to all this drama. My life is actually quite boring, Wendy. I can't cope with all this.'

'Jesus, that chat with Tiggy must've been bad,' Wendy replied, looking concerned.

Jessica stared at her reflection in the mirror as she washed her hands in the sink. 'Let's head back to the table. Is it over? What happens now?'

'Yep, it's just wrapping up. The fashion blogger Lauren Reynolds won the award for "Blogger of the Year" predictably. I mean, it was never going to be a parenting blogger, was it?' Wendy said, rolling her eyes. 'And listen babe, our babysitter has said she's fine to stay for a few more hours and we were thinking about heading somewhere for a few more drinks if you fancy joining us? Maybe you can fill me in on exactly what just happened?'

Jessica paused for a moment. Saying yes would be the sociable thing to do. It was probably the professional thing to do. And she'd love to chat things over with Wendy. She knew it would make her feel a lot better about winning this award and about the words Tiggy had just spat in her face. But just as she was about to accept her invitation, an image of Henny, Mel and Deena flashed into her mind.

She could picture them sat together on Mel's sofa, pouring glasses of champagne and waiting for Jessica to call with all the gossip. She could hear their voices. She could smell Mel's favourite cinnamon candle burning on the mantelpiece. She could hear the radio playing quietly in the kitchen. It was all so familiar to her – unlike this ballroom filled with people she didn't know, these shoes pinching her feet, these tummy-sucking pants squeezing her in places she really didn't enjoy being squeezed, and these awful, brightly-lit toilets that now smelt of her own vomit.

They were her tribe.

Her gang.

Her support network.

Her people.

And they were currently only a few miles south of the river, celebrating Jessica's win and hoping she might divert her taxi and let them see the award for themselves.

And in that instant, she knew where she needed to be.

'You in?' Wendy asked, with a smile.

Jessica smiled back.

'Thanks so much for inviting me, Wendy,' she replied. 'But there's somewhere that I need to be.'

21

(to be published at a later date)

Dear Bella,

I'm sorry for not writing a letter to you sooner, but it's been a whirlwind since I won that award. I will never forget hearing my name called out, or the feeling of camera flashes blinding me as I stood on that stage, nor the look on Daddy's face when I arrived back at the table clutching that award. It was wonderful, and surreal, and overwhelming, and crazy, all at the same time. To be honest Bella, it's taken me a while to come back down to earth.

But the night of the awards ceremony didn't end there. Not long after heading back to the table, I climbed into a cab with Daddy and asked the driver to drop me at Mel's house so I could spend time with my friends. He'd drunk far too much champagne by this point and was more than happy to head home and collapse in bed, reassured by the fact Granny and Grandad were around if you decided to wake in the night. So I made him promise to sneak in and give you a kiss from me and then I jumped out of the cab and knocked on the door of one of the places I have felt happiest since I became a mother.

After Mel opened the door, I followed her through to the kitchen – and there was Henny with a bottle of champagne in her hands, standing alongside Deena, smiling from ear to ear. And as I smiled back at them, the champagne cork suddenly popped and hit the ceiling above us and all three of them cheered, clapped, and ran over to hug me.

We spent the rest of that evening laughing, chatting, passing around the award to pose for silly pictures, and swigging champagne (or sparkling grape juice in Mel's case, which she told us was torture). And just as I was starting to think about calling it a night and phoning for a cab to bring me home to you, I felt another wave of nausea rise from my tummy right up to my throat.

'Oh Jesus,' I said. 'Not again'. And when I told the girls I had thrown up earlier in the evening, they all frowned and asked what I'd eaten at dinner. But the truth is that I had barely eaten anything at all.

I'd felt sick a few too many times recently for it to be nerves, or food poisoning, or drinking on an empty stomach. I was starting to wake up from the fog and stress and excitement of the previous few weeks to realise that these constant waves of sickness might be something else entirely.

Within a few minutes of airing my concerns to the girls, Mel had dragged us all upstairs to the bathroom and started rummaging in the cabinet. And she was suddenly holding out a box, containing a plastic stick that had the potential to change my life – and your life – forever.

Just three minutes later, I would know for sure.

So, I did a wee on that pregnancy test, Bella, with three friends waiting the other side of the bathroom door, yelling to ask if I'd done it yet. And when I stood up and replaced the cap, we all stood over that piece of plastic, four faces craning to see one line appear straight away, then squinting our eyes to see if another was joining it to make a cross. My heart was beating so hard and so fast that I could barely focus. But I kept watching, Bella. I couldn't drag my eyes away.

And do you want to know how it turned out? How this part of our story is going to end? Well, winning that award was never meant to be the biggest shock of the night – because as another line appeared and shrieks rang out all around me, I flopped down onto the bathroom floor to stare at that test. I clasped it tightly in my hand, and I realised that everything was going to change. Everything was going to start again – right from the swollen bump, to the contractions, to the pushing, to the moment I would stare down into two eyes for the very first time.

This is the start of a new story, Bella.

Not just for your little brother or sister – but for us, too.

And we started writing it that night.

Not in a glitzy ballroom.

Not on a stage, with my eyes blinded from camera flashes.

Not clutching an award in my hand, as every head in a ballroom turned to me.

Not arguing in the toilet with another blogger, who didn't think I deserved to win.

But right there on the bathroom floor.

Clutching that piece of plastic with two bright blue lines, surrounded by my three best friends.

Love from Mummy x

Note from the author

This novel is inspired by my own experiences as a blogger, but the characters are constructed entirely in my head. Tiggy does not exist as a single person, but is created from snippets of people I have met along the way that, let's say, made my path a little more difficult to navigate – as is Wendy, who represents the many friends I have made in the industry since I started blogging. It's not such a bad place to be, after all.

Acknowledgements

I would like to thank the following people:

My husband Charlie, who has only ever encouraged and supported me on both my blogging and writing journey.

Our children Stanley, Wilfred and Mabel - because without them, I would have neither a subject for my blog, nor a subject for my novel.

Our friends Alex and Graeme Thompson (and their children Oscar and Bea) for allowing me to write most of this novel from their kitchen table.

My parents, Roger and Sarah; my sister Rebecca, and my in-laws Paul and Penny, for all the offers of childcare and for the general support and encouragement (sorry about the swear words).

My brother Anthony, because I couldn't possibly write these acknowledgements without mentioning him. He never did like reading books very much, but he would definitely have been proud that I have written one.

My favourite English teacher, Mrs Lennox. Every time I write, her advice still comes into my head.

My agent, Caroline Montgomery from Rupert Crew, for believing in me from the beginning and helping me whip this manuscript into something worth pitching to publishers.

And finally to my editor, Hannah, and the whole team at Aria at Head of Zeus, for making my writing dreams come true.

Now read the first chapter of
Mum's Big Break

MUM'S
Big
BREAK

LOUISE EMMA CLARKE

Can one normal mum
survive life in the spotlight?

UNCORRECTED PROOF COPY

I

Followers – 93,350
Weeks pregnant – 26
Months pregnant – 5
Awards – 1
Free holidays – 1

Dear Bella and Bump,

I found out I was pregnant for the second time on Saturday, 1st September 2018.

Well, not exactly.

It was probably Sunday, 2nd September by the time I confessed how I was feeling to my friends and followed them reluctantly to the bathroom to wee on a pregnancy test. It was late, I was tired and I didn't expect to see that second line appear quite so quickly.

If I'm honest, I already suspected I was pregnant. But I hoped the test might break the news a little more gently. I expected to shout to the girls, 'Umm, I'm not entirely sure

actually? Can you come through and have a quick look?'
I expected that we'd have to hold the test up to the light
and squint to try and spot a second line. I thought I'd be
in limbo for a few days, re-testing, re-evaluating, recalcu-
lating – and during of all it, half-expecting it was all going
to turn into nothing but a fuzzy dream.

But as I stared down at that test, there was no doubt
about it.

The second line appeared in a flash. Bold and blue and
determined.

And that's when I knew my second baby really was nes-
tled somewhere deep beneath the silver sequins of my
evening dress.

As I sank to the floor with that test in my hands, everything started slotting into place. The nausea, the dizzy
spells, the exhaustion.

I was pregnant! It was obvious now.

A few hours earlier, I'd been oblivious as I climbed onto
a stage at a glitzy award ceremony in London to accept
the award for 'Parenting Blogger of the Year'. The fact
I'd won was a big enough shock in itself, given I'd only
started blogging six months earlier, and I knew that night
would be etched on my memory forever. I thought it would
be because I had heard a hush descend on the hall, followed by my name being called out as the winner – and

then I was standing on that stage in front of everyone, with camera flashes blinding me. And because I had woken up to the competitiveness of blogging that night, when the praise wasn't unanimous from my fellow nominees. It was a crazy, brilliant, terrifying, stressful and surprising night. And I was never going to forget a single moment of it.

But sitting there on my friend's bathroom floor just a few hours later, it all suddenly made sense. That heavy, gold award felt good in my hands, of course it did, but it didn't cause fireworks to explode in the pit of my stomach in the same way that that piece of plastic did.

It wasn't even close.

Because that was the moment my story as a mother started all over again.

Right back to the very beginning.

And I promise that I will tell you all about it.

Love from Mummy x

Finishing the letter, Jessica rested her pen and looked up from her sunbed. It was hot today – she guessed at least thirty degrees – and Chris and Bella were still splashing around in the pool. She smiled, watching them for a moment.

This was their first family holiday since Bella was born nearly two years ago, and after a long, wet winter, the feeling of warm sunshine on her skin was very welcome indeed. Jessica sighed and shut the notebook, moving it to the table alongside her sunbed. She closed her eyes and allowed her mind to drift away, listening to the sound of the waves breaking on the shore behind her. This was the life.

'Mrs Holmes?'

Her eyes shot open.

'Sorry to disturb you, Mrs Holmes. I trust that you were expecting me?'

Jessica blinked up at the blonde lady stood over her sunbed and nodded. 'Of course, yes, hi Annika,' she said, pulling off her sunglasses.

Annika was wearing a formal chocolate-brown skirt suit and thick black tights with heels. Jessica couldn't help feeling immediately self-conscious in her swimsuit, reaching for the kaftan that was slung over the back of the sunbed to cover herself up.

'I hope you are still enjoying your time at The Merrygold Hotel and Suites?' Annika asked in an accent Jessica hadn't quite managed to place, but she guessed was German or Scandinavian.

'Oh yes,' Jessica said, pulling the kaftan over her head and wiggling from side to side to ease it over her twenty-six-week bump. 'It's been great, apart from the toddler still suffering from jetlag, but we're used to staying up most the night anyway so it's nothing new…' She laughed gently, trying to break the ice.

Annika cocked her head to the left and curled the corner of her lip into a slight smile. After a pause, she said: 'Would you like to follow me? We have a tour of the hospitality rooms scheduled for 10 a.m., don't we? I hope it is still convenient?'

Jessica did her best to keep the smile fixed on her face. 'Oh sorry, yes, silly me.' She swung her legs over the side of the bed and stood up slowly, pausing to find her centre of gravity. 'Should I change? Or am I OK in this? Sorry, I probably should've gone back to our room to get ready…'

'No, that will be fine. We will start with the conference room. Just follow me and I'll lead the way!' As Annika strode away with her clipboard in her hand, Jessica threw her phone, notebook and pen into her canvas beach bag and slung it over her shoulder. She hurried to slide her flip-flops onto her feet, turning to Chris in the pool as she strode past.

'Another tour!' she mouthed, rolling her eyes. 'I'd better go or I'll lose her!'

Chris rolled his eyes back and nodded, moving to the side of the pool. Placing Bella on the side, he called after her, 'So we'll just wait here for you then? How long will you be this time?'

Jessica turned back to him and shrugged, before disappearing inside the revolving doors to the hotel.

Jessica knew that Chris was rapidly losing patience with the tours, the personal greetings, the cocktail parties and the endless introductions since they had arrived in Dubai, but what could she do? She had been offered this holiday in return for posts on her social media feed and they'd hadn't paid a penny to be here, so she could hardly tell these people to go away and allow her to enjoy a quick snooze on her sunbed instead.

Truthfully, she'd been a bit surprised by how much time had been demanded by the staff at the hotel, but it was too late now. She'd accepted the holiday and she had to do the work – even if that meant being dragged away from her sunbed to listen to a monologue about the interior design decisions behind an overwhelmingly brown conference hall.

It was a few hours before she was able to say her goodbyes and scurry back to the pool, but when she arrived, Chris and Bella were nowhere to be seen. Looking down at her phone and realising it was now midday and Bella had probably been tired and grouchy, she made her way up to their room.

Suite 3008.

Floor 20.

She'd never set eyes on a hotel suite before this holiday, let alone stayed in one, and when they first arrived and were shown to their room, it had taken them a good five minutes to explore, eyes wide with shock. There were two bedrooms, joined together by a large lounge. Wardrobes opened up to reveal storage space the size of small rooms just for their clothes and shoes. Everything inside the suite was perfectly matched in hues of dark wood and warm tones of caramel-brown, and vast, floor to ceiling windows showed off the view to its absolute best.

From their balcony, they could see the whole of Jumeirah Beach stretched to the left and right of them. The white sand, the colour of the sea a perfect reflection of the cornflower-blue sky above, hotels dotted along the coast, the impressive Burj Al Arab hotel shaped like the sail of a boat to their right, and a big wheel that seemed to be sat on its very own island to their left.

Looking directly down from their balcony to the hotel grounds, a series of pools stretched invitingly in front of their hotel.

'Seven pools, to be exact,' their concierge had informed them on that first night. 'Three general pools that everyone can use, one saltwater pool, one shallow pool for children, one adult-only pool, one pool for swimming laps, and a swimmable canal that connects them all.' The biggest pool was directly below them, with the words 'THE MERRYGOLD' stamped on the bottom in large, black letters. And as swimmers disturbed the surface of the water, the letters shimmered and danced in the sunlight.

It was, without doubt, the most impressive hotel that Jessica had set foot in.

In fact, the room alone was so inviting that Jessica was quite tempted to spend the full week inside it, relying on room service and gawping at the views, but with a nearly-two-year- old in tow, that was never going to happen.

Jessica made it back to the room and stood in front of the heavy mahogany door with 3008 monogrammed in gold letters, pulling her key card from the pocket of her bag to unlock it. As the light flickered green, she pushed the door as gently as possible.

CLICK.

'Sssshhh,' Chris hissed, turning towards the door from his armchair. 'Fuck's sake, Jess, please don't wake her!'

'Seriously?' Jessica whispered. 'What was I supposed to do? Beam myself through the door?'

Chris rolled his eyes.

'You know,' Jessica continued. 'This hotel room is nearly as big as our house. She's got her own room, Chris! You're sat out here lording it up with your iPad and she's fast asleep in her own room, with the door closed. How was I ever going to wake her?'

'Lording it up with my iPad?' Chris repeated slowly. 'Good one. That's obviously what I've been doing while you've been swanning around conference rooms for the last couple of hours...'

'Oh whatever,' Jessica said, shaking her head. 'Anyway, what have you been doing while I've been gone? Has she been OK?'

'No,' Chris said. 'She's been a bit of a bloody nightmare actually. She was tired and hungry, and she wanted Mummy as soon as you disappeared. We waited for as long as we could, as I thought it would be nice to have lunch together, but I needed to give her something to eat in the end. Not that she enjoyed the chips I ordered her... Most of them ended up on the bloody floor, so she's probably gone to bed hungry.'

'That isn't my fault, Chris!' Jessica said, her mouth dropping open in shock. 'I got away as soon as I could!'

'You didn't tell me you were going to disappear for most of the morning!' Chris snapped back, the volume of their argument steadily increasing. 'And you didn't mention that would be the case every bloody morning of this holiday! Because if you had, I probably would've told you it was a shit idea and suggested we holiday in Greenwich instead!'

Jessica walked over to him and looked down. Their

eyes met, each daring the other to spit the next line. But just as she was about to reply, Jessica burst into tears.

'This is shit,' she sobbed, taking a step backwards to sit down in the armchair opposite him. She sniffed and wiped her face with the back of her hand. 'I agreed to come on this holiday as I thought we all needed a break, but it's been fucking pointless.'

Chris sighed and stood up, taking the few steps towards her and pulling her into a hug.

'Sorry honey, I'm sorry. I didn't mean... Sorry.'

'It's not your fault,' Jessica replied, a single tear rolling down her cheek. 'This is crap for you! You're looking after a toddler the whole day while I have to tour bloody conference rooms, or walk round the kitchen of the restaurant that is going to cook us dinner that night, or sit opposite a hotel manager in his stuffy office while he bleats on about what a brilliant job he's doing! It's not a bloody holiday! It's bloody hard work!'

'Well, judging by the size of this room, they're making you work the room rate.'

'I'd happily take a tiny room with just enough to room to squeeze a bed and a cot, if it meant I could have a few hours by the pool with my family.'

The two of them sat in silence for a moment, their heads turned towards the window as they watched waves rolling in the distance.

'I knew there were going to be strings attached,' Jessica continued, not taking her eyes away from the bright blueness of the Arabian Gulf. 'I mean, who offers a blogger a holiday to Dubai, clearly worth thousands of pounds, without wanting something in return? But I didn'tthink they'd make me work quite so hard for it.'

'It's not exactly been relaxing,' Chris added. 'For either of us. Although I'm not sure a pool holiday could ever be relaxing with a toddler intent on throwing herself in the pool every waking moment. I've had far more relaxing days at work.'

Jessica laughed as she sniffed. 'Oh, bloody hell, what a disaster! And do you know the thing that pisses me off the most?'

Chris shook his head.

'It's the fact you've used up five days of annual leave to be here! Those days are so precious now and we've wasted them.'

'Well, we were both craving some sunshine... Maybe we'll be surprised when we get home and realise it's done us both some good?'

Jessica raised an eyebrow. 'Nice try, but I think this holiday is going down in history as the least relaxing holiday we've ever been on. We'll probably laugh about it eventually.'

Chris cleared his throat and turned to her. 'So next time what's-her-name...'

'Annika?'

'Next time Annika disturbs you on your sunbed, why not tell her it's not a convenient time? Why not start calling the shots?'

Jessica shivered – and she wasn't sure if it was down to the chill of the air-conditioning or the thought of having to stand up for herself.

'I mean, what would Tiggy do in this situation?'

Jessica's head snapped round. 'Oh, don't bring her into it!'

'I know you don't want to think about her, honey,' Chris replied. 'But she's a good example, because I don't think she'd stand for this shit.'

Jessica slowly blew out a breath to try and calm herself. She didn't want to give Tiggy a moment's thought. She didn't want to picture her face. She didn't want to imagine her on holiday. She didn't want to say her name. And she most certainly didn't want Chris to imply that she would handle this whole free-holiday-situation with far more professionalism than her nemesis would.

'I'm having a nap,' she said, standing up. She walked over to the master-bedroom door of their suite, simultaneously rubbing her bump and biting her tongue. 'Wake me up when Bella wakes.'

'What about lunch?' Chris asked.

'I'll have something when I wake up,' Jessica shot back, feeling the tiredness drag at her eyelids.

She shut the door and lay down on the bed, appreciating the coolness of the crisp, expensive bed linen against the soles of her tired feet. Lying flat on her back, she could feel the baby start to kick in her tummy, just the gentlest pops at this stage of pregnancy, but reassuring, nevertheless.

'Hello, little one,' she said, placing her hand over the lowest part of her tummy. A few kicks later, she turned onto her left side and drifted quickly into a deep sleep.

Jessica had made a conscious effort not to think about Tiggy Blenheim recently, fully aware that just a fleeting mention of her name would send her blood pressure rising. It had been five months since the two bloggers came head-to-head in the toilets at the blog award ceremony, Jessica clutching her award in her hand and Tiggy struggling with the humiliation of losing. The words spat during that argument had knocked Jessica's confidence in the weeks and months that followed, and whenever she caught a glimpse of that heavy, gold award (displayed upstairs on her dressing table ever since that night, in fear of Bella doing some serious damage with it) she found herself wishing it hadn't been her name called out as the winner at all.

It wasn't that she hadn't wanted to win it. Of course, she had! Back in September, she had been shocked but genuinely delighted to hear her name called out to a hushed banqueting hall. But she hadn't expected the backlash that followed. She certainly hadn't expected the competitiveness, the jealousy, the comparisons, the accusations or the character assassinations that seemed to come hand-in-hand with success in mummy blogging. She just wanted to write – but in doing so, she'd walked into a world she'd been quite unprepared for.

Finding out that she was pregnant with her second baby was the perfect excuse to step back from it all for a while. Jessica and Chris had both agreed in the early stages of her pregnancy that she wouldn't share the news with her blog followers until they were safely through their twelve-week scan – and as she always wrote her letters straight from the heart, she didn't see the point in putting pen to paper until she had the freedom to be honest again.

She kept her social media feed ticking along as usual, posting photographs from the award ceremony initially and then photos of family days out as the weeks and months passed by, but she hadn't published a letter to Bella since she'd won that award five months earlier.

The other problem was that she'd lost her notebook. That precious yellow notebook, which was monogrammed with her initials and filled with the letters she'd written to Bella since she'd first found out she was pregnant in August 2016. She knew it was somewhere in their house, as she'd never taken it beyond the front door – but despite fruitless hours of searching, it was still nowhere to be seen. By the time the calendar had flipped over to October, she'd given up the hunt and treated herself to a new notebook, choosing one with the same soft leather cover, but this time in an emerald-green. She imagined lining up a rainbow of notebooks on a bookshelf one day, filled with letters to her children. But even with a new notebook in her hands and a photo from their twelve-week scan stuck to the fridge, she couldn't find the motivation to start writing again.

She needed a break – and so that's exactly what she did. She battled through the first few months of nausea, attended appointments with her doctor and midwife, and tried to summon up the energy to get through the day when her toddler was, quite literally, running rings around her.

She would never describe her first pregnancy as 'easy' but faced with an entirely different scenario for growing her second baby, she felt pricks of jealousy towards the person she used to be. With her first pregnancy, she could enjoy lie-ins every weekend to catch up on sleep, she could sit at her desk all day and gaze out at the stretched lawns of Blackheath whenever she needed a moment to breathe, or collapse on the sofa as soon as she made it home from work. She wore skinny maternity jeans, stylish tunic tops and flattering dresses, all purchased new from the likes of Topshop, H&M, and ASOS maternity sections. She had time to sit and stroke her bump, letting her mind wander to the little person who was growing inside it. She asked Chris to take pictures of her bump regularly, stood side-on against a white wall in the landing upstairs, comparing the size to the photo before. She had an app downloaded on her phone that counted the weeks, likening Bella to a piece of fruit of the equivalent size. She had time to carefully plan Bella's first wardrobe and the décor in her nursery. And when Bella arrived, albeit a month early and not how Jessica had planned in her mind at all, she felt like she already knew the little girl who stared back at her with big, green eyes.

But this time? Jessica barely had time to think about the pregnancy, let alone the baby that would follow. There were no lie-ins, no moments of calm gazing out of the window, and no lazy afternoons on the sofa. Her clothes still fitted her, but this time they were dotted in unidentifiable splodges caused by a hug from a snotty nose or the remnants of that morning's bowl of porridge. When people asked how many weeks she had reached in the pregnancy, she had to open the app on her phone to get a reminder – and she would have no idea, literally no idea, whether the baby inside her tummy was the size of a grape or a lychee or a watermelon. She'd only taken two pictures of her growing bump since she found out she was pregnant, and those were only once she realised in a moment of panic that she'd completely forgotten to take any at all. They'd chosen not to find out the gender this time (a compromise, as Jessica had wanted to find out with Bella and Chris had relented, despite preferring to keep it a surprise) which meant she didn't know if Bella was getting a sister or a brother. The truth was that at twenty-six weeks pregnant, Jessica didn't really know who she was expecting at all.

She hadn't had the energy to write letters, to compete with other bloggers for campaigns, or to attend launches. But here they were in Dubai, on a holiday she had promised to tell her followers about, and for that reason, she knew she needed to start blogging again. She couldn't appear in photos in a bikini with her bump on show without some kind of explanation to her followers. So she'd unpacked that emerald-green notebook, and taken it to the pool each day, finding that the words spilled out far more easily than she'd imagined.

And as she slept on that hotel bed that lunchtime, Jessica's first letter was drafted on the first pages of the notebook lying in the bottom of her beach bag. And later that day, she would pull it out, dust off a layer of sand, start typing it up into a blog post, and press 'publish' to send it out into the world.

And just like that, she would be blogging again.

Hello from Aria

We hope you enjoyed this book! If you did, let us know, we'd love to hear from you.

We are Aria, a dynamic digital-first fiction imprint from award-winning independent publishers Head of Zeus. At heart, we're committed to publishing fantastic commercial fiction – from romance and sagas to crime, thrillers and historical fiction. Visit us online and discover a community of like-minded fiction fans!

We're also on the look out for tomorrow's superstar authors. So, if you're a budding writer looking for a publisher, we'd love to hear from you. You can submit your book online at ariafiction.com/we-want-read-your-book

You can find us at:
Email: aria@headofzeus.com
Website: www.ariafiction.com
Submissions: www.ariafiction.com/we-want-read-your-book

f @ariafiction
🐦 @Aria_Fiction
📷 @ariafiction